Faking It

Riley Hart
&
Devon McCormack

FAKING IT
(METROPOLIS, BOOK 1)

Riley Hart
Devon McCormack

METROPOLIS SERIES, BOOK I
Copyright © 2016 by Riley Hart and Devon McCormack
Cover Photography by Allan Spiers Photography
Cover Design by Jay Aheer
Editing by Flat Earth Editing
Proofing by Judy's Proofreading

Other Works by Riley Hart

Wild Side Series
Dare You To (Wild Side Series Prequel)

Crossroads Series
Crossroads (Crossroads Series #1)
Shifting Gears (Crossroad Series #2)
Test Drive (Crossroads Series #3)

Blackcreek Series
Collide (Blackcreek Series #1)
Stay (Blackcreek Series #2)
Pretend (Blackcreek Series #3)

Broken Pieces Series
Broken Pieces (Broken Pieces Series #1)
Full Circle (Broken Pieces Series #2)
Losing Control (Broken Pieces Series #3)

Rock Solid Construction Series
Rock Solid (Rock Solid Construction Series #1)

Other Works by Devon McCormack

Romance
Filthy Little Secret
Tight End
Weight of the World (Devon McCormack & Riley Hart)

Bastards Series
Cheating Bastard (Bastards #1)
Lying Bastard (Bastards #2)

Young Adult Titles
The Pining
Hideous
When Ryan Came Back
The Night Screams

1
Gary

"What's wrong with you?" Derek asks. He slaps my arm as we make our way down the sidewalk, toward the condo building we both live in. After spending a couple of hours at Flirt, the local gay bar, we're hammered. We downed vodka sodas and Fireball shots before tearing it up on the dance floor. Well, in my case, I bobbed my head slightly on the dance floor while Derek forced every hottie he could find on me. His version of therapy.

"There was sooo much hot man-beef out tonight," he says.

I try to ignore his rambling, but he grabs my arm and pulls sharply.

I stop walking and turn to him. He glares at me. The long blond bangs of his undercut falls over his eye. He slaps at it, which makes the hair rise and fall right back where it was before. Despite his failure, he continues staring at me, but I'm hardly intimidated by a guy who's five foot four and wearing a T-shirt that says "dumpster" across the front. If anything, his expression is pretty adorable as he purses his lips and bats his long lashes repeatedly—surely thinking somehow this fierce look will help him get his point across.

"I just wanted to hang," I say.

"You still don't want to move on." He shifts his weight to one leg. He loses his balance and starts to fall. I grab him and help him regain his bearings before putting his arm over my shoulder.

"Okay, buddy," I say. "Let's just keep walking. Get you some water."

"I want Chinese. Can we order Lucky Buddha? Please...please...pretty please?" This sounds more like the Derek I'm used to.

"That's fine."

Although as soon as I get him back to my place, I doubt he'll be conscious long enough for us to order out.

"Don't patronize me!" he shouts. "You're a sexy guy. You need to own that. You got that nice muscular build. Not super ripped, but like muscly and sexy. It's a very vers look. Is he gonna want to bottom? Top? Who knows? Let's find out. And this short crewcut is like Sean-Cody-cute. Totally all-American. It's perfect for this sandy-blond hair you got. Will be great for hiding the grays when you need to worry about that. I think you have seven years before you have to worry."

Derek's a hair stylist, so I'm used to him assaulting me with critiques like these.

His expression turns serious again. "Don't get me wrong now. You're not like hot stuff. You don't got the jawline people like. And that freckle under your right eye is like all I can look at right now. Just saying, you're not like a cover model or nothing. But like...porn hot."

He must sense my confusion. "Like I wouldn't mind watching you sit on a guy's face for five to ten minutes of a thirty-minute scene. I'm just saying you have to own it and get back out there. Guys will date some ugly dudes, and you're not ugly, which means you're pretty much a hot commodity. It's science."

Before I have a chance to make sense of anything he just said, I notice a couple of guys heading down the street, making their way from Cypress Street to Flirt. I pull Derek aside to let them pass.

One of the guys, in a backward baseball cap, wears a tight, green T-shirt that sculpts around his fit body.

I appreciate the view and smile politely to him and his friends as they pass. They have that sort of dazed look in their eyes—one that suggests they pre-gamed before coming out.

"*Hey, sexy thing*," Derek sings, turning his head and watching the guys pass.

The guy in the cap turns back to us, gazing at Derek with interest—the kind of interest that makes me think, if I'm not careful, I might lose my buddy in a few minutes.

"Show me your dick!" Derek shouts.

"Holy shit," I say, turning away from the guys. A gut reaction. Maybe because I hope they won't see me when they look back.

But I'm too curious not to glance over my shoulder. Cap spins around, grabs either side of his khaki shorts and yanks them down with his underwear, revealing an impressive length...especially for being soft. His friends laugh and gaze at each other with wide eyes, clearly as shocked as I am by his reaction.

Derek pulls away from the arm I have around him. I grip his shoulder.

"I've gotta go," he says, his expression stoic, dead serious.

"I don't think that's a good idea," I say, forcing him to turn with me back toward the condo building.

"That's my boyfriend," he whimpers, glancing over his shoulder and shouting, "I love you!"

"I love you, too!" the guy shouts back.

He resists me even more.

"We're going the wrong way!"

"No, we're really going the right way."

"Why won't you let me have sex with him? I'm sorry for getting mad. You can be a prude and abstain from sex while you figure your stupid shit out about that asshole Peter. Go. Lie down in bed. Dream about what it'll be like in ten years when you finally decide to get over him. I honestly don't care right now. Just let me have my boo."

He fights me again, but he doesn't resist enough for me to believe he wants to follow through with this horrible decision.

"How about we get back to my condo," I say, "and we can discuss how you aren't able to consent right now."

"Consent? I would consent to anything that man wanted."

"That's what concerns me."

He pouts. "This sucks. I am *so* clean right now. I took a laxative two days ago. I fucking cleaned the hell out of this thing this afternoon."

"That's...incredible information to be aware of."

I continue guiding him back to the building. We live in separate towers of Metropolis, which people refer to as the only unofficial gay building in Atlanta. Straight people live here, too, but we have an unusually high demographic of young, gay tenants. Derek lives in the North Tower, while I'm in the South.

I take him up to my unit on the fifteenth floor. I'm fine with him crashing on the couch tonight as he sometimes does, so we can run out in the morning and get donuts and coffee...or as Derek calls them, "carbs and happy."

We stumble into my place.

I'd be a little worried about my new roommate, but we saw him on the dance floor less than thirty minutes ago, and he was on the prowl. I doubt he'll be home before Derek passes out.

"You so should have fucked one of those guys," Derek says as he makes himself cozy on the couch. "Gary...Gare...Garusula...listen to me." He runs his fingers through his lengthy bangs again. "Peter was a douchebag to you. He was seeing a guy for two years of your four-year relationship."

"Five years."

"You guys were together five years? Really? I would say that's impressive, but I know a little too much now to be impressed."

"Can we just go to bed?"

The room is spinning, and all I want to do is climb into bed and pass the fuck out.

"No!" Derek shouts. "Not until you promise me you will move the fuck on."

"It's been three weeks since I broke up with him."

Three weeks since I found the message on his Facebook Messenger. Three weeks since I found the vids on his phone. Three weeks since everything I thought was safe and secure blew up into the biggest fucking catastrophe ever.

"Most people need more time than three weeks," I insist.

He rolls his eyes—a big dramatic roll—before falling back on the couch.

He pulls his phone out of his pocket and scrolls across the screen.

We chat a bit more, Derek's energy fading as he lectures me about needing to move on. When he passes out, I make my escape into my room, adjacent to the living room Derek's sleeping in. I take off my clothes.

Just gonna take a quick shower. But the bed is too tempting to resist—I'll take a shower after a brief nap. I need a minute to rest.

***

My head. Oh, my fucking head. The pressure is so intense it feels like I need to dig a knife into my skull to relieve it.

The night returns to me in a series of flashbacks: a wide-eyed Derek shouting "shots" at the top of his lungs before downing Fireballs, the music blaring so loud I thought my eardrums were going to pop, and the awkward feeling that everyone was watching and judging me while I was on the dance floor.

The comfort of Peter's arm around me is the only thing that brings me some ease.

I scoot back across the bed, tucking my ass against his pelvis.

He clings to me a little tighter.

Wait a second. I'm not with Peter anymore.

Must be Derek. He's only slept in the bed with me a few times and definitely never cuddled with me before, but it's gonna be funny to give him shit about it before we go out for carbs and happy.

I roll around to face him, a grin sweeping across my face. He's going to feel so fucking silly. But it's not Derek. There's someone else in my bed. *There's someone fucking else in my bed!*

"Holy shit!" I exclaim, crawling across the mattress and jumping off the foot of the bed. I land on my feet, and in my rush to get away from the stranger, I hit my heel against the metal frame of my desk.

"Fuck, fuck, fuck!" I say, before losing my footing and falling on my ass.

The guy in the bed sits up quickly, his eyes wide, as though he's as surprised by all this as I am.

All the craziness in my brain settles as I realize I know this guy.

His dark brown hair. Those jacked arms, stacked with muscles. The dip between his abs that hints at the incredible six-pack I know is concealed under those covers.

The guy lives in the tower across from me, two floors below. I've caught him a few times working out on a mat in his living room, doing Pilates and some sort of ab workout video. His body would glisten with sweat as he committed hardcore to whatever exercise he was in the middle of.

Wonderful as he is to look at, what is he doing in my bed?

"Where the fuck am I?" he asks, glancing around uneasily. "You're not Jacob."

Oh, shit.

"Jacob's my roommate," I say. "Let me guess. You came back with him."

And likely came with him, too.

Jacob's six-foot-something with strawberry-blond hair and a body thick with muscles. His sweet, southern charisma never fails to charm the pants off the guys he's interested in. He's only been living with me for two weeks—since I gave Peter the boot, but in that amount of time he's let me know just how much sex I should be having as a single, gay man. And not like one trick a night. Like multiple sessions throughout every day. I've managed to get a handful of Grindr and Scruff tricks, but I'm no Jacob.

I definitely couldn't get a guy like this.

Sharp lines stress the definition in his thick muscles, and he has that jawline Derek was talking about last night—the kind everyone thinks is so hot. His full, pouty lips push forward as he glances around my room. His eyebrows shift together as his forehead scrunches up.

"What the fuck? I went to the bathroom and when I came out, I was heading back to what I thought was the right room, but there was this twink on the couch. Just said, 'wrong room,' and pointed me to this one."

Of course. Thanks a lot, Derek.

"I'm so sorry," I say. "He was really drunk. I think he got confused."

Confused about how totally inappropriate that was.

His gaze shifts, and he looks like he's thinking about something, but it only takes me a moment to realize he's looking at my crotch.

Fuck. I'm still naked.

2

Travis

I've seen this guy around, but I can't for the life of me remember what his name is. Garrett, maybe...? Whatever his name is, he's cute. He's got a little flush to his cheeks, especially now that he's realized where my eyes keep traveling. His dick lengthens, and I can't help but take in the show. I mean, he's here, I'm here, and he's not moving to cover himself up. He's got a nice cock, heavy balls, and neatly trimmed brown pubes.

I can't see it, but I know his ass isn't bad either since I kept my cock nudged against it half the night.

When I meet his eyes, it's clear he's going to lose it. I'm pretty sure his body is cemented in shock, and a little embarrassment—because if he could move right now, I have no doubt Garrett would run and hide.

"I'm sorry. I didn't mean to make you uncomfortable. I was drunk as shit last night. The twink told me this was the right room." Kicking the covers off, I turn so I'm sitting on the edge of the bed, facing Garrett. As soon as I do, my head begins to spin.

"Oh fuck," he rushes out as his eyes dart toward my dick.

"Yeah, I know. It can be intimidating the first time you see it, but I promise, I'm good with heavy equipment." I wink at him, hoping to relax him a bit. Jesus, he's wound up tight.

"Come here." I hold out my hand to him as he's still laid out on the carpet.

"Huh?"

"Come here," I say again. "I know I should leave, but I'm afraid if I try to stand up right away, I'll be the one on the floor. My head is like the fucking Gravitron or something. I need a minute, and you shouldn't have to be naked on the floor in your own room." Unless he wants to be naked on the floor. Sometimes the bed is just too far away.

There's a short pause before Garrett reaches out his hand and grabs mine. I pull him up easily. Once he's on his feet, I pat the bed beside me. He's smaller than I am. Not real twinky, but I don't think he spends much time in the gym. I've seen him there off and on. He's timid, almost like he does just enough to get by. He's cute though, in an awkward way. "Are you going to stand in front of me with your dick out, or are you going to at least sit down?" He looks like he wants to crawl under the bed and not come out.

"Let me grab some clothes."

"So, I'll be the only one naked? Don't think so," I reply.

"You're the one who ended up in my bed, not the other way around. And look at you...you're..." He attempts to shield his cock, cupping it with one hand. The other hand he uses to try and cover his stomach, which is ridiculous considering he can't really hide either one, and there's no reason to. "I'm just going to get some clothes on."

"And ruin my view?" I grin at him. I'm not flirting because I plan to fuck him. He just seems like he might need to hear it.

"Are you being serious right now?"

"As a heart attack. Or as serious as your head exploding, which mine feels like it might do right now. Jesus, I drank too much last night. Please, sit down, Garrett. I'll apologize again, then we'll make small talk on even footing because we'll both be naked. Eventually, I'll slink out of your room, and when we see each other at the mailboxes, we'll laugh about the time I hijacked your bed."

"Gary," he says, his voice suddenly tight.

"Huh? My name is Travis."

"No. Me. I'm Gary, not Garrett."

Fuck. But can the man really blame me? We've never been properly introduced, and it's not like he's the guy who tries real hard to make an impression. Plus, I didn't go home with him last night. If that was the case, I could see him being taken aback. "I'm sorry. I'm really fucking this up. I'm just...I'm going to go." Before I make this anymore awkward than it already is—which honestly, I could have easily laughed off what happened, but I'm not sure Gary can. His unease is what's causing me to continue to make an ass out of myself.

I force myself to my feet, close my eyes as my brain pulses against my skull, and my legs are wobbly, like I might still be a little drunk. "It was a pleasure waking up naked with you. You don't have to be so shy. You have nothing to be concerned about."

Gary opens his mouth. I wait, but then he closes it again, without saying a word. Taking that as my cue to leave, I manage to stay on my feet well enough to stumble out of his room. As soon as I hit the living room, I recognize the man sleeping on the couch, and suddenly a whole lot of shit makes sense. Derek is always up in everyone's business.

"Have fun?" he asks without opening his eyes, making me realize he's awake.

"You're a dickhead."

"What? Me? Why? What did I do?" he feigns innocence, but I ignore him. I'm too fucked up to deal with Derek right now.

I make my way back to Jacob's room and fall into bed with him. The mattress feels lumpier than Gary's did—or than it felt last night. I had my mind on taking his ass when I was in his bed before and not where I did it.

"I thought you left," he mumbles into the pillow.

"No. I got up to take a piss and then ended up in the wrong room. I woke up naked with Gary. I don't think he liked being naked with me as much as you did."

"Oh, shit." Jacob's blue eyes pop open, full of mischief. "I bet he freaked out."

"What's his deal?" I ask, because it's going to be weighing heavily on me. It was an accident, and though it wasn't a big deal to me, I think it was to him. The last thing I want is to make someone feel uncomfortable, especially considering it's my job to do just the opposite and make them comfortable.

"He was dating some guy named Peter for a few years." As soon as he says it, things start fitting into place. Peter and Gary. I've heard people talking about them at the Midtown Flex—the best place to nab a few tricks and catch up on the latest local scandals. Still, I let Jacob confirm what I've been told. "Gary found out Peter had been cheating on him with some guy in North Tower. They were fucking behind his back for years. He kicked Peter out and Peter moved in with the guy. I didn't know him before, but he doesn't seem like he's ever been a real confident guy. That obviously didn't help."

Oh fuck. I didn't realize it had been years. That has to be shitty, especially when everyone in the damn building probably knows his business, and he has to worry about seeing Peter around. You can't trust anyone. That's exactly one of the reasons my ass will never give someone power over me like he did.

Still, I tell myself I'll make a point to find Gary to apologize again. Then my hangover wins, and I pass out.

***

When I wake up later, Jacob is knocked out in bed beside me, so I try to be quiet as I rummage around for my clothes. I find them, pull them on, and make it to the door of his bedroom before he says, "Thanks, man. I had a good time. It's a shame Gary didn't at least get a blowjob out of the morning. You have a magic fucking mouth."

"So I've heard," I tell him. I'm good at sucking dick, and I take pride in it.

Jacob laughs and then I make my way out of his room. It was a fun hookup. We both got what we were looking for, so it'll end there.

Derek isn't on the couch when I get to the living room. Something tells me Gary is gone too, but still, I go to his room and knock. When he doesn't answer, I leave their condo and take the elevator to the seventh floor, where I can cut across the pool level to get to North Tower. There, I jump on the elevator again and head for my floor.

I really want to walk my ass to the gym and exercise, but I have some work I need to do before my meeting tomorrow with an investor I hope will decide I'm worth dishing money out on.

I love what I do—fucking love it—but traveling around to people's homes to give them massages is getting old. There's nothing I want more than to have my own space— a place where people can come to me.

I'd tried like hell to do it on my own, but money doesn't come easy. Cash is one of the things my parents held over my head when I got caught just before I took a really nice cock at twenty-one—in my own apartment, I might add. As Mom had told me, they paid for it, which made it theirs. And when they realized I was gay and tired of hiding it, of trying to do everything to make them proud, they reminded me they had a lot of money to give me. That if I didn't *do what was right*, then they would have nothing to do with me and I'd never be able to do it on my own.

Fuck what they think is right.

Fuck living your life for someone else.

Fuck not doing what you want and not being damn proud of the person you are.

That's what I took from the moment, and I've been living my life that way ever since.

Only they were right about some of it because here I am asking for someone's help, which means even if it's mine, it won't fully be *mine*—the same way my apartment at twenty-one wasn't.

It's just a logical step, I tell myself. You have to do what you have to do, and I'll be damned if I let them believe they were right about me. It might be taking me a whole lot longer to get my shit together than I planned, but I'm doing it on my terms, and my way, and that's all that matters.

3
Gary

"Nice work ditching me with the hottie this morning, asshole," I say to Derek as I step onto the treadmill beside the one he's running on.

I can't believe he did that to me. Travis is hot as fuck, and if I'd run into him in a bar, I would have been fortunate to hook up with him. But he wasn't in my condo to fuck me. He was there to fuck Jacob. And considering how awkward I was, if there was ever a chance of anything happening between us, I've killed it. Murdered it violently.

Derek turns to me, beaming. He hasn't broken a sweat yet, so I don't figure he's been here long.

This morning, he left without any word other than a text that read: *Gym. 2.*

I typically work out at the fitness center in our condo building. Not as crowded and I don't have to worry about getting cruised. I only started frequenting the popular gym again because Derek thinks it's a necessary part of my assimilation back into the world of gay singledom. I tried to convince him I'm not ready to work out at the Midtown Flex, where I'm surrounded by muscle-bound Adonises.

"It'll motivate you," Derek kept saying when he first dragged me here the other day. Yeah, motivate me to sit on the couch and spend the rest of my life eating pasta and cheesecake, since no amount of exercise will ever make me look like one of these muscle-bound gym rats.

"I heard you talking to him when he left my room," I add. "So, you must've dashed out of there real fast because you knew I was gonna beat the shit out of you when I came out."

"I don't know what you're talking about," he says, shifting his eyes about as he wears a guilty expression.

"And I noticed you didn't respond to any of my messages," I say as I hit the button on the machine and program a mild three-mile-per-hour powerwalk.

"I had a date." When Derek says date, he means he met up with some guy on Scruff, and the guy tossed him around in bed for a few hours. If not a bed, a car, a bathroom stall, a cluster of trees on the side of the road—any place that would offer the flimsiest amount of privacy. "It was good, but I doubt it was as good as the beefcake you hit the sack with."

"We didn't do anything."

"Why not?" He gives me a judgmental look—one that reminds me of how my parents used to look at my sister whenever she'd get into trouble, the sort of look I've always dreaded them turning on me if they found out I was gay.

I glance around and lean toward him, whispering, "In what universe do you think if you send a hot guy into my bedroom, we're magically going to have sex?"

"The universe of mortals," he replies without even thinking about it. "He walked to the bathroom butt-naked. Or should I say, cock-naked, because damn. *Damn.*"

I notice a few people looking our way. The guy on the treadmill on the other side of Derek, beefy with his iPod earphones in, eyes us, looking more interested than annoyed.

Derek continues, "How did you see that ginormous corndog and not mouth-worship the meat right out of it?"

"How are we even friends?"

He turns to me and runs the back of his hand down the side of his face. "Because you think I'm pretty. Plus, you're the only guy who can repair my PC whenever I've bogged it down with porn and nude selfies. And I'm the only hair stylist in the city who's willing to work around your cowlick."

I pick up the speed on my machine, starting into a light jog.

"Fine. Next time, I won't send you a beautiful cock of the gods," Derek says. "If I'd been smart, I would have gotten down on my knees and blown that thing myself. Somebody's gotta do it."

"You're such a trooper."

"The guy knew your name, for Christ's sake."

"He called me Garrett."

"You should feel blessed a guy that hot, who you've never met before, *almost* knew your name. You're so ungrateful. Whatever. So, what are you wearing to the Second Chances pool party tomorrow?"

Second Chances, a major nonprofit organization, hosts a variety of fundraisers throughout the year to raise money to house people affected by HIV and AIDS. It's a great cause, but Peter's on the board.

"I told you I'm not going," I reply.

"You have to go! You have to show him that his asshole behavior isn't going to keep you from being at one of the hottest pool parties of the summer. Plus, you have to show every other guy who'll be there what you look like in a speedo."

"I look terrible in a speedo."

"You know what *doesn't* look terrible in a speedo, Gary? Your dick. And that's all anyone'll care about. Okay, your ass also, but you've got that covered pretty well. Not saying you should skimp on the squats, but you'll be fine for tomorrow."

I want to refuse to go, but there's no point fighting Derek. He's already made up his mind, and he's right. I can't spend my life hiding from Peter and Evan. A successful prosecuting attorney, Peter is an incredibly active member of several boards for a variety of LGBT causes. On top of that, since most of my life as an out, gay man has been spent in Atlanta with him, we also share a lot of the same friends, meaning the only way I could possibly avoid him would be to become a hermit—something I was tempted to do when I discovered what he was doing with Evan.

I take a breath and pick up speed on the treadmill so I'm jogging a little faster. Derek and I build into an intense run. When the treadmill really gets moving, I find negative affirmations are the best way to keep me going, reminding myself: *You're a failure. You're disgusting. Keep going if you ever want anyone to like you.*

It's how I've always approached working out. I've never strived to look like one of the guys at this gym. I don't need to look like a model. In fact, I'd rather not. It's a thin line I've always treaded. Never wanted to look out of shape enough that people would think I was lazy, but never so fit they'd call attention to my body.

When I was little, I didn't ask for attention. I think a part of it had to do with my troublemaker older sister, who was always getting primarily negative attention. While my parents scolded her for everything from bad grades to destruction of property, I lay low. I didn't swing the other way like some people might have done. No, I didn't need them to praise me. In fact, I think I was afraid if they ever did praise me, it might set me up to disappoint them. But if their expectations were always average, I never had to worry about upsetting them. I could keep them happy, and they'd never have a reason to fuss at me.

That's why I never came out to them. That would have disrupted the normal image I'd worked so hard to create.

Normal's still all I want to be. A normal guy who blends in and never has any attention called to him for any reason, which has only amplified all the shit that went down with Peter and Evan because it's called so much attention to me. Made people notice me and point to me as they tell the story of what went down...or their version of the story, at least. Of how long he was seeing Evan. How stupid I was for not knowing anything was going on.

I had to be stupid to believe he was being honest with me every time he said he was heading to the gym, or to the office, or to meet with a client...when really, he was sneaking over to a unit directly across from me. A unit where he and Evan could have fucked while watching me work on my computer in the bedroom.

When Derek and I finish breaking our sweats, we hit the showers. As I'm about to get out, I realize I didn't grab my towel from the locker room.

Shit.

Most of the guys I know aren't shy about their bodies. Peter and Derek have never given any shits about being naked at the gym, but it's something I'm still self-conscious about. I can put on the act like I don't care, but I'd rather not walk around, displaying my junk like I did with Travis this morning.

Plenty of guys walk around showing their dicks at the gym.

I walk out and act casual as I pass a few guys on the way into the locker room.

My face has to be bright red right now because my cheeks are on fire, but I keep playing it cool.

When I reach my locker, I open it and retrieve my towel.

I notice someone within my periphery looking at me.

I instinctually turn and see Evan a few lockers down. Fully clothed, his duffle bag at his side, he nods to me politely.

I play it cool as I wrap my towel around my waist. While he throws his duffle bag in the locker, I pretend to keep busy with my bag until he leaves.

My cheeks tremble. My eyes water.

I'm glad I was able to keep my shit together while he was here.

I've run into him a few times since it's happened. At the grocery store. At the gym. At the bar. It has to happen because we live so close to each other and run in the same circles, but considering how little time has passed, it's still a lot for me to handle.

I wish I could crawl into this locker and cry. But I have to keep it together. There's nowhere to run.

"Hey, Gary," I hear someone say behind me.

I turn and see a guy I run into occasionally at the bars. I smile and wave. He's always nice whenever we chat, but for some reason, right now, I can't for the life of me remember his name. And it's killing me having to smile and act like everything's fine when I want to curl up on the floor and burst into tears.

"Hey, man. Good seeing you," I say.

Just keep it together. Keep your shit together, Gary.

After Derek finishes showering up, we walk back to Metropolis together. When I get back to my unit, I hurry into my room and close the door, my chin quivering and my eyebrows twitching violently before I totally lose it and burst into a fit of tears. I fold my arms as I collapse onto the bed.

I can't. I can't do this.

It's a thought I've had a lot since I discovered the truth. It's so hard to face the world when it seems like everyone, especially Evan and Peter, is laughing at me.

But Derek's right. I have to get back out there. I can't hide from the world, tempting as that may be.

4
Travis

I'm nervous as hell. I don't usually let shit get to me, but right now, it is. Every time I sit down, my leg starts bouncing like I'm a dog and getting a really good scratch. When I stand up, I can't stop pacing the fucking room. It's incredibly frustrating.

This is my life, though. Sure, I'm not going to lose my business if Steven decides not to front me for my retail space, but it'll be a giant kick to the balls I'm really not interested in feeling. I like a little pain now and then, but that's going overboard.

It doesn't help that the meeting was set for today of all days. You'd think after all these years I wouldn't give a shit, and in a lot of ways I don't, but it's still a crappy situation to be in.

I push off my dark-gray couch for the tenth time in about that many minutes before making my way to the large living room window, my treadmill next to it. South Tower is across the way—a courtyard below, separating it from North. I let my eyes travel up two floors, and I wonder what Gary is doing over there. For some reason, he's popped into my head a few times since yesterday— probably because I feel like I owe him a sober apology. I'd be lying if I didn't admit I enjoy waking up in beds that aren't my own after a fun night, but it's also pretty fucking vital that the man I'm in bed with knows and wants me there.

My phone vibrates against my thigh. I pull it out of my pocket. I have my favorite tight, gray swimming shorts on beneath them for luck.

It doesn't surprise me to see my brother Malcolm's name on the screen. I'm pretty sure I'll hear from Martin, the youngest Waller boy, at some point as well. My gut twists into a knot that I honestly could do without right now. The last thing I need is to stress myself out even more.

Running my finger across the screen, I read Malcolm's text: *I'm sorry.*

I close my eyes and think about the family getting together to celebrate Mom's birthday. They'll go to lunch, or maybe have a houseful of Mom and Dad's friends over, who they'll talk badly about afterward. It's such a fucked-up situation, the way they treat other people and look down on them, yet feel like something is wrong with me. There's not. I know there's not, so fuck them if they can't see that.

Don't be. I'm sure I'll have more fun today than you will, I reply.

What are you doing?

Malcolm and Martin don't know I'm meeting with an investor. There isn't a doubt in my mind my brothers will try to give me the money to get my own space, but I don't want it because even though they both have their own careers, their money is still attached to Mom and Malcolm Senior. It paid for their college educations. They each got inheritances at twenty-three. Everything I have, I earned for myself.

Pool party, I tell him, which isn't a lie, then I shove my phone into my pocket, and damned if someone isn't at my door.

"Jesus fucking Christ," I mumble. I have an hour until I have to meet with Steven, and apparently no one will leave me alone before then.

When the door pushes open, I know who it is. I fall to the couch, force my legs to chill out, and say, "What do you want, Cody?"

He lives in the unit next door to me and is the only person at Metropolis I can honestly say is a good friend. Everyone is fun, nice to say hi to in the hallway or party with at Flirt, but Cody is different. The motherfucker forced his way into my life, and I haven't been able to get him out since.

"Are you nervous?"

"No," I lie.

"Would you tell me if you were?"

See? The bastard knows me too well. "Of course. You know I tell you everything. I can't wait to see you so I can give you a rundown on my day-to-day life."

He pushes a hand through the red waves on the top of his head and sits next to me. "One, you're a liar because two, you didn't tell me you fucked George from South Tower."

Ha! I'm not the only one who fucked up his name. "Gary. And I didn't fuck him. I fucked Jacob—are people saying I fucked Gary?"

"Do you know where we live and the places we frequent?" Cody asks, and I drop my head against the back of the couch.

"Damn it." Not that I give a shit what people say about me, but I believe Gary might.

"I heard it at the gym. Some guy named Peter was there. I don't know him, but I've heard about him, and I've seen him around. Apparently he's Gary's ex, and he was sort of losing his mind over the fact that you and Gary slept together."

"Fuck him." I roll my eyes. "He cheated on Gary with Evan for years, and then moved in with him. He doesn't get to say shit about who Gary gets down with. Evan's probably nearing his expiration date, so he's jealous Gary's getting new dick."

"Because everyone wants you," Cody teases me.

I nudge his arm. "Of course." My nerves hit me again, and I let out a deep breath. "I can't deal with this shit right now. I hate gossip."

Cody drops his head to my shoulder. "You know...it would be okay if you were nervous, T."

I shrug, moving his head. "But I'm not. I'll be fine. If it doesn't happen, it doesn't happen." *Please fucking happen.*

"Mr. Macho gay man who doesn't talk about his feelings. That's why you have all the boys begging for your cock. Sexy, slightly brooding but also sarcastic and outgoing. You're like the trifecta. Good thing I'm immune to you."

Even though I try to fight it, a smile pulls at my lips. "You said four qualities, not three, and you even missed a few: muscular, vers, and the ability to deep throat like a fucking champ."

"Oh, God. I remember. That's the only thing I hate about being your friend."

Cody and I hooked up once a few months after he'd moved in next door. It was fun. I try not to deny myself things I'll enjoy. I spent too many years doing that, too many years denying myself or hiding who I was or what I wanted. But with Cody, it had been awkward the next day. That's when I realized that somehow in the months leading up to the hookup, we'd become good friends, and there was no attraction. Don't get me wrong, Cody is fucking beautiful—soft features, all sinewy and flexible, with killer blue eyes he knows how to use to his advantage. But the physical attraction for him just isn't there.

"You need to go. I'm going to finish getting ready, and then head to my meeting." Where I'll find out if Steven thinks I'm worthy of investing in.

"Okay. I can take a hint. Good luck."

"Are you going?" I ask him. Steven and I are meeting up before the Second Chances fundraiser, where quite a few people from our community will be. He shakes his head, blows me a kiss, and then walks out.

***

A good pool party is pretty high on my list of favorite things. Music, drinks, men showing a lot of skin. What's not to love? Meeting with someone who has the ability to help you change your life and realizing it's not going well, puts a pretty big damper on things.

There isn't a part of me that thinks Steven is impressed.

He's a nice man—looks to be about in his fifties, attractive with graying hair at his temples. He has the whole daddy, silver fox thing down well.

I discovered he's been with his partner since he was twenty. He worked his way through college on his own, same as me, only he started at eighteen. He didn't start one degree and suddenly change his mind and drop out— take a couple of years off, which is what it looks like I did. What it doesn't tell him is that I'd gone to school for years for what my mom and dad wanted. That once I wasn't their perfect son anymore, I had to figure out who I was, which included some time off, yeah, but that was because of finances. I'd had to put money away before I started my training to be a massage therapist.

But what I refuse to do is use my past and the shitty things that have happened to me to secure this deal. I want to earn this because he thinks I'm qualified, not out of pity.

"So, you've said you've only been practicing massage for about a year and a half?" Steven asks. People are swimming and dancing and talking all around us. Might as well call this meeting a wash now and join them.

"Yes, sir."

"Steven. Call me Steven."

Fuck. I forgot he'd told me that already. "Yeah. I worked at a shop for about a year, and then I went out on my own." Translation—I don't always work well with others. "It's been six months, and I'm doing well. I have a steady clientele. I have an eighty-five percent return customer rate."

I wring my hands together, waiting for him to reply.

"Considering how many clients you said you're averaging per week, that's an impressive rate. Very promising." Steven pushes to his feet. "Walk with me for a second."

Fuck. This isn't going well.

I stand and head his way. Steven crosses his arms. My eyes scan the crowd, and that's when I see him—Gary, standing off to the side by himself. He's wearing a red speedo that I'm pretty sure he's not comfortable in if the way he's trying to hide against the wall says anything. He has no reason to worry. He really is fucking cute, in a quiet Gary way.

"I like you, Travis." Steven's words pull me out of my thoughts of Gary before he continues. "I do, but I'd be lying if I didn't say I'm a little nervous. I'm where I am in my life because I take my business seriously. This is a lot of money, and I have a few concerns. Looking at your experience, you haven't done anything long-term. What happens to me if you decide this isn't what you want?"

"I won't," I tell him. We stop moving and I face him, attempting to plead with my eyes. I'm not good at asking for help, at asking for anything, so I try to do it the only way I know how. "There's nothing I can say to prove how I feel. I get that. And I know this is your money, and you have to make the best decision for yourself, but I believe I'm that. I wouldn't be here if I didn't. I love what I do. It's the only thing in my life I've ever wanted, and I'm good at it. I'm good with people. On paper, I know I don't look like an ideal candidate. All I have is my word and my future actions that can prove it. I work hard. I'm honest, I'm loyal, and I know what I'm doing. If I wasn't sure this would be a good deal for both of us, I wouldn't be here right now."

"I'm not saying no," he tells me, and I finally feel like I can breathe. "I'm saying, I need a little more incentive. I need a little more time to make sure this is a good deal for both of us."

"I wouldn't want it any other way. If you jumped in headfirst, I'd have reservations of my own."

Steven smiles, showing me that was the right response. "Come on. Let's enjoy this fundraiser a little bit."

"Let's do it." I'm not sure why, but my eyes find Gary again. When I follow his intense stare, I see Peter and Evan on the receiving end of it, and I feel bad for the guy. He hasn't seemed to learn that most of the time, people let you down.

5
Gary

I'm so fucking old.

Twenty-six isn't old, but compared to twenty-two-year-old Evan, who looks like he could be in college, I'm basically ninety. I never had a chance competing with that. Peter's thirty-eight, and he's always had a thing for younger guys. Guess that's why I attracted him when I was twenty-one and fresh out of college.

I try to stop looking Peter and Evan's way. I don't want either of them knowing I still give a damn, but I can't help it. Even worse, Robyn's playing. I guess the universe knows I'm in the corner, watching Peter kiss him...oh-oh-oh. I figured Derek would offer me some sort of protection in all this, but he threw himself to a pack of bears right before my dickhead ex and his child-lover arrived. In an emerald-green speedo, Derek flaunts his twink body as he backs his ass up to the biggest bear of them all, who has a gray beard and a chest full of matching curly hair. Derek's abs shift about as he dances, his bangs flipping side to side with his movements. He knows how good he looks. Every time there's a costume or pool party, he picks out the skimpiest outfits that will be as revealing as possible. "Gotta show off the goods," he always says.

Derek can jump into every situation with any group of people and act confident. I'm not like that unless I get a good bit of liquor in me. Even then, I'm still reserved. This vodka Red Bull will help, but I figure it'll be another thirty minutes before I'm comfortable in this tight speedo that leaves me feeling like I did when I was bare-ass naked at the gym yesterday. Once again, I'm trying to act confident, but my discomfort must be easy to read.

With Peter being on so many boards, I'm no stranger to events like these, where I have to strut around in the tiniest speedo possible to fit in with everyone else's outfits, but I've never gotten used to dressing like this in public. I don't like feeling exposed. Vulnerable. And when Peter and Evan walked through the back door of the mansion-of-a-house hosting this event, I felt even more vulnerable.

I remind myself to breathe but also to suck in my stomach like Derek kept telling me to do before he wandered off.

"Hey, Gary," I hear someone say beside me.

When I turn, I'm relieved to see it's my friend Hayden. He looks incredible in a white speedo with light-blue polka dots. He wears a pair of thick, black-rimmed glasses. Between those and the six-pack abs, he's got the hot nerd look down. We've never hooked up. We met while I was with Peter, who's friends with Hayden's boyfriend. Hayden and I are the guys who chat and dance while our men work the room, pretending to enjoy conversations with people they'll talk smack about the moment we leave the bar.

I search around for Hayden's boyfriend, Lance, the sociable one of the two—the one everyone loves to be around because he has this power to make someone feel like they're the most important person in the world when they talk to him. Hayden's the same way, but much quieter about it. And unlike Lance, when Hayden listens to you, he genuinely cares—isn't pretending to care so that he can get people's attention.

"How's it going?" I ask as we hug.

"Pretty good," Hayden says. "We've been working on renovations on our place over at Viewpoint."

He talks about the changes they're making and how stressful it's been working with contractors before I notice something within my periphery.

In a gray box-cut swimsuit, the hottie I woke up with yesterday morning—Travis—chats with a small group of equally hot studs. He laughs and pats the ass of one of the guys beside him. Another young guy in front of him backs his ass up against Travis's pelvis and gyrates it about. Travis grabs the guy's hips and pulls him close, whispering something in his ear that makes the guy chuckle.

I blush.

I could never do something like that. There's a good foot between me and Hayden, and the closest I'd ever get to him or Derek...or any guy I wasn't with...would be for a hug.

I envy guys like Travis. How can he be so at ease in public? So comfortable about who he is? I've spent my life trying to hide that from everyone. He's not even like that here. He's so comfortable about being sexual. I can't help but wonder: if I'd tried something in the bedroom, would he have gone for it? If I'd been as forward as Derek had wanted me to be, would he have rolled with it?

Not that I would have had the balls to do that...not with a guy that hot. But he seems more like the kind who— had I done something wild...something so not me—would have thrown me on the bed and had his way with me.

Travis laughs with the guy who shook his ass against him. Travis now has both arms wrapped around him. His gaze shifts to me.

Fuck. Caught. Bail.

I turn back to Hayden.

"So, I was hoping to stick it in the back," he says.

I have no fucking clue what he's talking about, but now I'm imagining Travis's dick in my ass, and I realize my dick has been growing this whole time.

Fuck me to hell.

I turn so my hard-on is facing the wall beside me. Hayden doesn't seem to notice, and I'm hoping no one else will catch on.

"That sounds good, right?" Hayden asks me. "Just put the shoe rack in the back of the closet?"

"Yeah. Sounds great."

"Hey, stranger," a voice comes from beside me.

I tense up.

Hayden eyes me uneasily before I turn and see Peter approaching with Evan at his side.

For once, my anxiety around them works in my favor because it doesn't take my dick long to recover from what thinking about Travis did to it. I wait for it to settle before I turn the rest of my body toward the lying cheat.

I can understand Peter coming over, but with Evan? Evan can fucking go find a buddy to chat with. I don't need to be ambushed right now.

I search for Derek, who's still busy entertaining the bears. Fortunately, as I look to Hayden, a wink assures me he's got my back. I move close to him, shifting my body to face off with Bastard and Bastard's Lover.

"Glad you made it out today, Gary," Peter says, offering a smile.

I can tell he's shaved his chest and torso for the event. The longest he ever lets the grays grow out on his chest is a half inch or so. He usually cuts it the night before events like this. His jet-black hair is, like so much of our relationship was, a lie. I used to help him dye the spots he couldn't see in the back of his head. Guess that's Evan's job now.

Evan's about my size but blond with gorgeous hazel eyes. He's shorter than me and a lot prettier. His smile, filled with perfect teeth that must've cost someone a fortune, reminds me of his modeling past—something Derek and I learned when we Facebook-stalked him after I discovered Peter's betrayal.

I never stood a chance against this guy.

"Derek wasn't going to miss this for the world," I say, stressing that my reason for being here had nothing to do with him.

"How you been?" I can tell by the way Peter asks that he's reaching for something. It's the way he'd talk to me if he wanted me to tell him why I was having a hard day at work.

Why do you think I'm having a bad day, asshole? You think that having to confront my ex and his new guy is easy for me?

"I'm fine," I say quickly, hoping the shorter I am with him, the sooner they'll leave me alone.

He studies me, and I worry he's sensing my uneasiness. Then he asks Hayden, "How's the new place working out for you guys?"

Hayden launches into his spiel about his and Lance's place. He doesn't go into great detail. He talks to Peter the way he would if some stranger was asking about the same thing. But he still manages to drag it out like he's working to keep Peter's attention off me, which I appreciate. After a few minutes, Hayden starts chatting Evan up.

"I'm a little concerned about you, kiddo," Peter mutters.

Kiddo? That's his pet name for me. I never liked it, but now I really don't like it.

"Why are you concerned?" I ask.

"You know, people talk."

"Are there rumors about me that don't involve you and Evan?"

He looks slightly shocked by my confrontational response.

"Gary, I know you're still hurt about what happened, but you don't have to act out."

"How am I acting out?"

"Yesterday morning, Evan and I saw you from his place. You were with a guy. That kid, Travis."

Evan's unit is on the sixteenth floor in the opposite tower. I usually keep my blinds cracked during the day to let a little light in. I close them at night since I can see into the bedrooms on the lower floors in the North Tower when people leave them cracked open. Figure if I can see into theirs, other people can see into mine. But I was so drunk the other night, I didn't even think about it.

He totally thinks we were messing around, and I'm not going to lead him to believe otherwise, especially if it's bothering him, which it must be if he's bringing it up now.

"What does that have to do with you?" I ask.

"Nothing, but, Gary, the guy's trouble. You know he's a massage therapist, right?"

I didn't, but apparently he's even more handsy than I'd previously considered.

"So...?"

"Guys talk about the kinds of things he does for them sometimes. And it doesn't surprise me, considering he's not exactly a saint around town. I'm just saying...he's not the kind of guy you can trust. He's—"

Heat flashes to my face.

"The kind of guy who'll cheat on me?"

"That was different. I fell for someone outside of us. I was a coward. I didn't have the balls to tell you that. This Travis guy. He's bad news."

"He's been nothing but good to me."

Which is true. Just not in the way I make it sound.

"He uses guys for sex."

Who is he to tell me this?

The rage he's stirred is too much for me to contain. I spit out, "Maybe that's what I needed to get over you. A guy who uses me for sex. Travis gives me the incredible, mind-blowing sex I needed...the kind I never got when we were together."

I'm enjoying leading him to believe I'm already running around, having all this awesome sex. That I'm so over him that I'm having this incredible affair with someone as hot as Travis. He'll find out soon enough that there's nothing going on, but it gives me some satisfaction right now.

Peter starts to say something, but before he can get anything out, I notice someone approaching me from my side.

I turn and see Travis, a broad smile across that gorgeous face of his. I'm looking directly into his beautiful hazel eyes—greener toward the center and browner on the edges.

He wraps an arm over my shoulder.

"Hey, sexy," he says before kissing me.

Fire fills my cheeks.

What the fuck is happening right now? Did he overhear what we were talking about?

What does he think about me implying that I was hooking up with him?

Although, with our lips locked, it's obvious he doesn't mind. Is he helping me out?

These thoughts race through my mind in a moment before I abandon all concern and enjoy his wet tongue as it slides between my lips.

He hugs me and strokes up and down my back, his fingers pressing into my muscles. Considering how it feels to have him caress me like this, I imagine he must give people some incredible massages. I'd pay for this shit.

My dick stirs to life again, but I don't care because right now, the only thing in the world that exists is Travis and the hottest fucking kiss I've ever had in my life.

6
Travis

Gary moans softly into my mouth. I swallow it down, tighten my hold on him as his blunt nails bite into the skin of my back. His tongue sweeps my mouth, and his body presses against mine. He's all fucking hunger and need, and all I can think is, *Christ, he can kiss*. They always say it's the quiet ones, and I've never seen it until now. He gives me another sexy, little groan. Nips my lip, and fuck if I don't wish we were somewhere more private so I could see if he would really let loose.

I press another quick kiss to his lips before I pull back, put my arm around his shoulder and tuck his head against my neck. I have no fucking clue what I'm doing here. All I know is I glanced over and saw Peter and his boy talking to Gary. The tenseness rolled off him, showed in the stiffness of his body and the way he took a step back, almost like he wanted to disappear.

Steven had excused himself a little while before and told me to relax and have a good time, which I'd tried, but then I'd seen Gary over here, and I'd had the urge to save him—which is a pretty fucking foreign emotion if I'm being honest. When I got close enough to hear Gary talking about the mind-blowing sex I gave him, I decided to go for it, hoping I didn't take a knee to the balls, even if it was just out of plain shock.

Now that the kiss is over, Gary's like a board against me. Peter looks like he wants to hit me but also has his mouth wide open like he can't believe Gary's out getting dick instead of weeping over him. Forget the fact that Gary might very well be weeping over Peter. I have no fucking idea. All I know is, I'm pretty sure he's a smug bastard who really needs to be put in his place.

"Jesus, that fucking mouth. I can't get enough of it." I drop my hand and swat Gary on the ass, and he lets out a sharp squeak. "I love it when you make that sound."

Letting my eyes wander Peter's way, I say, "Oh, hey. I'm Travis," and reach out my right hand. My left arm is still wrapped around Gary, who sounds like he's slightly hyperventilating beside me.

He doesn't grasp my hand right away, looking at Gary and then back at me. Jesus, this guy is a stuck-up motherfucker. Is this the kind of dude Gary is into?

Finally, he grabs my hand and shakes it. "Peter. This is Evan. How long have you known Gary?"

This gets Gary's attention. "It's none of your business, Peter."

"Yeah. It's none of your business, Peter," I add and wonder what in the fuck I'm doing. I sound like I'm twelve.

Just then, I see movement out of my periphery. Instinctively, I know exactly who it is, and I'm caught between wanting to pull away from Gary because the last thing I need is for Steven, who already has questions about my character, to think I'm randomly fucking Gary, but also not wanting to hang Gary out to dry.

"Travis, I was looking for you." Steven zeroes in on the man beneath my arm. When Gary nudges my side, I realize I'm squeezing his shoulder.

"You know him?" Peter asks, and fuck my life for trying to help Gary out. All it's doing is creating a mess for me.

"Peter. It's good to see you." Steven holds his hand out for Peter, who shakes it a whole hell of a lot quicker than he did mine. "Travis and I are considering doing some business together." He turns his attention back to me. "I didn't realize you had a...friend here."

My pulse begins to slam against my skin. A bead of sweat rolls down the side of my face and stings my eye, but I force myself to ignore it. What are my choices here? If I say Gary is just a friend, then I give Peter's smug ass the satisfaction I don't want him to have and also, risk him telling Steven that basically I'm using Gary as a fuck-toy, which he no doubt believes. And no, there's nothing wrong with fuck-toys if both parties want to play, but it's not something that's really going to make Steven confident in dishing money out on me.

And I really want this fucking money. I need it.

So...I wing it. "I'm sorry. I wasn't sure if it was appropriate for Gary to be around while we spoke. Gary, this is Steven, the man I told you about. Steven this is my..." *Oh fuck. I am so screwed.* How did I get myself into this situation? "...My boyfriend, Gary."

Gary doesn't move. Doesn't breathe. Doesn't respond. I'm going to fucking kill him if he calls me out on this lie after I came over to save his ass. This is basically all his fault.

Speaking of ass...I lower my hand again and give his a gentle pat that I'm hoping says, *Play along. You owe me.* "Sorry. I think I rendered him speechless with the kiss I gave him a few moments ago. He does that to me every time I look at him."

That seems to shock Gary into action. "Don't be ridiculous, Travis. *You're* the one who nearly knocks me on my ass every time I see you."

Once. He fell on his ass once and that was Derek's fault for sending me to his bed.

"Hi, I'm Hayden," the other man, who I'd forgotten was there, speaks up. "Peter, Evan, you guys look great," he adds, and I'm pretty sure he's trying to take the attention off us.

"You get speechless when you look at me? Laying it on a little thick, don't you think?" Gary whispers tersely out of the side of his mouth.

"Fuck off. I'm going off the fly here."

Steven's attention zeroes back in on Gary. This time, he manages to shake the other man's hand. Peter's got his arms crossed, giving me a hard stare, and I really think I fucking hate this guy.

"Peter, let's go swimming," Evan tells him, which is a great idea if you ask me. I want them to get the fuck out of here as quickly as possible.

It's Steven who speaks next. "How would you and Gary like to have dinner with my partner and me next week, Travis? There are a few things I'd like to think through, and then the four of us can meet again and take it from there."

He's testing me. Not because he thinks I'm lying about being with Gary because who in the fuck really does that? But I think he's trying to see how much I want this. If I'm willing to be patient. Hell, judging by what he told me about his relationship, maybe being with Gary shows him I have some kind of stability that he thinks I'm lacking. "Yeah, that'd be great. What do you think, Gary?"

I look down at him and see a wild, sort of frantic look in his blue eyes. Luckily, he recovers quickly. "Of course. That'd be great. We'd love to."

"Good, good," he replies. "I'll get in touch with you on the date. Now have fun; go swimming, you two." Steven turns toward Peter. "I wanted to run a few fundraising options by you when you get a chance, Pete," he says, making it painfully obvious the two know each other well, at least through their fundraising work.

So, I've just tied myself into a relationship with the ex-boyfriend of someone who knows the man I'm trying to get money from for my business. What in the hell just happened here?

"That'd be great, Steve," Peter replies. "I'll talk to you soon, okay, Gare? I'll call you. There are a few things I want to talk to you about."

"Okay," Gary replies, still stiff as a door beside me.

Steven, Evan, and Peter walk away. Hayden chuckles, pats Gary on the shoulder, and then gives us space by leaving.

"You can loosen up a little you know? You kiss me like a man starving for my lips—fucking hot, by the way—and now you're standing here like someone shoved something up your ass and not in a way you enjoy."

"Excuse me if I'm trying to figure out what in the hell just happened!"

We must look at least a little suspicious. We're standing together awkwardly, my arm around him, both of us facing forward and speaking quietly out of the sides of our mouths.

"I kissed the hell out of you—and you kissed the hell out of me right back, I might add—after hearing you tell your ex how good I am in the sack. Things went downhill from there."

"Oh, fuck. Peter...he thinks..." He seriously sounds like he's on the verge of passing out.

Gary tries to pull away, but I don't let him get far. I lock his hand with mine and pull him so he's facing me. "Play it off for now, please. We can figure the rest of it out later. This is important to me." Fuck, if I don't hate admitting that, but it's true. Whatever it takes to convince Steven he can trust me, I'm willing to do.

Gary opens his mouth to reply, but Derek's voice cuts him off. "Christ on a cracker. Turn my back for five minutes and look what happens. You guys know you owe me one threesome with you."

"Derek, now is not the time," Gary rushes out.

"Fine. At least let me watch, but that's my final offer." He steps up to me, lets his hand roam down my chest, traces the lines of my abdominal muscles with his finger. "Fucking hot. You're welcome, Gary."

With a parting grin, Derek walks away and the two of us are alone again.

7
Gary

I study Travis's torso of fit, toned muscles. So many lines, so many curves—all of which, given the opportunity, I would eagerly worship with my tongue. The thick veins in his biceps, obliques, and shoulders push forward as they struggle to be contained by his beautiful, smooth flesh.

The fact that I can appreciate his body after everything that was just thrown at me speaks to how hot he is.

He narrows his eyes as he looks at me like he's deep in thought.

I'm glad one of us can think right now because I'm still reeling from the thrill of that kiss. Excited as it made me, it also terrifies me. Our lip-lock knocked the thoughts right out of my head, and something within me took over—something hungry for wild, uninhibited sex. I wanted to fuck Travis right then and there. Forgot about everything, even my d-bag ex and his new boyfriend. I was consumed in the moment, not caring why Travis was kissing me, only that he was. The taste of whiskey on his tongue, the sensation of his breath rushing across my face, and his hot touch were the only things that mattered to me.

I'm sure it was only a few moments, but it felt like we were lost in each other for hours. Well, I was lost in him. Even as he stands before me, thinking through what just happened, I know I was the one who was blown away. This is likely just another day for a sexy-as-sin guy like him.

"We're in a bit of a jam here, Hot Ass," he says, moving even closer, his torso rubbing up against mine, his lips inches from my face. I could easily lean forward and kiss him again, so I'm forced to fight every impulse in me to take advantage of the opportunity.

Act like a fucking human, Gary!

"Who was that guy you were talking to?" I ask. That came out way more defensively than I meant because there are too many questions running through my brain for me to process at once.

"A guy who can get me the cash to make my dreams come true. And a guy who thinks I might not be reliable enough to make good business decisions because I don't have much of a track record with anything long-term. He seems to think being able to hold down a man means something about my skills as a businessman. Don't get me wrong. I am good at holding down a man."

I'm blushing again. Fuck him for oozing sex and charisma.

I force myself to pay attention to the issue at hand. "So, you were using me—"

"You told your ex we hooked up to make him jealous, so who was using who here?"

I was right. He heard me and then he pitied me. That's the only reason any of this happened.

My face fills with heat, but now not from the passion of his hot kiss. Just 'cause I'm embarrassed that I'm the guy he had to bail out of an awkward jam.

"Thank you," I say.

He scrunches up his face.

"Thank you? I need a little more than a thank-you right now."

If he wanted it, he could have a lot more than a thank-you.

"You gotta come to this dinner thing with me," he says. "I assume you have a good suit to wear. Maybe a few too many because you seem uptight enough that you probably wear one for work occasionally."

True, but it doesn't keep me from being offended.

I pull away from him. Hot as he may be...and hard as my dick still may be from that kiss...I don't have to take this.

"This is how you ask for a favor?" I keep my voice low, despite wanting to shout at him for being such an ass.

"Come on. I'm kidding. Trying to get you to ease up a bit. You're all tense, not to mention hot and bothered. I helped you out of a jam, so I'm asking you to help me out of one."

"I'm sorry, but this is crazy, and I can hardly even think right now."

I turn to walk away.

This is the stupidest situation I could have gotten myself into, but I'm getting out of it right now.

A few people glance our way. We obviously created quite a few scenes together at this party.

I try to yank my hand free of Travis's grasp, but he holds on tight and pulls me back to him, forcing another kiss.

The explosion happens all over again. Everything I'm pissed about, everything that's bothered me disappears as I'm left with this hot moment and my desire to have him all to myself. To taste every part of him. To give him the sort of pleasure a guy like Travis must need. To work that fat cock of his until he blows his load in my mouth.

I hate myself for how much I want him. My body's betraying me.

And my dick is hard as a fucking rock.

His tongue greets mine, and I accept it. I won't fight this. *Can't* fight this.

My body trembles with excitement as Travis releases my hands and strokes up and down my back, down to my ass, cupping both cheeks. He must be a good massage therapist. Every touch, every stroke feels so perfect—like he knows just how much pressure to apply to each muscle. Like he fucking took a class on The Art of Making a Guy Horny as Shit.

If he gets to enjoy my body, I don't see why I can't enjoy his, so I grab hold of him. Quickly. Desperately. Like this might be the last chance I ever get. I pull so close to him that his ripped torso is pressed against mine, and his hard cock—that big fucking cock—is against my pelvis.

He pushes me back against the cement wall before breaking our kiss.

Every nerve in my body is on edge, but my muscles are surprisingly relaxed.

"Why the fuck did you just do that?" I ask. Not that I have a problem with it, but I'm curious.

"In case you haven't noticed, we got a lotta people watching us right now, so if we're going to keep this up, we need to put on a good show. Plus, you're a whole lot more agreeable when I have my tongue down your throat."

He gives my ass another squeeze. "Now can you do me a solid here and help a guy out? I'm not asking for much. Just one dinner. Please."

"I don't think we're going to be able to pull this off. I'm not a fucking actor, for Christ's sake."

"You didn't need to be an actor to make them believe you a few minutes ago. Why is it any different?"

He's right. I've never done anything like this before, but we were able to convince all those guys that we're an item, so maybe I can.

"Which would you rather people think?" he asks. "You're moping around, feeling sorry for yourself because that asshole who didn't deserve you to begin with was a sleaze and moved in with another guy? Or that you're so fucking over him that you've already fallen in love with a hot new piece of ass? That's why you started lying to him earlier, isn't it? You wanted him to think that you'd moved on. Why not throw this in his fucking face, and give a guy who could use a break a little help?"

I should think this over. I should consider the consequences of my actions, but with his body pressed up against me as he practically pins me to the wall, offering something I so desperately crave—getting to throw this all back in Peter's face—I can't deny him.

"I'm in," I say, surrendering to this sexual spell he has me under, as so many other guys have done before me.

The way his lip curls into his dimple is sly, reminding me this isn't a guy I can trust. I need to remember that. With a pretty face like his, it seems like something that'd be easy to forget.

He leans forward and kisses me again.

I figure he's going along with our act, so I kiss him back, enjoying the taste of his mouth, the sensation of his flesh against mine. I nip at his lip again. I imagine him turning me around. Pulling my speedo down to my ankles. Pushing within me. He would be like an animal, biting at my ear as those skilled hands probed my body.

He pulls away, and I find myself leaning toward him, trying to make the experience last a little longer.

I notice how many people are looking at us now.

"Guess you did a good job convincing everyone," I say.

He glances around, his eyes narrowing before he looks back at me. "I wasn't trying to convince anyone of shit. That one was for fun."

He grips my ass. "I got a few appointments I got to get to, so let's ditch, and we can chat more later."

"Works for me."

As we walk side by side to the main house, his hand on my ass, I'm left wondering, *What the mother-loving-fuck did I get myself into?*

8
Travis

We exchanged numbers before I told Gary to meet me at my place at six. I want to confirm we're on the same page with this whole fake relationship thing because while it'll be fun to fuck with Peter's head, this is actually extremely important to me.

Life changing.

Tilting my head to the right, I take my eyes off the steering wheel in front of me and look at the massive, white Colonial style house across the street. My brothers' cars are parked out front, along with others I don't recognize. It looks quiet from the front, but I know them. I know everyone is out back in Mom's prized gardens she loves to show off so much. They'll be drinking wine and chatting. The event will be catered, of course. Malcolm and Martin will play their parts perfectly, even though inside they'll hate every fucking second of it.

The thought makes my skin feel too tight and my jaw go so tense it hurts. It's bullshit, having to play a part like that. Having to be someone you're not so people love you. Who the hell needs love if it's conditional? I sure as shit don't.

Still, I'm here, and I don't want to let myself think about why that is. Instead, I grab the bouquet of flowers off the passenger seat and get out of the car.

The grass surrounding the custom walkway looks like synthetic turf, it's so damn green. It's not, of course, because Abigail Waller won't be bested by anything, even if it is fucking grass.

Once I get to the porch, I set the bouquet down, with the unsigned card inside that simply says, Happy

Birthday, before I put my sunglasses on, and then make my way back down the walkway again.

My whole body is buzzing—not the good kind either. Almost like I want to break out of my skin. I make it to my car, turn it on, and peel away from the curb. All of this because I ruined her idea of the perfect family, just because of who I like to fuck.

Speaking of fucking, I let my mind go back to Gary and the sexy little sounds he made when I kissed him. There was a second I thought he was going to climb me like a tree right there, and I would have let him. There's a beast in there waiting to break free. Has he let him out before, or does he always keep himself locked away?

There's a part of me that really wants to find out, wants to make him let loose, show me what that sexy ass of his can do. But even though I think he's got a closeted, kinky freak living inside of him, I'm not sure if I should be the one to let him out to play. Would it be fun? Fuck yes, but Christ, he was with that prick for five years. Gotta admit that makes me want to run the other way. That sure as hell isn't what I'm looking for.

The only thing I'm focused on right now is getting Steven to put up the money for me to get my place.

After finishing my errands, I stop by this little café down the street from Metropolis. I order two salads to go, dressing on the side, and then make it back to my condo in time to change into my workout clothes before there's a knock on my door.

I pull it open to see Gary, looking like the all-American boy-next-door, with his sandy-blond hair, shorts, and a polo shirt. I don't know why in the hell I think it's so fucking cute, but I do.

"Hey, Hot Ass. It's good to see you." I lean toward him and take a taste of his mouth. Just tease him a little with my tongue to earn one of his sounds. He's holding back. I feel it in the press of his lips. *Who are you hiding in there, boy?*

Once we part, Gary steps inside. "Can you just please not call me *Hot Ass*?"

"No." I close the door behind him.

"Why not?" He shakes his head like he doesn't understand me, and it makes me smile. "No one is going to believe that. You're going overboard."

Huh. That's interesting. "Why wouldn't anyone believe it?"

He cocks his head and lifts a brow like I just asked the stupidest question in the world.

Does he really not see it? "You have a hot ass, Gary. Own that shit." I nod toward the bar. "Sit."

He takes two steps...then stops. "I'm not a dog."

"So, no puppy play for you? Got it. Glad we're getting the parameters of our relationship set up now."

"Oh my God. I can't do this. I changed my mind." He moves toward the door again, but I reach out and grab his wrist.

"Nope. You already agreed. Plus, it was a joke. You know, ha-ha. Not that I would be averse to playing around. I'll try anything once. Will you?"

His blue eyes blow wide and his arm goes stiff. "What...I...are you..."

A laugh jumps out of my mouth, one I'm unable to hold back, and then Gary jerks his arm away and says, "I fucking hate you."

"Is this our first fight?"

He sighs, and I have a feeling I'm exhausting him. I don't know why I enjoy that thought. It's fun messing with him. I like getting under his skin.

"Fine, whatever. But no one was in the hallway. You didn't have to kiss me."

"Kissing is an underrated activity. I like to kiss, and by the way, you nearly lose it every time I kiss you. I think you like it, too. Nothing wrong with a little practice so we make it realistic when we're around people. Sit," I tell him and nod toward the bar again. He opens his mouth, making it obvious he's going to refuse me, so I add, "I got you a salad. Have you eaten?"

Something flashes in his eyes, an emotion I can't read. "You got me a salad?" he asks as though he's surprised I thought of him. That doesn't make me real confident on how well Peter treated him. By the sound of it, I'm a better fake boyfriend than he was a real one.

"Yes. It's just a salad, but if you don't sit and eat the fucking thing, I'm going to get my feelings hurt." I walk over to one of the bar stools and sit down. Gary pauses before he walks over and takes a seat beside me.

We eat in silence for a few minutes. When I can't take it anymore, I tell him, "Now, as soon as I get a date from Steven, I'll let you know. And for your part, to really fuck with Peter's head, I think we need to be seen together—gym, coming and going from each other's condos, shit like that. It would be beneficial if you didn't do that initial freeze-up when I first kiss you and just go straight into the part where you kiss me like you want to rip my clothes off and mount me."

Gary coughs, following it with a pat to his chest before coughing again.

"Are you okay?" I ask.

"Lettuce." He says before coughing again. I grab my bottle of water and hand it to him, and he swallows half of it down.

"You gonna live?"

"I don't kiss you like I want to mount you!"

Deciding to have a little fun with him, I lean close. "Oh yeah, Hot Ass, you do. Lips don't lie, and neither do dicks. Let's not pretend you weren't hard as stone when I had you against that wall."

He looks at me out of the corner of his eye like he's trying to be annoyed with me, but damned if I don't see him trying to bite back a smile. "And you weren't?"

"Never denied it." I wink at him. "Now finish your salad because we're going to the gym." I could use a little weight time to keep my mind off my family. It's going to be that or fucking.

"Already?" he asks.

"No time like the present."

For a moment, I think he's going to argue with me, but he doesn't. We eat and then head to his condo for him to change. It's the perfect opportunity to make a show, so I keep my arm possessively around him like I couldn't keep my hands off him if I wanted to.

When we get to his door, he says, "Oh, fuck. What about Jacob?"

"Are you worried he'll tell people we aren't dating? He won't say anything." I make a mental note to talk with Jacob about Gary and me. He's a cool guy. I know we don't have to worry about him spilling the truth.

"You know that, why? Because you fucked him?" He doesn't sound convinced.

"Yes, actually. My cock has the ability to control even the strongest of men. Once you've had it, you'll listen to me a whole lot easier than you do now, too," I tease and again, watch his eyes go wide.

"How did I get myself into this mess?" he asks and opens the door. Jacob doesn't seem to be here, which I think makes it a little easier on Gary. Gotta slowly work him into this stuff.

He heads for his bedroom, me right behind him. "What are you doing? I need to get changed." He looks absolutely scandalized.

"I'm enjoying the view. It's nothing I haven't seen before, remember?" I say as I walk into his room, sit on the bed and wait for the show.

9
Gary

Here he is again. In my room. Looking hot as ever in a navy-blue tank with a pink stripe across the chest. He's the kind of guy who could wear a fucking pink tutu and he'd still look like the most masculine guy in the world. I slide the door to my closet open. My Ikea shelves are packed—folded tees and polos at the top and shorts, jeans, and underwear at the bottom. Not enough space in my closet to change, so the only way I can get some privacy is to head into the adjoining bathroom. That's what I should do—that's what I would normally do—but I don't want to leave.

I already know he likes what he sees. I keep acting like this is all one-sided, but he's already made it clear that it's not. I recall his little joke about how if I didn't eat the salad, he'd get his feelings hurt.

His words were dripping with sarcasm, as if there was no way that could ever happen. I imagine he's never had to live through the sort of grief I experienced with Peter. I envy him. I've always gotten attached. After I'd hook up with a guy, there was always the lingering question, "Should we see each other again?" It's been about finding a relationship for me. Was the guy interested in more? Was I interested in more?

I'm not worried about that with Travis. I've seen him at Flirt and know how he is with guys. He'd fuck anyone with a pulse...and I've already seen that he wouldn't be totally against fucking me.

I grab a pair of gym shorts and a tank top. I feel him watching me. He's waiting for me to chicken out. Waiting for me to race out of the room because I'm too much of a coward to handle him seeing me naked.

But he's already seen everything and by now, groped everything.

In the back of my mind, a part that's always so loud seems faint as it cries out, *Don't do it!*

I can't deny what I'm feeling right now or that it only seems fair that if Peter's moved on, I should be able to as well. And I know that's partially what this is all about. Yeah, he's hot as fuck, but knowing it would piss Peter off excites me. Just knowing this would irritate him. That it would make him feel even a fraction of what he made me feel when I found out about Evan.

I throw my tank and gym shorts onto the bed and strip down. Even knowing he's seen it all before, I worry he might suddenly realize he's been wrong about thinking I'm attractive. About calling me Hot Ass—a nickname that, even though I pretend not to like, excites me. A lot more than kiddo.

His gaze is right on me, and soon I'm in my boxer briefs.

Now that faint voice in the back of my head has gotten even quieter because I just had a wicked thought—one that will likely wind up embarrassing me. But what do I care if Travis thinks I'm being ridiculous? I hardly even know him.

I grab either side of my boxers and drop them to the floor.

"Oh, really?" he says. "I didn't figure you'd need to change those."

I smirk, feeling particularly clever. "It's my good underwear."

There's that look in those hazel eyes. Pure, animalistic desire. When it comes to sex, he's easy to read. I can't imagine being as transparent as him, letting the world know how horny I am, letting everyone know just how much I want them.

It's reassuring.

He doesn't make a move, which is strange. I was kind of expecting the big porn scene where he leaps at me and ravages my body, takes me the way I clearly need to be taken. Instead, he keeps his gaze fixed on me, and standing here, naked before him, I realize I have total control of this moment. I can make this go either way. Grab some fresh underwear or take this somewhere else...somewhere different. Do something crazy. Something I wanted to do when we kissed at the pool party.

Stop being a coward for once in your fucking life, I scold myself.

"You might want to cover up before I decide to do something real bad to you," he says, his mouth hardly moving as the words slip past his lips.

"What did you have in mind?" I ask.

This isn't like at the gym or the pool party, where I felt so uneasy. I felt like people were going to judge or scrutinize me. He doesn't seem like he'd do that, and I feel oddly at ease standing like this in front of him—probably because I can see the interest in his expression. A look that seems to tell me how much he wants to bend me over and fuck the hell out of me right now.

He rises from the bed and starts toward me, scanning my body in a way that lets me know how interested he is. His lips curl upward as his gaze meets mine, something predatory in his expression.

"Just so we're clear," he says. "I'm not exactly the five-year relationship kind of guy."

"Perfect. I wasn't any good at that anyway."

He rushes me so quickly I back up against the wall beside the closet before his lips smack against mine.

As I kiss him, my thoughts scatter.

What the fuck?

A wave of heat flashes across my face and relief wells within me as his kiss assures me that he wants this as much as I do. I'm lost in the passion...in gropes and sweeps of his tongue. I'm blinded by how good it all feels. By how my face is on fire and a powerful sensation stirs in my chest.

He pulls away, offering a stern look as he wipes his thumb across my cheek. "I warned you about what would happen if you didn't cover up."

"I wanted to show you something," I say.

He scans me up and down. "And what is that?"

I lean to him, whispering, "Why I deserve the name Hot Ass."

The lust in his eyes returns. It's beyond interest. It's something feral. Something wild. Something I'm not sure he can control.

He kisses me again.

I slide my hands under his tank and claw at his back.

My cock is hard as stone, sliding up against the fabric of his shorts. My balls feel full. They ache like I need to rub one out. And it's nice knowing I have Travis to help me with that.

"Please...tell me you...have condoms," he says between kisses.

I guide him toward my nightstand, continuing to kiss him. I grip his hair and tug.

I don't know what's possessing me. Don't understand half the desires within me. But I don't care. I want to explore. I want to experiment, and I want Travis to help me.

We make out as he kicks off his shoes on the way to the nightstand, where I fish around for the box of condoms. It's clear we both use Magnums, which is a relief. Sometimes, a moment like this isn't so easy. Peter always needed a much smaller size.

As I pull out the box, Travis snatches it from me and throws it on the bed, the condoms sliding out and scattering across the covers.

I shove Travis. Hard. He falls back onto some of the gold wrappers on the comforter, and I yank his shirt up and bury my face in his abs.

I can't control myself right now. Primal impulses consume me—force my hands up and down his sides, feeling his muscles as my tongue takes in the taste of his flesh.

He removes his shirt and tosses it off the other side of the bed. I kiss down to his gym shorts, trailing my nose along his dick, dreaming about having that giant cock inside me. I lick my tongue across the fabric, along his shaft.

As I become impatient with the barrier between us, I yank off his gym shorts, removing them hastily, exposing that beautiful, fully-erect, vein-covered dick.

I realize how much I've missed that since I saw it yesterday when Travis woke up in my bed.

I gaze up at Travis, who looks back with narrow eyes, a curious expression on his face.

"Well, aren't you full of surprises?" he says.

I smirk before burying my face in his balls, licking them, teasing them, allowing my instincts to guide me as I slide my tongue around them, delighting in how he tastes like a fucking man and how I'm making him leak onto his abs right now.

I take in a whiff of his pubes before I surrender my work here and crawl onto the bed over him, my knees on either side of Travis's hips as I settle onto his waist.

"I need this, Travis," I say. "I need you to shove this fat cock inside me and make me come."

What is possessing me? I guess just because I know this is what he does with guys. And if I'm going to pretend to move on from Peter, why not actually do it? And if we're going to do this, I want it all. I deserve it after all the mediocre sex I had with Peter.

He grabs the back of my head and pulls me down to him, kissing me hard. I break it for a moment, whimpering softly.

He grabs my hair, clinging to it, keeping me from leaning back down to kiss him.

"I'll give you something to whimper about," he says.

He grips his arms around my thighs and twists his body, rolling so he ends up on top of me.

He licks my neck as he grabs one of the condoms beside him.

He suits up and leans over to the nightstand. He retrieves a bottle of lube from the open drawer and dispenses some before lathering it over his shaft.

I can't help but smile knowing that in a moment this nagging emptiness within me will be filled.

He's teased me too much. He's brought me too far to leave me hanging now.

His chest expands and compresses with heavy breaths.

"Jesus, you're a fucking animal." He sounds like he's impressed. And I feel proud, knowing it must take a lot to impress a guy like him.

He pushes my legs back as he walks on his knees to me. He presses the head of his dick against my hole, and I throw my head back, preparing for his entry.

I'm filled with this inexplicable hunger that's made me this needy bottom for him.

"Get inside me now," I say.

"You've got to be a little patient."

Fucking logistics. My body's too greedy for logic right now.

I need him shoving that cock inside me right now. Making me scream out. Bringing to life all those fantasies I've been playing out in my mind, ever since he first stirred desire in me when I'd watch him exercise in his living room.

When he pushes in, the pressure is intense. Even more than I was expecting, which makes me relieved that he opted to take his time.

Still, it feels so good. I can't help but make that sound again, and as I do, I see his eyes fill with eagerness.

I point my toes as I work to relax my body to allow him in me.

He's slow enough for me to adjust but quick enough that I don't get impatient.

Soon he's bringing to life all those nerves that he awakened at the pool party—some inexplicable chemistry between us that sets fire to everything within me.

It's like I haven't lived until this moment.

I grab his arms, bulky with muscles, as he pushes inside and works up into a stride.

I'm lost in his touch, in constant motion around my body, feeling his kisses, licks, nips, and bites across my flesh. Nipping back. There's a playful light in his eyes but also something furious—that same hot desire to reach the end of our destination.

We go until he's dripping with sweat and panting like he's run a marathon.

Every thrust hits my prostate, and a puddle of pre-come has collected on my abdomen.

His fingers make another sweep over my body. It's like he's grabbing at something that isn't there. "I can't fucking touch you enough," he says.

As much as I've tried to relax my muscles, I'm still tensed up because I've never had one this big inside me before.

But that sweet spot he hits makes it all worth it, sends the rushes of energy surging throughout my body.

I cry out.

"Fuck, Travis!"

He leans back, and like a champion...like the fucking sex god he is...he rams into me.

"Give me that cry. I want to hear you scream," he demands.

And I do. I unleash all the passion I've bottled up all these years.

Letting him know how much I love the feeling of having him inside me. I've never made these sounds before. No. These are from whatever this is that Travis has awakened within me. Whatever this thing is he's bringing out of me.

His movements are powerful and leave me trembling beneath him as my body works to keep up with all that he's giving me.

He leans down and kisses me.

"I want you to come," I tell him. "I want you to fill that condom while you're inside me."

But as soon as the words escape my lips, he pulls out.

"Get on your knees," he instructs.

I obey. I face the wooden headboard, on my knees, my palms before me, ready for him to take me.

He gets behind me, slides back in, grips my hair, and yanks back forcefully.

I submit, arching my body with his pull, and the position makes his entry hit all those sweet spots within me just right.

I grip the headboard with my right hand and reach back and cling onto his ass cheek with my other.

I fight his pull on my hair to glance down at my cock, which continues spilling pre-come across the covers.

I keep making that noise that reveals how good it all feels, and I can tell by his frenzied movements, it's making him even harder.

"God, you're gonna make me blow my load," he says.

"Do it."

"Uh-uh. Not until I get you off."

He leans forward so his torso is flush with my back. He reaches around with his free hand and jerks me off.

His face is right next to mine. He kisses my cheek furiously as his hand brings me closer and closer. Strings of pre-come drip from my cock.

"Goddammit," I say. "I'm gonna....Fuck..."

I spill across the sheets and then feel him violently rocking within me before his movements become a series of forceful jerks forward as he slams against my now-sensitive prostate.

Heat swells in my face and sweat drips down my body as he wraps his arms around me.

We pant and occasionally quake together as our bodies twitch, recovering from our climaxes.

"Ready to...hit...the gym?" he asks, panting.

I chuckle.

10
Travis

I sure as shit hadn't expected that to happen. Yeah, I knew Gary had a wildfire raging beneath the surface, just waiting to blaze uncontained, but I hadn't been real sure if he would be able to give in to it. Certainly not so soon. But he had and Christ, that fucking ass. If we continue to play together, this whole fake relationship thing might be a little more fun than I thought it would be.

As long as he isn't looking for anything more serious, we'll be good.

We'd gone to the gym like planned. He'd returned to being a little more reserved. He's a contradiction I haven't quite figured out. Despite the desire that had flared in his eyes, Gary had seemed fucking scandalized when I'd woken up in his bed the other morning. Add in the way he clearly wanted to fade into the background at the fundraiser—and again at the gym—with the way he let loose, begging me to fuck his ass and I don't know what to think.

I'd played my part well while working out—fucking and exercising are two of my favorite things—so the evening had worked nicely for me. I touched him often when people were watching and witnessed the confusion of how to act play across his face. When I'd kissed him good-bye, he went Greedy Power-Bottom Gary again, and I thought he would try to take me right there.

So yeah, quite the contradiction.

It's been three days since the fundraiser. I've played boyfriend every morning at the gym, gotten all the queens and everyone else at Metropolis talking, but I haven't heard from Steven yet, and it's starting to piss me off.

I glance at the time as I tap my thumb on the steering wheel. Traffic is fucking brutal, and I have to make it from Midtown to Sandy Springs for appointments today. I left one of my older male clients twenty minutes ago, and if shit doesn't change quickly, I'll be late for Vincent, one of my regulars.

"Fuck," I grit out as I look ahead of me with no end in sight. I usually try to keep my appointments a little closer together, but it doesn't always work that way.

I arrive fifteen minutes late to Vincent's town house. Luckily, he's an easygoing guy and understands. By the time we're in his room, my massage table open in front of the second-floor window that overlooks the city, I feel like I'm the one who needs to be rubbed down.

But the second my hands begin to knead his back, I'm in the zone. The tension begins to seep out of me while I work on him. There's something about this that I love, that just feels right for me, which is why Steven's money is so important.

"My lower back has been giving me some problems. Can you pay extra attention there?" he asks.

"Of course." I push the edge of the blanket covering his ass down slightly and begin to dig my thumbs into the small of his back. When I find a knot, I focus on it, trying to work it out. "Yeah, I can feel tension in here. We'll get you taken care of."

"Thank you," Vincent says and then lets out a long moan. It's deeper than the sounds Gary makes—which I have no clue what the fuck he has to do with anything, but there you go. "Jesus, your hands are like magic."

"So I've been told," I say playfully but then focus on the job at hand. An hour later, I'm packing up my supplies, and Vincent is watching me, wearing a pair of sweats and his arms crossed. We met when Vincent used to live at Metropolis, but he moved a few months back.

"I was at Flirt the other night. I miss the old neighborhood," he says.

"I'm sure you do. It's a whole lot easier to stumble down the block with a trick than it is to come all the way out here."

He smiles. "Are you calling me a slut?"

"Fuck yeah," I reply.

"Just making sure." We laugh. I finish packing my shit, and then I'm on my way. I have three more massages today. Luckily, those are all near one another.

Still, all I can think about is how much easier this would be if I had my own place.

***

By the time my day is over, I feel like shit. I make it back home, take a shower and then realize I haven't eaten since breakfast. After grabbing my cell, I head for the door. For some reason, I don't feel like eating alone. I start to head for Cody's unit but then keep going and make a call instead.

"Hello?" Gary asks timidly.

"You have my name in your phone. Why do you sound like you're not sure it's really me whenever I call?" It makes me chuckle.

"Because I'm still getting used to the fact that you call?"

"Are you hungry? I need dinner. Let's grab dinner. That's what boyfriends do." Stopping at the elevator, I push the button and wait.

There's a pause before he asks, "Has Steven called yet? I feel bad. You've been meeting me at the gym for the past few days, and now you want to go out to eat. I mean, it's working for me. Peter keeps trying to call, so he must be annoyed as fuck now that he thinks I'm actually moving on, which is awesome. But I feel like I'm just wasting your time. We don't have to make an appearance together every day. People aren't paying that much attention. They have a life outside of us."

"Fuck that. No one has a life outside of me," I tease. The elevator doors open, and I step inside, realizing that I *want* to meet Gary for dinner. It's fun trying to figure him out, trying to discover how he can be so wild in the sack and timid in his daily life.

And it's also easier to focus on Gary's shit than driving myself crazy and wondering why Steven hasn't called. "Just eat with me. I'm heading down."

"You're bossy."

"You like it."

"Ugh. I'll meet you downstairs." He hangs up the phone, and I realize another smile has spread across my lips. I don't know why he fights himself so damn hard or why I seem to be making it my business. But he does, and I am...and yeah, I'll scratch those thoughts too.

It takes him about ten minutes to meet me. When he arrives, I realize his hair is wet. He must have either just gotten out of the shower or he wet it to meet me. He's got this shy, unsure look on his face that presses my buttons in ways I wouldn't have thought. "You're cute," I tell him when he stops in front of me.

"I'm..." His brows pull together, and he gets this twitch under his right eye. "Why?"

"Don't ask *why* if someone says you're cute. Own that shit, Gary. Let's go." I open the door for him. He doesn't move, just stares at me before I signal for him to go out. When he does, I'm right behind him, and we're making our way down Cypress Street.

"Is Mike's okay?" I ask him. It's only about a block up the street. "We can eat on the patio up front. We'll be sure to be seen."

"Yeah, that works. I...thank you for doing this. You're going above and beyond."

I shrug, don't tell him that part of the reason we're heading to Mike's right now is because I find him intriguing. I've never known someone like him before, and the thing is, it's obvious he's a good guy. It pisses me off what that fucker Peter did to him, and that he's so in denial when given a compliment. He deserves better than that. "No problem."

It doesn't take us long to get there and be seated. We both order sweet tea before the waiter has a chance to get away from us, and then we're browsing the menu.

"You didn't answer my question on the phone," he tells me.

Without taking my eyes off the menu, I ask, "What question?"

"If Steven has called."

My stomach clenches tight. *No...no, he hasn't called, and it's driving me out of my fucking mind.* What if he doesn't? What if he changes his mind? "Nope." My eyes are still browsing the sandwiches.

Gary has a concerned tone to his voice when he speaks. "He will. Try not to worry about it. I'm sure he's just been busy. It'll all work out. It's obvious he wants to give you the money."

It's impossible to keep my eyes from darting his way now. I want to tell him I'm not worried because I hate feeling out of control, like I'm being given some kind of test to tell if I'm good enough because that's always what my parents did. But the truth is, I'm really fucking worried it won't happen. That I'll fail. There's also a part of me that wants to know how in the hell he realized I'm bothered, but I don't say that either. Instead, I answer with, "I'm thinking about getting the roast beef sandwich. I deserve some bread today. What about you?"

Gary gets a frown on his face, and there's something almost endearing about it. Like he's worried about me when he really doesn't know me all that well. Gary's got a big heart, and people tend not to waste theirs on me. He is, though.

The waiter shows up and asks if we're ready to order. I wait for Gary, who is still fucking looking at me like I'm a goddamned puzzle he's trying to figure out. Forget that I likely see him the same way—I don't make it as obvious as he does.

He orders a BLT, and I ask for the roast beef sandwich. When we're alone again, I lower my voice and ask, "How did we meet?"

"Huh?"

"If anyone asks, how did we meet?"

"I don't know. How everyone meets? We were out at Flirt, went home together."

I roll my eyes. "Yeah, but that happens all the time with everyone. I've gone home with a shit-ton of men from Flirt, and my ass has never dated any of them."

"You've never been serious about anyone?" he asks.

"Nope. And don't plan on it. So, back to us—why were you different? How did you tame the beast?"

He nearly snorts sweet tea through his nose. "Tame the beast?"

"Obviously. Now answer." I'm curious how he'll respond. Gary doesn't seem like the type who has a whole lot of good things to say about himself.

He shakes his head. "I don't know. You tell me."

"Could be because you're a hot piece of ass." I lean back in my chair and stretch my legs out in front of me.

"There you go. There's your answer, though I doubt I'm the only good lay you've had."

"It could also be because you're shy and not cocky, and that's so fucking different from me that I find it interesting." That one seems to surprise him, which makes me want to keep going. "Hmm...but you're not completely shy. You're like the wolf in sheep's clothing—quiet and submissive on the outside but a fucking beast on the inside." I'm enjoying this, I realize. The banter we have together.

"I thought you were the beast?" he asks.

"We both are." He looks away, takes a drink, and I add, "Maybe I just thought there was a lot more going on with you than you showed the world, and I wanted to find out what those other pieces were." Which is more truth than fiction, but he doesn't need to know that.

His eyes get intense, emotions flashing through them that I don't understand. It makes me shift uncomfortably. "I'm good at this game. If massage therapy doesn't work out, I can be a boyfriend-for-hire—oh, food's coming." The waiter brings our plates. I avoid Gary's eyes because I'm nervous he'll see those things I said were true. That I do think there's more to him than he shows the world, only I don't know what it is...but there's a part of me that wants to.

We eat in near silence. Even though he argues with me, I pay for the meal, and then we walk back to Metropolis.

"I'll walk you up," I tell him.

"You don't have to do that."

"I know." When we get to his door, my phone buzzes in my pocket. I pull it out and see Steven's name on the screen. *Thank God.* I close my eyes because I really thought he wouldn't call. "It's him," I say, then answer the call. "Hi, Steven, it's good to hear from you."

My pulse jackhammers. Just because he's calling doesn't mean he still wants to meet. He could change his mind. What the fuck would I do if he changed his mind?

"Travis, sorry about the delay. Things have been crazy. How does next Friday night look for you and Gary?"

Fuck, yes! "He's right here. Let me ask him." Turning to look at Gary, I say, "Steven wants to meet next Friday night. Does that work for you?" Then I add, "babe," because I'm obviously an overachiever.

Shock flashes in Gary's expressive eyes. "Yeah...yeah, of course."

Steven gives me the time and says he'll text the address. The second we get off the phone, I'm picking Gary up and squeezing him in my arms and spinning us around. "Oh my God! I can't believe I'm going to admit this, but I was scared as hell he would tell me he changed his mind! I'm one step closer, Gary!" And then I'm sandwiching him between my body and the door. His legs are around me, and my hands are on his ass. "I just..." *I'm so happy...hopeful...*but those things feel too close for me to speak out loud. I don't know what to say so I let my lips slam down on his. My tongue sweeps his mouth, and he shudders against me. His hands go into my hair and now he's Sex-God Gary again. I knead his cheeks and think about dipping my finger into his crack. Rubbing that tight little hole of his and opening it up for my cock.

But at the same time, I feel like I'm going to burst out of my skin with anticipation for our dinner with Steven.

The door next to his opens and someone clears their throat. I look at the blond man and let my first thought burst free. "Sorry. I can't keep my hands off him. He just made my fucking night."

Gary nearly chokes on his tongue. I press another kiss to his mouth, set him on his feet and then head down the hallway, hope zipping through my insides. "Thank you, Gary!" I yell as I walk away, knowing he's probably bright red behind me. "I don't know what I would do without you!" Doors start opening, everyone wondering what the hell is going on.

"Holy shit," someone says, "he's got it bad."

No. I've got a chance. That's all I've ever wanted. A chance to make my dreams come true.

11
Gary

"This is fucking ridiculous," Derek exclaims as I watch the green bar inch across the screen, letting me know how close we are to the end of this virus scan.

"Derek, I'm pretty confident it's from watching all that free online porn."

I sit in front of his laptop at the desk in his bedroom, facing the wall-length window that overlooks the pool deck on the seventh floor.

"I need to fucking use that tonight," Derek says.

"Why? To watch more porn?"

Derek glares at me. He just got home from work, so he's all dressed up, wearing a short-sleeved button-down with a black bow tie. His hair's gelled into an arc over his head.

He groans and stomps away from the desk, walking alongside his bed. "I think I might be able to schedule in a ten o'clock and a two thirty."

Tomorrow's Saturday, so he's obviously talking about tricks, not clients.

"This is why I came over here? So you could line up your weekend fucks?"

He approaches the dresser on the other side of his bed, opens the top drawer, and retrieves a set of powder-blue binoculars before returning to the window.

"The blinds aren't even shut," I say. Not judging him for the binoculars since I have my own pair. Just for how obvious he's being.

"Whatever. They can all do the same thing. I'm not ashamed."

He looks down at some of the hunks in speedos who lie across lounge chairs around the pool. Hard not to look down when there are so many abs and bulging packages to enjoy. This view is basically an amenity.

"Not all of us have a fake boyfriend we can hit up anytime for a booty call."

I told Derek right after the fundraiser to keep his big mouth shut about our lie because I'm not interested in becoming the next featured story in *David Magazine* or *Project Q* or some other Gay Atlanta news source as the freak who made up a convoluted lie so I could convince my d-bag ex I'm not the pathetic miserable loser I am.

"Speaking of which," I say, "we have that big dinner tonight."

Strange to think we've already been doing this for nearly two weeks.

"Oh, yeah," he says, not pulling the binoculars from his face as he continues perusing the hotties below. "Speaking of which...you're being careful about this, right?"

"Yeah. We used condoms."

He lowers the binoculars.

"That's not what I meant. You're not exactly the kind of guy who hooks up, and then calls it quits. You were in a relationship for five years."

"Trust me, the last thing I want is to get involved with a guy like Travis."

He eyes me suspiciously. "But you are involved with him."

"What are you talking about? This is all just an act."

And a convincing one, considering we've seen each other every day this week—hitting up the gym and grabbing meals together. We're doing all those things couples do in public, including holding hands as we make our way down the street, which is awkward as hell to do with a guy I'm not actually in a relationship with.

"Intellectually, I get it's pretend," Derek says. "But you're still having sex with him."

"Once. We had sex *once*."

"Okay. Whatever. Had sex once. Going on dates with him. God knows, every gay in town knows you guys are always at the fucking gym together. I'm surprised you don't look like the Hulk already. Although, I'll admit you have a nice little bump in your biceps right now."

I glance at the sleeve of my polo, noticing it fits slightly better than before.

"Guess someone's upping those weights now that he has to impress people."

"Whatever. I don't know. It's strange. We had dinner the other week and—"

"Check," he says as he makes an imaginary check mark in the air before him.

"What?"

"I'm going to check off my imaginary list every time you say something super boyfriendy about this guy who you're not going to develop feelings for."

"No. We were at Mike's and—"

"Check."

"He said something about needing to have a story for how we met."

"Check."

"Stop! He said some things that I couldn't really tell if they were compliments or not. Like they sounded like the kinds of things you'd only say to someone if you were interested, but I could tell he wasn't, and it was just...very weird. I was actually kind of surprised at one point because I realized he was saying all these things, and the thought of something happening between us kind of freaked me out. Not that anything would happen because he wouldn't want me like that, but I don't know. I'm used to things heading that direction, so it's what popped in my mind when he was saying that shit. If anything, I like to think we could be friends after this...who maybe have sex occasionally."

"Check, check, check!"

"How is any of that *check*?"

"A guy you had impossibly hot sex with who you also could be friends with? Isn't that what a boyfriend is?"

"No. A boyfriend is a lot more than that, and you know it."

"Whatever."

"And as fun as it can be, he's kinda full of himself."

"But you like it."

I feel my cheeks redden. "Yeah."

His blond brows rise as though he's wise to some secret I'm keeping.

"No," I say. "It's nice to have fucked and still be able to hang without having all those awful things that come with being in a relationship. Having someone check up on you constantly. Texting to see where you are. Wondering why you didn't bring them back anything from Starbucks. Shouting because you forgot to pay the electric bill."

"How does anyone forget to pay the electric bill anymore? Don't you auto draft that shit?"

"I forgot to renew it *one time*," I say, my irritation with Peter from our past argument resurfacing.

His eyes are wide, as though he's surprised by how much that bothered me.

"Hmm. Maybe I can see your point now," he says. "But you had to have thought about it."

"Derek, if a guy so much as glances at me on the street, I guarantee you five minutes later, I've dreamt about our future life together with kids and a *Notebook*-style happily-ever-after. So, yeah, I've thought about it, but it's not what I want right now, so this thing we're doing kind of works out perfectly."

"Okay," Derek says with a shrug. "I'm eager to see how long you guys can keep this up. I actually see it as a great experiment. Let's put two, incredibly attractive...well, one moderately attractive and one insanely attractive guy together...who don't want to kill each other...who have mind-blowing sex...and let's see what happens, shall we?"

"I'm not fighting with you about this."

He smirks. "Only thing you're fighting is *lurve*."

"I hate you."

"No, you don't. Now, is my fucking laptop good to go or what?"

I finish removing the viruses, and as usual, there were a shit-ton, so it takes another hour, meaning I need to dash and scramble to get ready for dinner tonight.

I sweat as I'm getting dressed because I'm a little nervous about perpetuating this act with Steven and his partner. It's one thing to parade around town as a couple. Even if we were just friends, people would make their own assumptions, so that hasn't been hard. Actually having to lie to people face-to-face is a whole other thing.

I button up my shirt in the mirror behind the sink in the bathroom before fixing my hair.

We're meeting at Two Urban Licks. It's a nicer restaurant, so I have to dress up a bit, and I think it'll be good for Travis to be dressed up for the occasion. I bet when Steven sees him looking more professional for a change, it'll instill some confidence in him about investing in Travis.

While I'm texting him about coming over, my phone starts ringing. It's Dad. I answer quickly.

"Hey, just checking in to see how you are," he says.

"I'm good. Look, I have this thing tonight I'm getting ready for. Do you mind if I call you guys back later?"

"What are you going to?"

"Just out with some friends."

Another lie. One of millions I've told my parents. To keep them from knowing about this life I live. About who I really am. To hide everything I know they'd be ashamed of. God, to think what they'd say if they knew the truth about tonight.

"Your mother and I would love it if you could make some time to swing by and have dinner with us this weekend. Your mom wants to hear about how things are going at work and with your friends."

I love my parents, but dinners with them are exhausting since most of my energy is spent on crafting lies to keep them from ever suspecting the truth about who I am. "I don't know about this weekend, but we'll catch up soon."

A knock at the door. "Oh, that's my friend, Dad. I'll call you back later, okay?"

I tell him good-bye before answering the door. Travis stands in the hall, looking adorable in black slacks, a pink button-up, and a black tie. He has his hair combed slightly to the side, making him look really sharp.

"Don't you clean up well?" I say.

"Not looking too bad yourself." He winks before rushing in and pushing me back against the dividing wall in front of the kitchen. I assume he's excited about this meeting, but it feels so good that I don't care.

I snatch his tie and pull him closer to me as the door closes behind him. I take control, switching places with him, pushing him back against the wall.

Fuck, I'm getting hard as a rock, but we have to be at dinner.

"We...should...go," I say.

He breaks our kiss. "We have a sec."

"No. You keep doing this and I'm not going to stop."

He looks me right in the eyes, wincing slightly. I wonder what he's thinking.

"There's always time for a little celebratory fuck later." He grabs my hand and starts for the door. "Come on, babes."

My gaze drifts down to his ass. His slacks sculpt around it so well they leave little to the imagination. It's a butt that's hard not to look at when he's doing squats at the gym. I notice a gray spot over the fabric—dust that must've come off the wall when I forced him back against it.

"Shit."

I tug on his hand and pull him back into the condo.

"What is it?"

I lead him around the dividing wall and guide him into the kitchen. I retrieve a wash cloth from a drawer and dampen it in the sink.

"Just something I did when I was trying to ravage you," I say, exchanging a knowing look with him. "Turn around."

He obeys and I wipe the spot off and inspect for any other messes I might have made.

"Perfect."

"Thank you, honey," he says—clearly a joke—as he whirls around and kisses me on the cheek. "I've never had someone take care of me like that before."

I tense up, reflecting on my conversation with Derek. I know he meant it as a joke, but a part of me naturally recoils from even the possibility that it could have meant more.

Stop being ridiculous. He doesn't give a shit about you other than to get this money.

But I know that isn't true. He's a good guy, and he cares about me as a person. In the short amount of time we've been doing this, I know that much.

"You good?" he asks.

"Totally. You're gonna do great. And if you're real good, you might get a little hot ass later."

"And if I'm not real good?"

"Then you'll get some pity hot ass later."

He beams, though I think he's more excited about this opportunity than anything I've said.

We head out the door, my nervousness about fucking this all up for him intensifying as we head to his car.

12
Travis

I'm a nervous wreck. Of course, I'll never admit it to Gary, but the way his eyes keep darting in my direction, I'm pretty sure he can tell something is up. I'm wishing I had gone to his place earlier to fuck before we left. There's nothing like an orgasm to relieve tension...or to sidetrack me from tonight. He looks adorable as hell. The way he keeps moving around in his seat tells me he's as nervous about this as I am.

"We'll be okay, right? We can pull this off?" I ask, surprised by the need inside me for an answer, and the tremble in my voice that probably makes my fear obvious.

"Yeah, of course. We've had almost two weeks to practice being boyfriends."

"By working out at the gym together, fucking once, and eating together a few times? Is that all boyfriends do? Hell, my neighbor Cody is my boyfriend too, then." I hope for a chuckle but don't get it. He turns his head in my direction, and I can see Uptight Gary making an appearance.

"Are you fucking Cody right now?"

"What? No. But it would be okay if I was." Because this thing between us is a charade.

"Travis, that wasn't me being weird and possessive. I just don't need everyone at Metropolis thinking I've lost two boyfriends to other assholes in the building."

I see his point there. "You don't need to worry about that." *Fuck, this fake boyfriend shit is going to change a lot in my life.* "While we keep this up, I'm good with just you, Hot Ass." I wink at him, and the left side of his mouth teases me with the hint of a smile. "Speaking of, has Peter tried to talk to you since the pool party?"

"No." Gary slinks down in the seat. "He called a couple of times right after the fundraiser. I assumed he just wanted to press for details about us, so I ignored him. I'm surprised he hasn't tried again, even if it's just to apologize."

Oh, Jesus Christ. "Do you want that motherfucker back?" I ask, making a right turn.

"What?" This makes Gary jerk upward into a straight position. "No!"

"Good. He's a stuck-up dickhead. You can do better."

"By better, you mean like you?"

"Yes, exactly like me. We make a hot fake couple."

We both laugh, and it helps relieve some of the tension.

It doesn't take us long to arrive at Two Urban Licks. When we do, I drop the car off at the valet and meet Gary on the sidewalk. His eyes are a little wider than they were in the car, and I have a feeling the reality of this is starting to hit both of us.

What is going to happen at this dinner? How long will it tie us together? And how fucking ridiculous will we look if what we're doing gets out?

"We got this," I tell him. "We're in it together." And then I lace my fingers with his and hold his hand. As I open the door, I realize this is the first time I've held a man's hand like this.

***

Gary takes a drink of his Chardonnay and sets his glass down. "Oh my God. *Les Mis* is incredible! I can't believe you don't like it! I don't know if I can continue this friendship with you." Gary playfully turns his back on

Steven's partner Raymond. They became best fucking friends in about two seconds flat—which is a good thing. I know that, but hell, they're going to like Gary more than they like me. That's a little scary since Gary is temporary.

"Uh oh," Steven says.

Raymond laughs. "I didn't say I don't like it. I just think it's overrated."

"I feel like I don't even know you right now." Both Raymond and Steven chuckle at Gary this time. He's a fucking hit. Reaching over, I wrap my arm around him and squeeze his shoulder.

"It's okay, baby. I know it's your favorite, but remember, we all have different tastes and that's what makes everyone special." Really, I had no fucking clue it was his favorite until Raymond brought the subject up. "I'll see it with you anytime you want."

"Thank you for restoring my faith in humanity." Gary looks my way and smiles. We haven't talked business at all yet tonight. I haven't wanted to be the one to bring it up, but I have to admit, I'm feeling a little on edge. It's obvious they're having a good time, though. The conversation hasn't slowed at all, and Gary has played his role well. There's a part of me that thinks if this happens, it will be because they like him so much, and I'm not sure how I feel about it. Thankful, obviously, but there's a little twist of discomfort there too.

Steven asks about family. I tell them I'm the oldest of three boys, and my parents and siblings are all in Atlanta. It's not a subject I'm real excited to discuss, and the nerves eating away at my gut just spread more. The last thing I want is pity. If I get this investment, I don't want it to be because my parents—well, mom and stepfather—want nothing to do with me because I won't deny who I am. I want it to be because they respect the work I do and have faith in my ability...or I guess because they think I have a boyfriend they like.

"What about you, Gary?" Steven asks. I feel him briefly tense up and wonder what that's about.

"My mother and father are just outside the city, up in Ashwood County. I have one sister." I didn't know that about him. He also probably didn't know about my brothers. It makes me realize that, in a lot of ways, we're still strangers. We live in the same complex and were thrust together into this partnership, but we don't really know anything about each other.

This shit could go really fucking wrong.

More than that, I realize I'm curious about the set of his shoulders when family was mentioned. Does he love theater or just *Les Mis*? Why the hell is he like Jekyll and Hyde when it comes to sex?

Gary and Raymond break off into their own conversation. Steven watches his partner for a moment, and I can see the love and devotion for him in the way he looks at him. It makes me shift in my seat to look at Gary. He's smiling bigger than I've ever seen him smile, talking animatedly with his hands. Raymond reaches over and touches his hand and laughs at what Gary said.

I've never seen this side of him before, though I guess I haven't seen most sides of Gary. It makes me curious about him, makes intrigue dig its claws in a little deeper. For some reason, I want to know more about him. What makes him tick?

"They get along well," Steven says, pulling my thoughts from Gary and Raymond.

"They do. Raymond is great."

"He is." Steven grins. "As is Gary. I know the two of you haven't been together long, but you make a lovely couple."

We're not a couple. We're lying, drifts through my head. My hand tightens on Gary's shoulder.

"I know it may seem like I'm dicking you around—making you come here tonight, but I wouldn't do it if I wasn't interested in doing business with you, Travis."

For the first time since dinner started—hell, maybe for the first time since the pool party, I feel like I can breathe.

"Thank you. It means a lot to me to hear that. I love what I do. There's nothing I take more seriously than my career. If we move forward together, and I hope we will, I want you to know there's not a harder worker than me. I don't care what I have to do. I'll make sure it's a worthwhile investment for you. I've...I've given up a lot to be where I am."

"You should be proud of what you've accomplished so far," he says, and I am. I really fucking am, but, Jesus, does it feel good to hear someone else tell me that...and there's a part of me that feels like it's not enough.

"I'm proud, but I want more."

He winks at me. "Most good businessmen do. That's a good sign. I have a proposition for you."

My first instinct is to tell him it sounds kinky because I've always had a dirty mind, but I hold back. "I'm listening."

"Raymond and I are putting together a fundraiser that's happening in a few weeks. It's in your neighborhood, at Flirt. Fundraising is incredibly important to Raymond—well, both of us, but him especially. He had it hard when he was younger, and this is his way to give back."

"That's very honorable," I tell him, meaning it.

"I agree. It's why I love him so much, but anyway, I have some information, if you'd like to look it over. I was thinking we could use this as a sort of trial run. Maybe you—and Gary if he's interested"—he looks Gary's way, and I glance over to see Gary turn to Steven as well—"if you're interested, we can work on the fundraiser together. I have upcoming business trips, so it's a lot for Raymond to handle on his own. If everything goes well and if the way we do business fits well with one another, maybe we'll be able to come to an agreement to move forward with your venture."

For a second, I'm not sure if I heard him correctly. *This is it. My chance. I fucking know it.* I know jackshit about fundraisers, but I'll do whatever I need to prove myself.

"Absolutely. I can help in any way. What do you think, Travis?" Gary asks and damned if there isn't sincerity in his eyes. I don't know if it's because this is something he really wants to do or because it's important to him to help me, but I see it there.

"Yeah...yeah, I think that's a great idea. Whatever you guys need, Gary and I are in." Then I pull him toward me and press a quick kiss to his forehead, hoping like hell I look like a good boyfriend, but also really hoping to show him how grateful I am...and maybe I'm realizing that I just like kissing Gary too.

Damned if he doesn't almost look like he's blushing.

13
Gary

It's just Travis, I remind myself as he pulls away from the kiss on my forehead. It stirs this warm feeling within me. A feeling I might have had when I was with Peter. It's not something I can control. Just some knee-jerk reaction my body has to the seemingly affectionate kiss. It's part of his act, but I'm certain he can see me blushing.

I'm not like him. I don't like people knowing what I'm feeling.

I try to play off my awkwardness by grabbing my glass of Chardonnay and taking another sip.

Empty.

It's only my first glass, but I feel lovely right now.

I guess I got so absorbed in my conversation with Raymond I forgot about drinking.

"Here, I've got you," Steven says, pouring me another glass. He chuckles and looks to Travis. "Don't you worry. I've been topping your boyfriend's drink off all night."

I exchange a worried look with Travis, who appears not to have noticed either. I'm sure he was so busy trying to impress Steven that he didn't see him steadily pouring wine to the point that I'm now feeling really good. Really, really good.

I pretend to take another sip but then set the glass down quickly.

They're going to think I'm a wino.

But as I look to Travis, his smirk suggests he's amused more than anything.

Fortunately, we only stay a few minutes longer before Steven pays the bill and escorts us out to the front. I'm not stumbling or anything, so I couldn't have gone too far overboard with the drinking.

When the valet brings Steven's Audi around, Raymond fishes through the back and grabs a packet about the fundraiser. He passes it to Travis, who he says he'll touch base with over the next few days. After they drive off, Travis turns to me and says, "Sorry to rope you into the fundraiser."

"Oh, no. Not at all. Peter was always the sort who helped out because he found fundraisers were a great way of being social or being seen by the right people. It was very insincere...self-serving. Kinda made me sick when he'd talk about them because he made it clear he cared more about who was bringing the most money to the party than he did people's desire to help out with an important cause. I didn't get that impression with Raymond, and considering how much behind-the-scenes work I did with Peter to help put together fundraising events, I feel like some of these skills could actually come in handy and help out someone who's passionate about all this."

He appears impressed by my long-winded response.

"Sorry, I'm kind of drunk," I say. "Not like really drunk but a little tipsy. I think that's why I started harassing Raymond about the musicals. I mean, he's great and all, but who doesn't like *Les Mis*?"

"How well does Peter know them? I mean, he's on the board with them, right?"

"Yeah, but they're not the kind of guys he would hang around. I mean, he would be impressed with their money, and he probably plays kissy-face with them when they're out, but Steven and Raymond are pretty down-to-earth, and from what I can tell, they have a pretty good bullshit detector."

"Obviously not that good," Travis says.

That's right. I forgot the entire dinner was about duping them, and now I feel bad. They're really nice guys. The kind of guys I'd enjoy hanging out with outside of our farce of a relationship. It'd be fun to talk to Raymond about musicals, but it makes me sad knowing this entire dinner was based on a hoax. I try to remind myself it's not a terrible lie. Travis isn't a bad person. Just a guy who needs some cash to start a business that will end up benefiting Steven, too. But this whole idea was a lot easier when I didn't know how cool Steven and Raymond were.

I try to suppress my guilt while the valet fetches Travis's car. As Travis drives us back to Metropolis, I pump my mouth full of breath spray, anticipating where this is going. Travis swipes it from me to refresh as well. Clearly, we're on the same page.

***

"I didn't know you were such a fan of musicals," Travis says as we head down the hall toward my unit.

I start into my rendition of "I Dreamed a Dream." I turn to him, and he looks at me as if I've lost my mind.

"What? You don't know *Les Mis* either?"

"I know the song but never seen the musical."

"How is that even possible? Oh, I love the Ruthie Henshall version the best. Such passion. Such power in her voice."

His brows pinch together. "I don't know who you're talking about."

"Really? Your mouth-speak isn't making sense anymore. *Les Mis* isn't just a good musical. It's a look at the world as it really is. Warts and all. It's love and happiness and joy and misery, hopelessness and grief all in one. It's the total expression of the human experience."

"Oh, okay." I can tell by the way Travis is looking at me that he doesn't believe me, and I'm slightly overenthusiastic about this right now. "Don't get me wrong. It's cute that you're into musicals. Just never been my thing."

"You might as well be speaking another language," I say as we reach my unit. I retrieve my key, continuing "I Dreamed a Dream" under my breath as I start to unlock the door. Travis sets his hand on my shoulder.

"Thank you," he says softly in a sincere voice that doesn't hold the cocky swagger he often speaks with.

He pulls on my arm, and before I know it, I'm facing him, and he's kissing me, pushing me back against the door.

A powerful heat fills my cheeks—a sensation I'm sure is being helped along by the Chardonnay.

I'm even less inhibited than the first time we fucked. I'm curious to have another go and appreciative that Travis wants to explore that intense passion with me again.

His mouth opens wide as he offers powerful kisses like he's determined to show me how good a kisser he is—something that's self-evident. As my thoughts dissolve, I'm totally immersed in this experience, only able to focus on his subtle movements—his nips, the flick of his tongue, his nose running across my cheek.

When he finally breaks our kiss, he gazes into my eyes with the same intensity we shared that first time. "If you're going to sing, I'd rather it be in the bedroom."

"Yes, sir," I say, and I can't help but raise my eyebrow.

I like how free I feel around him, especially about sex. How I can let loose without having to worry about him judging me or thinking I'm this guy who goes around fucking everything that moves. He likely doesn't care considering that's his thing anyway.

He's so fucking hot all dressed up in that pink shirt and black tie. But right now, these clothes are fucking obstacles. Annoying fucking obstacles.

I lunge at him, kissing him powerfully. He stumbles to the other side of the hall, slamming back against my neighbor's door.

I'm hardly thinking about that as I loosen his tie with one hand. He doesn't fight me as I hastily open his shirt, moving from the top down. As I get a few buttons undone, I kiss from his neck to his chest.

His flesh tastes so good—tastes as good as the first time I got to enjoy it. I'm so fucking frustrated that there's so much of this shirt left to unbutton.

"Fuck it," he says.

He yanks the bottom of his shirt out of his pants, grips the placket and rips it open. His buttons shoot across the hall as I slide my hands around his torso and kiss down his body.

I can see why he's fucked around town as much as he has.

This body, these muscles…it would be selfish for anyone to have these all to themselves—at least for more than a night—and I'm glad that tonight's my turn.

God, why are we wearing so many goddamn clothes?

I grab my bow tie and yank it off before undoing the top of my shirt and pulling it open forcefully like he did, the buttons popping off in every direction.

I stand back briefly as I work to get out of it as fast as I can.

I get it down back as far as the cufflinks, where I get stuck. I struggle with the lock on them, but they're not as easy to undo.

As I turn my attention from my failed attempts back to Travis, I see those eyes again. Filled with hunger and passion as he glances at me, up and down like he's totally shocked.

It takes me a moment to remember we're still in the hall.

In my obsession with his body—having him, being with him, touching all over him—I'd totally forgotten where we were and how wildly inappropriate this is. How anyone could walk out and see what we're doing at any second.

But as he rushes me again—pushing me back against my door, my wrists still bound behind my back by the shirt's cufflinks—I find myself lost in a series of passionate kisses once again.

He strokes one hand up my abdomen and reaches around, grabs the sleeves of the shirt, and twists so the cufflinks pull together.

He breaks our kiss and leans back. I'm lost in those hazel eyes, shimmering with the overhanging orange lights. There's something fierce in his gaze. If I didn't know from our other experiences how sexual that gaze was, I'd say he was about to deck me.

His mouth barely moves as he says, "You're gonna have to tell me if I cross a line."

I lean toward him, and I don't know what possesses me, but I take his earlobe between my teeth—gently. I nibble on it for a moment, his deep groan assuring me he's enjoying my work. I release his lobe long enough to whisper, "I don't bruise easily, Travis."

I start to back away when his lips meet mine again. He clings to the sleeves of the shirt, keeping my hands bound behind me as he kisses down my neck—licking, sucking. It's the same passion as the first time, but there's something even wilder about Travis now. Something I can't quite explain.

14
Travis

"Get inside." I reach around him, turn the key and unlock the door before shoving it open. My dick aches. My balls are so fucking full. My chest heaves in and out. He's got me so amped up, so goddamned hungry to watch the quiet, shy man transform into the whimpering, sex-starved boy who wants nothing more than a cock in his ass and to be rode hard.

He does as I say, stumbling into his condo. It's not fast enough for me, so I pick him up, kick the door closed behind me, and carry him toward his room. The position is awkward with his arms behind his back, but I think I like keeping him helpless like this.

"Oh shit," I hear Jacob say as we make our way down the hall. "Have fun!" he calls, but I ignore him.

"Next time, we go to my place." It doesn't escape my attention I'm telling him there will be a next time, but, Jesus, he's a hot fuck. It's like now that I've had him, I can't get enough. Why the hell shouldn't we enjoy the sexual benefits of our partnership?

"Holy shit. I can't believe Jacob just saw us." He leans forward, burying his face against me.

"I can invite him in to watch if you want."

I manage to finagle opening his bedroom door while still holding him when he says, "I can't tell if you're kidding or not."

"Funny. I must know you better than you know me because I can hear the interest in your voice and know you feel like you should hide it." I kick the bedroom door closed. "Fuck whoever told you that, Gary. Fuck whoever made you believe you should ever feel wrong or embarrassed about something you desire. You are who

97

you are, and fuck anyone who wants you to hide any part of that person." That's something I will never do again.

I drop him to the bed. His legs hang over the side, his arms still trapped behind him. My heart speeds up as I look at him—his eyes blazing with want, his swollen cock a bulge behind his slacks. His forehead already glistens with sweat. He's a combination of sex and innocence, looking up at me like he's not sure what I'm going to do to him next but really fucking wanting to find out. "Christ, you're gorgeous," I tell him, slightly surprised the words came out.

While standing between his legs, I reach down and begin to work the button, then the zipper on his slacks. Hooking my fingers in his pants and underwear, I pull them down, but leave them around his ankles. He still has his shoes on as well. "I'll just leave you trapped right there."

"Fuck...you're killing me over here. I just want you inside of me."

"I'm getting there. You're always so damned impatient."

His cheeks flush, but the look in his eyes tells me it's desire and not embarrassment. After pulling my shirt off my shoulders and dropping it to the floor, I make quick work of the rest of my clothes. Gary's prick jerks against his stomach, pre-come dripping down to a tasty pool on his abs.

"I want your cock," he says, eyes intensely on my aching erection.

"Patience. I'm taking a little taste first." I drop to the floor, my knees pinning his pants beneath me. They still won't come off with his shoes on. It traps him, the same way his arms are stuck behind his back. A rush of breath hisses out from between Gary's lips. I wrap my hand around his erection, rub my thumb in the pearl of pre-come at his slit. "You have a nice fucking dick. I might let you use it on me before this is over."

"Oh fuck," Gary grits out before I suck his cock to the back of my throat. I palm his balls, play with his heavy sac as he wiggles around on the bed, unable to move much because of the way I've imprisoned him.

Pulling off, I say, "I'm really good at giving head. Did I tell you?" before I continue to blow him, run my tongue along his thick, hot shaft. Gary makes those hungry little whimpers that drive me out of my mind as he thrashes more and more beneath me.

There's nothing I love more than driving someone wild, watching them come undone the way Gary is beneath me.

His dick falls out of my mouth with a pop before I bury my face in his sac. I run my tongue in the crease between his pelvis and his thigh and then trace it down the seam of his balls.

"Get your dick in me now!" Gary begs, still whipping around.

Yeah...yeah. I'm about to blow my fucking load too. I shove to my feet. Jerk his pants and shoes off and then say, "Legs up." Gary does as he's told. After sucking on my finger, I lean over him, take his mouth as I push my finger into his tight, little hole.

He says something into my mouth. Greedily I eat every sound as we rut against each other, and I keep fingering his ass.

It's still not enough, so I jerk away, grab a condom from his drawer, and get it on. After rubbing lube onto my prick, I roughly roll him to his stomach, his legs still hanging over the side of his bed. "This fucking ass," I tell him as I rub his globes. He pushes back toward me, begging me to take him.

Leaning over, I nip his ear with my teeth before saying, "You don't bruise easily, right?"

"No...please...do it, Travis. I need you."

Standing back up, I push his legs open farther with my foot. Put my hands on his ass, and spread his cheeks, my fingers digging into his flesh. His tight hole clenches and damned if I can't wait to fill it. "I'm gonna watch my cock open your hole." His body trembles beneath my touch. Letting go of him, I use one of my hands to angle my cock toward his asshole, push my head against his tight ring and watch it loosen for me, watch it let me inside.

"Oh fuck. Jesus fucking Christ," Gary mumbles, his hands still behind him.

"Nope. Just me," I tease.

"You are so going to hell," he tells me. I don't answer, just continue to work my way inside.

My balls nearly let loose the second I'm surrounded by all the heat. I promised him a hard fuck, and I intend to make good on that vow, so I grab his ass again to hold him open, tight enough that I could leave marks. Then I pull almost all the way out before thrusting hard again. His whole body jerks, bouncing as I rail him from behind. He has no control, not with the way his hands are trapped in his shirt. I don't have much longer before the position will be too uncomfortable for him, so I take advantage. He lets out a strangled shout each time I piston my hips.

My balls ache, feel so goddamned full they could explode. "Jesus, this is sexy, Gary. You should see my cock opening you up." I watch his hole, watch my dick disappear inside. His ass is squeezing me so damn tight, I'm not sure how much longer I can handle it, so I hold him more firmly, pull him closer to the edge of the bed, so he can stand up and bend over it.

I grab hold of his cock, stroke his thick meat as I speed up my thrusts.

His body starts to tremble. "Oh God. Right there, Travis. Right there." And then a guttural cry rips from the back of his throat as he shoots. I keep fucking, keep stroking his prick, which is now lubed up with his come.

Gary falls onto the bed. I go over on top of him. Let my teeth skin into his shoulder as my own orgasm tears through me.

There's a drop of sweat running down his neck. I lick it, taste the salt on my tongue before I pull out, ditch the condom, and go straight to work getting his arms out of his shirt. He doesn't talk. Doesn't move. Once the shirt is undone I toss it to the floor, lift him up and lay him correctly on the bed.

"That good, huh?"

"Yeah," comes out of his mouth, hoarse and rough. "That fucking good."

A smile pulls at my lips as I hit the light and climb into bed. "Scoot your ass over." He rolls to his side, away from me. I wrap an arm around him like I did the first night when I didn't know who I was in bed with, my dick right against his addicting ass. "This time, I'm damn sure you know who you're in bed with." I made certain of it.

15
Gary

I'm used to falling from the high of my orgasm after coming, but this time, there's this constant swirling sensation in my chest—one that, at times, climbs even higher. Like my body is celebrating how incredible it felt.

My ass is sore, something I couldn't be happier about. I enjoy Travis's arm around me for a moment, but I start to get uneasy about it. This isn't what we need to be doing if this is just pretend. I pull away and slide off the bed. I put on a fresh pair of boxers from the closet and grab the condom and wrapper off the bed before taking it to the bathroom.

"Why are you ruining my view?" Travis asks from behind me.

"Whatever," I say. I dispose of the trash and wash my hands before resting my elbows on the marble counter of the sink, taking a much-needed breather. My face is bright red from the experience. My inch of sandy-blond hair points every which way, disheveled from our fucking. The pain in my ass feels like a muscle I worked out too hard at the gym. I love the sensation, though. Peter sure as fuck never made it feel like that. No man has ever made me feel like that. And I know part of what makes it so much fun is that it's sex without expectations and without needing it to be anything more.

Why did I ever sacrifice this for a relationship?

Travis'll be leaving soon, I'm sure. He's not the kind of guy who spends the night unless he's drunk off his ass, so I figure I'll take out my contacts while I'm in here so I can crash as soon as he heads out. I remove and store them in the lens case in the top drawer. Then I put on a set of glasses from a case on the counter.

I only started wearing contacts because Peter used to make fun of what a dork I looked like in glasses. I don't imagine Travis gives a shit. He likes what he sees, and doesn't seem weird about shit the way Peter always was.

When I head back into the bedroom, Travis is stretched out across the covers, his dick laying across his leg. That big fucking cock that gave me so much pleasure a few minutes ago is semi-hard, and mine is, too. Clearly, he's enjoying mentally replaying the fuck-fest we had as much as I am.

His eyes widen as he notices me. "I didn't know you wore glasses."

I blush. I know it isn't from the sex now but from embarrassment. I didn't figure he'd say anything. Didn't think he'd care, but now that he's said something, I'm self-conscious. I remove them. I'll slip them into the nightstand.

"I normally wear contacts. I just—"

"No, no." He gets on his knees and approaching me quickly.

"I like it. Very Clark Kent."

He takes them from my hands and puts them back on my face before scanning me over.

"Clark Kent and Superass."

I chuckle. "Oh, now, it's Superass?"

He growls and my dick twitches.

"Yes, it is," he says. "You should wear these all the time."

Despite the sincerity in Travis's eyes and the fact that I know he doesn't have a reason to lie to me, for some reason, I can't take him seriously right now.

"Peter fucking hated these. I used to wear them all the time, but he would give me shit. Told me no one wears glasses anymore. I mean, he was right."

"Fuck that. They're part of what make you beautiful. Unique."

Beautiful?

No one's ever called me beautiful before. I turn from his piercing gaze.

He wraps his arms around me and pulls me so that our torsos are flush, his face inches from mine. "Peter sure did a number on you. Guess he was just trying to keep this hot piece of ass all to himself."

"Not as hot as that young thing he's got now." I'm trying to make a joke out of it because all this flattery makes me uneasy.

His hands drift down to my ass, which he cups, gripping securely as though he wants me to know that these cheeks were his less than five minutes ago.

"That little twink doesn't have anything on you," he says before his eyes narrow. "Why do you do that?"

"Do what?"

"Whenever I compliment you, your eyebrow twitches."

Now I'm really uneasy.

"It's cute as fuck," he adds before offering a kiss. It relieves the tension he stirred when he started talking like this.

Once again, I turn away from him.

He glances at the window.

"Hey, you can see my place from here, can't you?"

"Um...yeah."

He turns back to me, his right eyebrow raising quickly.

"Oh, someone enjoying the view a little more than he should?"

"You have blinds. If you don't want anyone to see, you should close them." I wink. I'm teasing him, but I like that the attention is off me for a moment.

"Such a contradiction," he mutters.

"What?"

"You didn't have any problem saying that to me, but I tell you how cute you are, and you get all weird and quiet."

"Now you're trying to make me uncomfortable."

And it's working.

"Stop being stupid and come here."

He kisses me, soothing me once again. I'd prefer to just do this. His touch. His caress. His fucking never makes me uneasy.

He slides his hands from my ass, up my back before wrapping his arms around me. He lifts me, pulling me onto the bed. He shifts his body, guiding me onto the covers until we're lying side by side. When he pulls away, I lie back while he remains on his side, gazing down at me.

He winces before saying, "So tell me about this family of yours."

"What?" *So much for feeling relaxed again.*

"I guess these glasses and that shit you were saying about musicals at dinner got me thinking about how little I know my fake boyfriend. You said that you had a sister—"

"I'd rather not talk about it," I say so fast and dismissively that I surprise myself, and Travis looks at me like I just shape-shifted in front of him.

"Now I've made it weird. It's nothing. It's just..."

I might as well tell him. I've signed up for a bogus relationship and now to help him with a fucking fundraiser, so he'll find out sooner or later.

"She's in prison," I confess.

"Prison?"

"Yeah. She was always getting into trouble when we were growing up. She had a very...outgoing personality. Very fun and loving and exciting to be around, but she wasn't the kind of kid that Mom and Dad could control. She would fight with them...a lot. When she was a teenager, that's when the sneaking out started. The fights about where she was began. And then she started getting into trouble with guys who weren't the best for her. Got arrested for shoplifting when she was sixteen. Did a little time in juvie and then when she was twenty-one, she was arrested during a drug bust on a meth house that she was at with one of her boyfriends. She got ten years. Now they have a diagnosis, at least. Borderline personality disorder. Well, they go back and forth between that and bipolar disorder. I can't really say what they think it is this week."

"Dude, that's some serious shit."

"And that's not even the half of it. Not exactly the best conversation for dinner parties," I say, reflecting on how many people in my life I haven't told this to. Reflecting on all the lies I tell to appear normal.

"It's not too bad for me," I add. "I only knew her really well when we were kids. She is three years older than me, and when she was old enough to start sneaking out, I didn't see her too much. She was always trying to get away from our family by then. It was worse seeing what it did to my parents."

He wears a serious expression like when we were sitting at dinner and he was stressing about whether he was going to win Steven's approval.

"Your poor parents. A convict and a gay in the family," he teases.

He's trying to make light of the situation, but it stirs up yet another sore subject.

"I'm not out to them, so—"

His eyes widen. "What? Really?"

"God, no. My sister was always causing enough trouble as it was. I didn't want to add fuel to the fire. They have enough stress to deal with already."

His gaze drifts, and it looks like he's thinking very hard about something. I can't imagine it's about my family, though.

"So, I'm assuming you're out to your family?" I ask.

"They found out the hard way. I fought it for a long time, and then finally, in college, I had my own place. I was like, 'Fuck it.' There was no way for my parents to find out, so I worked up the courage to set up a Grindr account. I found this hot frat guy at Tech. Had the biggest fucking cock, too."

"Bigger than yours?" I ask.

"It was insanely big. Like I don't think I had reasonable expectations for guys after messing around with him."

"Oh my God."

"I invited him over. Soon we were making out on the couch, taking off each other's clothes. I must not have locked the door or something because I don't even remember hearing it. Just turning and seeing Mom and Dad standing there, staring at me in horror. Like they were watching me kill someone. My dad lost his shit. He kicked the guy out, and my parents just started going off on me. Said they worked too hard to set me up with a good life for me to fuck it up like that. That what I was doing was wrong. They're both very Southern Baptist, so they saw that as sin. My dad did, at least. Mom was more concerned about it not fitting the pretty little image she'd worked so hard to construct for our family. They said I needed to do right or end up on the streets. From that moment on, I decided I'd never take another dime from them. That I didn't need their fucking help. Not if it came with the price of me being someone other than who I really was."

His jaw is tense, his gaze severe, as though he's looking back at that time of his life with judgment and contempt.

I'm surprised. I figured he didn't come from a lot of money, which was why he needed to work so hard to convince Steven to invest in him. I never would have thought he came from money but pulled away from it because his parents were such assholes.

"Sorry," I say. "That's a shitty way for your parents to find out."

"It worked out for the best. I'd rather it have happened like that so I could change my life for the better than to keep on living that lie."

"Don't know that you've completely given up on lies," I say.

"True." His lips twist into his dimple. Then he smirks. "But at least now I get all the dick I want."

He grabs my cock in my boxers and leans forward. I think he's about to kiss me, but he licks my lips.

He laughs and leans back, a broad smile stretching across his face.

"On that note, I better head out."

He rolls off the bed. I sit up as he hunts for his clothes. When he finds his pants and underwear, he slides into them before he approaches me, planting his palms on the mattress. I lean into him, and we kiss again.

He grabs the rest of his clothes and as he finishes tying his shoes, says, "Don't forget we have a fundraiser to discuss. I'll see you at the gym tomorrow, Superass."

16
Travis

I push my thumbs into the shoulder muscles of my last client for the day and try to work out the knot there. Gary and I are supposed to meet at my place this evening to talk about the fundraiser. *What a fucking mess.* I don't know how in the hell we got ourselves into this situation, but when I think about it, it's not as bad as I thought it would be.

I obviously enjoy fucking him. To my surprise, I like spending time with him as well.

He's...a good man. There's no two ways about it. Agreeing to help me with the fundraiser is fucking huge. He doesn't have to do that. It's going above and beyond grabbing a meal together so his ex will see us. I'm not sure many people would go as far.

There's something endearing about the way he flips from trying to blend into the background to the man begging for my dick. It's also pretty nice to have a consistent workout buddy. We spent close to two hours at the gym together this morning, and it had been hell to keep my hands off him in the shower. There's not a doubt in my mind that the feeling was mutual. He'd eaten me alive with his eyes, watched as my dick got hard and then looked like he'd nearly swallowed his tongue when I grabbed myself and nodded toward the back.

"What was that about?" my client asks, and I frown, unsure what he means.

"What?"

"You chuckled. You've never spontaneously laughed while massaging me before."

Huh. I hadn't even realized I'd done that. "It's nothing. My..." *Oh fuck. What do I call him?* I don't think my client knows Steven or Peter, but you never know. "Gary." *My Gary?* Christ, I could have come up with something better than that. "I just remembered something funny he said at the gym this morning. He's really just getting into working out with a purpose. He makes this funny little whistling sound sometimes when he lifts. I was giving him shit about it today. The harder he tries not to do it, the louder it becomes."

"Oh God. Not one of those," he says as I work my way down his back.

"No. He's not the guy who's doing everything in his power to draw attention to himself while he works out."

"Good. I fucking hate that...except when I'm the one who does it," he says and we both laugh. "You know how I like attention."

He definitely does.

I finish my massage, not quite sure how I ended up talking about Gary's whistle. Afterward, I head back to Metropolis. Just as I step through the door, Peter makes his way around the corner, his cocky smirk faltering when he sees me. I really fucking hate this guy. What in the hell did Gary ever see in him?

"Travis." He nods at me.

"Percy," I reply and watch his face immediately flush red.

"We'll pretend I don't realize you did that on purpose, shall we?"

"Think what you want." I cross my arms and wait.

"Just finish a massage?" he asks and I shrug. "I bet that job comes with its perks. Men throwing themselves at you left and right. Getting paid a little something extra for a special rubdown."

Motherfucker. My muscles tighten to the point where they hurt, but I fight hard not to let him see he hit a nerve.

My job being a cover-up for selling sex for cash is always one of the first things people assume—my parents included. A dirty queer like me can't possibly be professional enough to keep it in my pants.

"Aww, come on, Petey. Don't be like that. I know you gotta miss that ass. Jesus, it's fucking incredible. He's a goddamned beast in the sack, but remember, you're the one who wasn't man enough to handle him. I can, and he sure as shit is enough for me. I'm balls deep more than I'm not, and I'm sure you remember how much Gary is always hungry for cock....Or maybe you don't. He said you couldn't satisfy him the way I do."

I can see him working his jaw in anger. His fists tighten just like I knew they would. What a fucking joke.

"If you're trying to get under my skin, it's not working. Have you seen Evan? And my name is Peter."

"That's cute, pretending you're not thinking about all the times you fucked Gary and telling yourself you know how to work that dick better than you obviously do. It's okay. Not everyone can fuck as well as me. Now if you'll excuse me, I have a date tonight. I don't want to keep my man waiting. He can hardly keep his hands off me as it is. He has five years of mediocre sex to make up for. Catch ya later, Petey." Without another word, I turn and make my way toward the elevator.

A few minutes later, I'm in the shower cleaning up before Gary arrives. Afterward, I throw on a pair of basketball shorts and a tank top right as there's a knock at the door.

He's a few minutes early. A smile tugs at my lips as I pull the door open and..."It's like you're really in a relationship. I never see you anymore." Cody tries to step inside, but I hold my arm out against the doorjamb to block him.

"No, I just have shit going on—working and now this fundraising shit—and I'm fucking him, but no, it's not a relationship."

"Rumor has it you're at the gym together daily." Cody cocks a brow at me.

"Making an appearance. It's part of the gig. Come back later. He's on his way over so we can work on some fundraising shit."

Cody frowns at me.

"Why are you frowning?"

"I don't know. You're being weird. Why are you being weird?"

"Oh, Jesus." I roll my eyes at him. "Always seeing shit that isn't there. I'm not being weird." But for some reason, I don't want to hang out with both Cody and Gary at the same time. Honestly, I can't say why. Cody's my only real friend. Gary is...well, my new friend, but it almost feels like mixing two worlds.

"Fine, I'll go, but you and me?" He points to me and then himself like he's a fucking cartoon character or something. "We're talking later."

Just then there's a noise down the hall. I look up to see Gary standing a few feet away as though he's not sure what to do.

"I'll let you two get on with it." Cody winks at me and then turns toward Gary. "Sorry, your guy is ready for you now." He heads into his condo, but Gary still hasn't moved.

"Are you going to stand there all night?" I ask him.

"No...I hope I wasn't interrupting anything, though."

I wave him off. "It's just Cody. You know Cody, right?"

He finally gets his ass in gear and comes into my condo. I close the door behind him. "I've seen him around."

"He's like my Derek."

Gary seems to loosen up.

"Sit." I nod toward the couch.

"You're getting bossy again."

"I'm a bossy motherfucker, and it makes your dick hard, remember?" I wink at him and head toward the kitchen. "Are you hungry? I'd offer you something good, but unfortunately, I've eaten too many carbs lately."

When I glance over, I see Gary roll his eyes. "Like you have to worry about that."

"Everyone has to worry about that. Everyone but you, Superass." I grin at him.

"Yeah, right."

"Beer?"

"Wine?"

"Shitty wine."

Now it's he who smiles at me. "My favorite kind."

I grab the bottle, uncork it and pour us each a glass. This time when I nod toward the living room couch, Gary walks over. "Your ex is a dickhead, by the way...I fucking hate him." I hand him his glass and we sit down.

Gary's eyes go wide in this adorable, panicked look. "Why? What happened?"

"You're freaking out inside, aren't you?" I sit down beside him, not sure why I find him so amusing.

"Yes. I am. And you're enjoying it. Now, tell me what happened."

"What will you do for me if I do?"

"Suck your dick?" he replies.

"You'll do that anyway."

"True." He shrugs. "Tell me!"

For some reason, I want to keep it going, but instead I tell him about our run-in. His response is immediate. "Oh fuck. You really called him Petey?"

"Yeah. Cocky prick. I thought his fucking head was going to explode." We both laugh, but as I watch him, as I think about the things Gary has told me, I realize how different they are. Gary would never do the shit Peter has done or treat people the way he did. He's a genuinely good man. "What did you see in him?" I ask.

He sighs, taking a sip of his wine. "He didn't use to be the way he is now...well, I guess that's not true. Maybe I just didn't always want to see it. I'd never been in a relationship before. Like I said, I'm not out to my family, so I met this smart, attractive, older man who I thought accepted me in a way no one else had, and I fell in love. And I guess sometimes we wear blinders when we're in love."

There's a sadness to his voice I haven't heard much from him before. Peter doesn't deserve Gary's sadness. "Do you still love him?"

He takes another drink and pauses before saying, "No. I think I stopped a long time before we broke up. I just didn't let myself realize it."

I don't know why, but my chest gets lighter hearing that.

"What about you? Have you ever been in love?" he asks.

I can't hold back the laugh that jumps out of my mouth. "Fuck no. I would never give someone that kind of power over me."

He looks at me over the edge of his glass, curiosity in those expressive eyes of his. "Interesting...tell me more."

Not happening. "That would be another fuck no."

"What? I just admitted something to you!"

"I admitted something to you too." When he frowns, I add, "I'm mysterious. Mysterious is hot, right?" And then I down the wine in my glass. "Now what the fuck are we going to do about this fundraiser?"

17
Gary

"That's not really fair, is it?" I say, not trying to hide my annoyance.

His eyes widen with surprise.

"When you asked me a very personal question, I answered it," I continue. "When I asked you a personal question, you told me 'mysterious is hot'?"

He shifts on the couch beside me and cocks his head back before saying, "What's eating you tonight?"

I take a gulp of wine. I know this doesn't have anything to do with his response to my question, and I need to get this off my chest.

"That guy, Cody," I say.

"What about him?"

"Do you do the same thing that you do with me with him?"

His eyes light up.

"No, I didn't mean it like that."

"I think you did," he says like he's so damn proud of himself. "You're jealous."

"No. And yes. I don't ever do this. I know you're fucking around with other guys. I'm not delusional. I've never been in a situation with a fake boyfriend who I fuck occasionally, so I don't exactly understand the protocol."

He smirks and leans toward me. "I don't think there's a rule book for a situation like ours."

"I shouldn't have even brought it up," I say. "It's none of my business."

Travis sighs and scratches the back of his head as though he's nervous. "I'm not fucking Cody."

"But even if you were, it shouldn't matter. I'm going to be totally honest with you and say my mind is programmed for relationships. That's what five years does to you. I'm used to thinking of everything within the context of a relationship, so I see something like that and it mixes with this confusing thing we're doing and shit goes a little haywire in my brain."

He pauses for a second, as though he's thinking. "Okay. I appreciate you being real with me."

"Sorry, I made it weird, didn't I?"

He smiles. "No. You were being honest. Nothing wrong with that. Weird would be you telling me you're falling in love with me."

I laugh. That's one thing I'm definitely not worried about happening.

"Whatever," I say. "I'm gonna shut up now. I was saying I don't care what you do with Cody or any other guy. I'm still getting used to this whole situation."

That's not entirely true. While I would totally understand him fucking around with other guys, I get tense thinking about it, possibly because of the way things went down with Peter. Still, I don't have a right to be jealous, especially considering I know this can never really go anywhere.

He stares at me. Looks like he's trying to read my mind.

"What?" I ask.

"That's kind of adorable."

He's making fun of me. My cheeks are getting warm. God, this is embarrassing as fuck.

It's easy for a guy like him not to give a shit about stuff like that. He probably wouldn't even think twice about it if a guy walked out of my condo.

"I don't know why you look embarrassed all of a sudden. You shouldn't be...and truth is, Superass, I'm not going to be running around fucking like I normally do."

"It doesn't matter either way," I say.

But I can tell by the way his words brought me a sense of ease that it does matter to me.

"I think part of it has to do more with Peter than anything else," I add. "Finding out he was running around on me for so long made me feel like an idiot. I just...I guess I don't want to feel like an idiot again."

"You're not an idiot," Travis says and I'm surprised by how serious his expression is. "Smart people get cheated on as much as dumb people. You know it. I know it. You wanted to believe that Peter was a good guy because *you're* a good guy. There's nothing wrong with that." It's nice hearing him call me a good guy. I can't explain why, but I value his opinion of me.

"Maybe," I say. "I keep finding myself going back through every day. Remembering when he'd say he was going to the gym or the store. Trying to piece together when he was really going to the gym and when he was heading over to see Evan. Knowing I was sitting around the condo, working on shit or watching TV while he was tossing Evan around a couple hundred yards from me in the other tower. Hell, he was probably watching me from the window while he fucked him."

I'm lost in my masochistic fantasy about what was going on all along when I pull my attention back to Travis, whose expression is relaxed. I can see the pity in his eyes. I don't want his pity.

I take another sip of wine. "Life's shit, right?"

Travis slides across the couch.

He rubs his hand across my leg and leans toward me so his face is right before mine.

"If anyone's an idiot, it's Peter," he says, his voice low. My gaze is fixed on his hazel irises.

He rubs his hand up to my crotch, and my dick stiffens. He leans closer to me and slides the tip of his nose across my cheek. Goose bumps prick across my flesh. Soon, his lips are right beside my ear as he whispers, "He's the one who's missing out on this sex-crazed monster."

I reach out and caress his dick, hard in his basketball shorts.

He pulls his head back. "I'd feel bad for him if I wasn't so fucking greedy for it myself."

The heat in my cheeks isn't from embarrassment anymore, but arousal.

His gaze shifts to my lips. He looks like he wants to kiss me right now. Or shove his fully erect cock down my throat. I'd be fine either way.

"We're gonna have to wait for this," I say. "We have a fundraiser to talk about."

"Fair point. Let's get this out of the way so we can get on to more important things."

"Deal."

"Raymond told me they need ideas for the event they're hosting. Flirt is letting them host that night. He wants a good money-maker idea. I told him we'd brainstorm."

"That should be easy enough."

Travis's eyes narrow. "I think I have a fun way to approach this. For every good idea you think of, I remove an article of clothing. For every good idea I come up with, you do the same."

"How do we know if it's a good idea or not?"

"The person who's removing their clothes has to agree."

"It doesn't sound like there are any losers in this game," I say.

He grins as he rises to his feet. "Doesn't that make it the best sort of game?"

He steps back and folds his arms, his gaze trailing off.

We both think for a few moments.

I reflect on fundraisers I helped Peter with.

"Drag shows are always popular," I say. "Peter would sometimes convince the nonprofits he worked with to put on one when he wanted to make some quick cash."

I wait for his approval.

He nods and grips the hem of his shirt, pulling it off and tossing it onto the coffee table.

I take another sip of wine, enjoying the view.

"You gonna keep helping?" he asks. "Or just look?"

"I was going to stare for as long as I could get away with it."

He flashes his teeth as he offers a crooked smile. Cocky, conceited...hot as hell.

His long, thick dick shifts steadily in those basketball shorts.

How is this supposed to help me brainstorm when all I want to do is yank them down and stick that hard-on in my mouth?

"Focus," he instructs. "Otherwise, you won't get to any of the good stuff."

I force myself to think, but before an idea comes to me he says, "You know, drag shows are fairly specific. They make money, but for the people who aren't into it, they don't have a reason to show up."

"Is that an attempt to get your shirt back on?"

"Wouldn't dream of it. But you know, I've been to a few fundraisers where they had guys strip for money. That always goes over well."

I take off my shirt and set it next to his on the coffee table.

"Oh, you like that idea?" he asks.

"The more clothes that come off, the better. Everyone loves hot guys."

This sparks an idea.

I hop to my feet. I'm about to grab my glass of wine off the coffee table, but I'm distracted as I try to think this through.

"What if we had a drag queen hosting this big gay strip-show? We get a bunch of guys together—hotties who'll help us raise money. We can make it a competition. Like hottest ass or hottest whatever. They do like a little version of this at Burkhart's occasionally, and it's always a hit. But we could do it on a bigger scale? Between the two of us, we know some pretty hot guys. We could make a Facebook page, promote the shit out of it and get the guys to do the same on their pages. Hell, half of the people who show up will be there to see their buddies strip down."

I'm getting all sorts of ideas of how we could coordinate this, but before I have a chance to take it further, Travis pushes me back. I go with him until soon my shoulder blades are pressed against his balcony doorframe, and he's kissing me.

I'm pissed that he's distracted me, but just for a moment, until I'm lost in those same explosive kisses that make everything else in the world insignificant.

I wrap my arms around him and run my hands up and down his body.

As he pulls away, I find I'm out of breath, gasping for air, my body racing with adrenaline.

I look him over.

"Don't you have to take off something now?" I ask.

"For that idea, you get it all."

He kisses me again, pushing his firm body against mine, which feels a little tighter now that we've been hitting the gym together. I like to think he gets half as much pleasure out of it as I get out of his.

He yanks down his basketball shorts as I undo the button and fly on my shorts and push them down with my boxers.

He moves close, pressing his fully erect cock against my pelvis. Mine slides up the side of his leg. He kisses my neck, and I throw my head back, enjoying the hot sensations that pool through me and set my cheeks on fire.

Fuck, that was a good idea.

18
Travis

"This is incredible, Travis. I really think it will work well. You should be proud. I'm impressed," Steven says to me through the phone after I finish telling him about the fundraiser idea. I'm sitting in my car outside of Adelle's, where I'm meeting my brothers for lunch.

There's almost nothing I want more than for Steven to think I came up with this plan on my own. I want him to be impressed by me, impressed enough to want to give me money, but I'm not a liar...I also don't take credit for shit that isn't mine, and Gary deserves the praise for this. "Thanks, but it was all Gary. He really ran with the idea. Once he came up with it, he couldn't stop talking about it." I'd fucked the hell out of him. He'd had an orgasm screaming my name, and as we'd lain in my bed covered in sweat and come, he'd started popping off with more ideas about the event. "It was pretty cute, actually. He doesn't typically let himself show how excited he is about something, but he had this burst of excitement pouring out of him like he couldn't contain it. I could hardly keep up with him, but it was cool seeing him so happy about it. I couldn't have come up with it without him."

Steven chuckles. "I'm sure you could have, but I also respect the hell out of you for being honest. I think you sound more enthusiastic over Gary's excitement than anything else."

"I do?" tumbles out of my mouth, and I immediately wish I'd been able to hold the question back. Of course, I'm not happier about how Gary feels than anything else. Pulling this off for Steven affects my whole fucking life. That's what's important here. But then I realize that as much as I want this because of my career, Gary's joy is also really fucking incredible to see. There's a part of me that's honored to be a part of it because of him.

"You do, and why am I not surprised you don't realize it? You're a good man, Travis, and Gary is lucky to have you."

Only he doesn't have me—not really. And if I'm being honest, I'm probably not that good of a man either. "Thank you, sir, though I think I'm the one who's lucky to have him." Guilt churns around in my gut. Just a few moments before I'd been saying I wasn't a liar, but I am. This whole damn thing is a lie, and I dragged Gary into it. The only thing I'm not lying about here is me being the one who is lucky in this whole scenario with him.

"You're welcome. I'm going to work on a few things on my end, and I'll speak with Raymond. I'll let you know what else I need from you and how things are coming along. You guys will handle getting the boys, right?"

"Oh yeah. That won't be a problem." Men are the easy part.

"You should participate, yourself. You'd be sure to be a hit." There's amusement in Steven's voice, but I can also tell he's serious. I'd basically promise this guy the moon right now if I thought it would get me what I want. Then I remember how Gary looked when he thought I was fucking Cody. Not that it should matter since this whole thing is a game. It's not as if he has a say in who I strip or don't strip in front of, but that fucker Peter did a real number on him. He's a relationship guy, and all I can think about is how it might affect him—how it might make him feel or if it will give Peter some kind of satisfaction to see me do something that he knows would hurt Gary.

"I really don't want to say no, but I need to talk to Gary first. I need to make sure it's something he's comfortable with before I commit." *Not because I have to,* I remind myself. No one has any say over my life but me, but I really fucking hate Peter and want nothing more than to help Gary show the fucker that he's over him.

"See? Good man," Steven says again and a strange warmth settles in my chest. My parents sure as shit have never called me a good man.

"Eh, I have my moments." I play it off.

We talk for another minute about our plans. When I see my brothers walk down the sidewalk toward the restaurant, I end my call with Steven and get out of the car.

"Hey, man. What's up?" Malcolm asks when he sees me. I step up to the curb and give him a hug.

"Not much. How are you guys?" We pull away and I hug Martin next.

"Good," Martin replies before we make our way into the restaurant. There were times when we were kids that the three of us didn't get along—or I guess, I felt out of place with them, which really, I was. They're blond like Dad, look like him when there's no way I ever could since it wasn't his swimmers that made me. That's not something we talk about, though. We pretend it's not the truth. The older we've gotten, the closer we've gotten as well. I wouldn't have anyone who shared my blood and also gave a shit about me if it wasn't for them.

We're seated, and they order sweet tea while I get a beer.

"How's work?" Malcolm asks.

"Good. I have some things going on. There's a real possibility I could get my own place soon." The words make me sit up a little taller, feel a little more responsible.

"You know we wouldn't mind helping you with that, Trav. I don't know why you don't let us lend you the money to—" My body stiffens, and I give Martin a hard look that makes him add, "I'd understand it more if it was Mom and Dad's money, but it's ours. Still, I respect you wanting to do it on your own. Forget I said anything."

"Yeah, but it came from your inheritances, so it's still from them." This isn't the first time they've tried to lend me money. I won't take it. I'll continue on the way I am now or work for someone else before I do that. It's different earning it from Steven than having my brothers hand it over to me in pity because our parents are homophobes.

"It's good you're looking into options. I have no doubt you'll figure it out." He's also just trying to make me feel better, and I let him.

The waitress returns and takes our order. I get a fucking salad because I definitely need to keep my ass in shape if I might be stripping at Flirt for the fundraiser.

When the waitress leaves, it's Martin who speaks again. "I'm going to ask Liz to marry me," he says. Malcolm's eyes go wide, likely because he probably assumed he'd be the first one to marry. I obviously won't.

"Congrats," Malcolm finally says.

"Why?" I ask.

"Jesus, Travis." Malcolm shakes his head, but he's smiling.

"It's a good question if you ask me."

"Because he loves her, you jackass," Malcolm replies.

"Love makes you stupid." They both look at me with eyes that tell me to shut up, so I hold up my hands in defeat. "I'm kidding. Congratulations." I still don't get why you can't love someone yet not want to marry them, though. When I think of marriage, I think of our parents. They get along, but they sure as shit don't look crazy about each other.

"Her birthday is coming up in a few weeks—first week in July. We're having a party at the Hartley Inn. Mom and Dad will be there—her family, our friends." Martin looks at me. "And both my brothers."

Oh, fuck. I should have seen this coming. "I appreciate the offer....Was that an offer by the way? It didn't sound like one. I'm going to have to decline, though." I didn't even hear a peep from her after her birthday when I left the flowers. Not that I expected to. Even though I didn't leave a card, there isn't a part of me that doesn't believe she knew they were from me.

"You should be there," Martin tells me.

"They hate me. Why would you want me there? It will just make things awkward. It's not fair to you, and it sure as shit isn't fair to Liz."

"Because the two of you are my best friends, and I want you there. Because Mom and Dad need to get over this shit. Because none of it should fucking matter. Because I'm tired of seeing you alone when the family gets together. Because if Liz says yes, you sure as shit will be at my wedding, considering you'll be standing beside me with Malcolm as my best men. Are those enough reasons for you?" Martin asks with a smile—the fucker.

"Shit." I groan and run a hand through my hair. "You have to go and get all sentimental, don't you?"

"Yes," he answers simply.

The truth is, I want to be there, but I don't know if I can be.... "I won't ever be anyone other than myself. I won't ever be who they want me to be. I won't lie for them. I won't hide who I am from Liz's family and friends."

"She knows you're gay, Trav. She doesn't give a shit. If she did, I wouldn't be asking her to marry me."

My pulse speeds up and my chest feels full. "You sappy motherfucker."

"You got him, Martin. There's no way he can say no to that," Malcolm adds and as much as I want to kill both of them...I'm thankful for them too.

"I hate you." I cross my arms.

"You love me," Martin replies. "And I know you don't date, but if there's someone you want to bring, you need to bring him. If Mom and Dad have a problem with it, they can leave. I love them, but they're wrong here. Not you."

I close my eyes, dropping my head back because how in the fuck do I say no to that? What I should say is thank you because I'm not sure Martin will ever know what those words mean to me.

And then...Gary fills my thoughts. I don't even know if we'll still be playing this fucked-up game when the time comes, but I realize that if I go to this party, I'm not sure I'll be able to go alone.

Cody...I can always bring Cody. He'd love the shit out of playing it up for my family.

"Say yes," Martin says.

"You really have no choice," Malcolm adds. "You're part of the family."

Those words are meant to make me feel better, but all they do is make anger shoot through me because it shouldn't matter. *Why can't they love me the way I am*?

"I'll think about it," I say through gritted teeth. It's then that the waitress brings us our food. The rest of lunch has a heavy tone to it. Martin and Malcolm can tell I'm pissed and I don't try to hide it.

When I get back to my car, my fingers automatically move across the screen of my phone, finding Gary's name. Maybe he'll want to go work out with me to help me get my mind off this shit. It rings and rings before Gary's voicemail picks up. I click end, not even sure why in the fuck I called him. What? To complain about my screwed-up family? *Why should he have to deal with my shit? Why is he the first person I thought to call?*

As I pull away, all I can think is, *There's nothing wrong with who I am. The only thing that's wrong is hiding who that person is. Fuck anyone who doesn't see it that way.*

19
Gary

"I loaded the page three different times." Eric's voice comes through my Bluetooth earpiece as I sit at my desk, my laptop in front of me. "I added the one tab to the header that they wanted for their new price promotion, and then everything just went to shit."

"Give me a minute," I say. I can't focus when he gets all worked up like this.

I scroll through the Notepad doc, checking over the code Eric was working with before the website for our biggest client, eSteem—a retailer for anti-aging products—started acting up. Eric typically runs codes by me before uploading changes, but he figured the adjustments were minor enough that he wouldn't have anything to worry about. At least, that was his excuse when he called me in a fucking panic over this new crisis. Of course, this issue had to come up on a weekend.

"I'm already getting emails from Eva at eSteem because the checkout cart isn't working," he says. "That means they're losing money...and that means fucking Alice is going to have my head when she finds out about this."

Alice is the CEO of the IT company I've worked at for the past five years. Eric's already on thin ice with her after he fucked up a major account we had with an online hardware retailer. It took me three weeks to repair the damage he'd done. The only reason he wasn't fired over it was because he managed to convince Alice it was a mistake anyone could have made. I had his back at the time, mainly because he's the contact who got me the job with the company. But it probably would have been better if Alice would have let him go then because more often than not, his issues arise from his carelessness and refusal to maintain his training with the major eComm hosts we work with.

He's not passionate about coding the way I am. This is just a job for him. Coding is my life. My art. It's having a vision and finding a way to bring it to life using my skills and knowledge. Keeping websites maintained and functional makes me feel smart. Clever even—although I sure as fuck wasn't clever enough to figure out what Peter was up to.

I recall what Travis said about smart people getting cheated on just like anybody else, and my gaze shifts to my phone sitting beside my laptop.

Travis tried to call a few minutes ago. I'm curious to find out what he wanted, but he hasn't texted, so it couldn't have been all that important.

I'll call him back as soon as I fix this issue. Because my actual life has to come before my fake one.

I keep searching through the code when Eric says, "So what's this thing with Derek and Luke Henley?"

"What?"

"Derek and Luke Henley. The guy he's seeing."

"He's not seeing anyone."

"I know for a fact they've been hooking up for at least a month now."

Has Derek seriously been seeing this guy without telling me? I'm used to him sneaking off to trick out with some random hookup from Scruff or Grindr. He's like Travis. He could have sex with everyone in town and then start all over again without giving any more or less fucks about anyone he was screwing around with. But if Eric's right, something's up. Derek's never been secretive about the guys he's fucked around with.

"He sure as hell hasn't told me about it," I say, replaying the past few weeks in my head. "And he was like two seconds from having sex with a guy the other weekend."

"They're not exclusive or anything," he says. "But Luke's a big relationship guy, and Derek, well...you know, I don't exactly see him that way. So I doubt anything's really going to come of it."

I've never known Derek while he was in a relationship. He was in one for three years with a guy he met during his brief stint at Georgia State University. That was before he dropped out and went to cosmetology school...before we ever met. But since I've known him, he's always waved that single-flag high and proud.

As I go back through the past few weeks, I try to recall him saying anything about a guy he was messing around with. *Have I been that shitty of a friend? Should I have noticed he was being secretive?* Although between recovering from the Peter and Evan shit and my new phony relationship, I've been a little preoccupied.

I return my attention to the Notepad doc, and I notice a piece of code Eric misplaced. As usual, it's just a careless error with major consequences...and a colossal waste of everyone's time. I make the adjustment, re-upload it to the site, and make sure it's functional.

Problem solved. Superass saves the day again.

A sense of ease fills me. Aside from Travis and Derek, coding has been the only thing that's distracted me from my breakup. Just like when I was growing up and it distracted me from Mom and Dad's constant worry and grief over my sis.

When I get off the phone with Eric, I return Travis's call.

"Hey, what's up?" I ask as soon as he answers.

"Not much." He says that like he doesn't have anything else to say, but I know he called for a reason.

Silence. Strange, uncomfortable silence.

"Did you butt dial me earlier?" I ask.

"Oh, no. I was just thinking maybe we should get together tonight and make a list of guys we can convince to work with us on the fundraiser. I was on the phone with Steven, and we need to make sure we have some guys good to go for the event."

"Is that an excuse?"

"What?" He sounds defensive.

"To stalk some hotties on Facebook," I joke.

He laughs. Although I'm wondering why he's on edge. Something's clearly bothering him right now.

"Oh, yeah. You know me," he says.

His response confirms my suspicion.

"You wanna swing by around six?" I ask.

"Sounds good. I'll pick up some food on my way over."

We hang up, but I'm uneasy. I should have asked him what was wrong, but it's none of my business. I don't know him like that, and if he'd wanted to talk about it, he would have. I continue working on my other major projects for work—the ones Eric pulled me away from to fix the clusterfuck he created. Before I know it, it's four fifty. I unlock the door and text him that Jacob isn't home and to just come in whenever he gets here.

***

The sound of the door opening and closing precedes a boisterous, "Honey, I'm home."

I turn off the water and open the glass door to the shower. "Be there in a minute, *darling*!"

He chuckles.

I grab my towel and dry off before tying it around my waist. I put on my glasses and head into the bedroom. Travis lies across the bed, eating from a plastic container with a salad in it. He has another placed beside him on the bed.

"Just make yourself at home, why don't you?" I tease.

"Don't mind if I do," he says as he checks me out. It's clear, as it always is, he likes what he sees. Makes me feel pretty fucking good about myself.

"You have a thing for salads?" I ask.

"I figured I might need to watch my waist."

"Why would you need to watch your waist?"

"I was talking to Steven and he mentioned I should participate in the fundraiser. I was going to ask you about that tonight."

My muscles tense up. We didn't say anything about him being one of the guys stripping.

"What? You want to be in it? Like taking your clothes off?"

"I won't if that's an issue. I figured it might actually be fun, though."

We hadn't really discussed either of us participating, and knowing he wants to be in it makes me uneasy.

"I'm fine with it," I lie. "It's not like we're actually together. I don't really have a right to have a problem with it."

Maybe I don't have a right, but the tension in my chest assures me I do have a problem with it.

"I won't do it if you don't want me to, though."

"It's fine. That's totally something you'd enjoy, and like I said, it's not like we're even dating, so it's not even something you should have to ask me about."

He purses his lips and sizes me up.

"Now that I think about it, you should be doing it, too," he says.

"Oh, hell no."

"Why? You look hot as hell and it is for charity, after all."

"Don't do that."

"What?"

"Act like I'm throwing people out on the street by not wanting to strip in public."

"You do a good job of stripping in private."

He scans my body, and I might as well not even have the towel on, considering he knows what everything underneath looks like.

"That's not the point."

I open my closet and retrieve a pair of boxers. I drop my towel and hear a soft growl behind me.

I glance back at him, enjoying the hungry look in his eyes.

"You know what I said about covering up." Judging by the look in his eyes, he's dead serious.

I pull my boxers up quickly, because we won't get shit done if we start with that now.

I fall down on the bed beside him.

He's still looking at me, his eyes filled with lust.

I open the container with my salad and grab the plastic fork Travis placed beside it. I look at his laptop screen. He's already in his Facebook account.

"Come on," I say. "We've got work to do. We need to find these hotties, but I'm not planning on being one of them."

"But I can be?"

Tension fills my chest. I shouldn't react like this. He should fucking be able to strip in front of or fuck whomever he wants without me giving a shit. It's none of my business. For whatever reason, though, the idea of a room full of horny guys watching him strip down to his underwear makes me uneasy. Not just uneasy...jealous.

"Of course," I say as I open a packet of Ranch dressing in the salad container and pour it over the salad.

I'm acting cool, but really, I'm irritated as fuck. If he can undress in front of a room full of people, I should be able to. I'm not the kind of guy who does shit like that, but why the fuck not?

Because I don't look like him, that's for fucking sure.

Still, if he's doing it, for some reason, I feel like I should. It's only fair.

"Maybe you're right," I say.

He takes a bite of his salad, and with his mouth full, asks, "About?"

"I should do it."

He covers his mouth with his hand as he finishes chewing and swallows. "Are you serious?" he asks.

"Well, it is for charity," I say.

"Changed your tune real fast, didn't you? You jealous?"

He eyes me suspiciously.

A little, but I don't have to fucking tell him that.

"I think it'd be nice to rub this in Peter's face. Hell, I wouldn't have done something like this when I was with him. Maybe it'd be good for me."

I was just trying to make up bullshit, but as I say it, I realize it's kind of true. And I'd love to see the look on Peter's face when he finds out I'm going to be stripping in front of a bunch of guys at Flirt. Although at the same time, I'm fucking terrified at the thought of having to take my clothes off in front of people.

"I'm gonna do it," I say.

I set my salad container beside me, grab his laptop, and sit upright.

I set the laptop on my thighs before turning and seeing an uneasy expression on his face. Like he's surprised by how I just grabbed his computer.

"Oh, sorry," I say, realizing he probably has private shit on here he doesn't want me to see. "I'm used to people handing their computers to me. Part of what I do."

I start to hand it back to him.

"No, no. It's fine."

"You sure?"

"Yeah. We have to go through these pieces of meat together anyway, right?"

Though he's talking about other guys, he's looking right at me, his lips twisted into a playful smirk.

I wish I fucking knew what he was thinking.

20
Travis

I could tell how uncomfortable Gary was, so I should have told him I wasn't going to do it. The thing is, I'm glad he's stepping outside of his comfort zone. It's good for him. He's keeping a part of himself trapped inside and as crazy as it sounds, this is another step toward letting him free. Or maybe I'm a fucking head case and want to do the show so I'm being a pushy bastard. Who the hell knows?

"Hey," I find myself saying as Gary sits beside me, going through my laptop.

"Yeah?" he replies without looking at me.

"Are you sure you're cool with me doing the show?"

Gary whips his head around so he's facing me. Yeah, I get it. The question makes unease slither beneath my skin. It sounds an awful lot like something someone in a real relationship would say.

"I don't have the right to say whether you can or can't do something. Especially if I'm...wait. Are you saying you're not comfortable with me doing it? You brought it up."

"No...fuck no." He winces and I groan. "Not like that. You're sexy as fuck, Gary. Stop trying to hide it. Show the world how fucking hot you are. You deserve it. And I also want to see Peter lose his head." I sit up straighter. "I just know things are a little different with you...because of what Peter did and I want to make sure my doing the show won't make you feel like you look bad." *See? Look at me trying not to be a pushy bastard.*

"Oh." He cocks his head slightly. "That's...that's really nice of you, Travis."

What the fuck? I grab a pillow and swat him with it. "You don't have to sound so surprised. I *am* a nice guy, you know."

"Do I sound surprised?" He laughs and I roll my eyes at him. I like it when Gary lets loose like this.

"Fucker," I tell him. "If you're good, I'll be real nice to your ass a little later. Now, let's pick some of these guys."

First, we make a Facebook page for the event. Then we go through profiles of some of the men we both know. We make a list of people we think would want to participate in the fundraiser and send out a few messages, link them to the page and ask them to share it. When we're finished, Gary closes the laptop but leaves it where it's sitting. "What was wrong with you earlier? You didn't sound right when we first spoke."

Oh fuck. This is the last thing I want to do. I wink at him. "Oh, you think you know me so well now, huh? Just a minute on the phone with me and you know my mood? What about you? Are you sure you're okay with doing the show? I know you'll be great, but how do *you* feel about it?"

He huffs. "Why do you do that?"

"Do what?"

"Always change the subject when I ask a serious question. It sounds like you're deflecting."

Jesus fucking Christ. "I don't know, doctor. It must have something to do with my scarred childhood." Turning, I go to get out of the bed, but Gary grabs ahold of my arm.

"I thought we had become friends." There's an innocence to his voice that does something to my insides—twists them up and pries my mouth open.

"We are." I sigh and sit back against his headboard again. "It's nothing. You're making a big deal about nothing. I had lunch with my brothers. Martin is planning on proposing to his girlfriend at her birthday party. He wants me to go, which means I'll be in the same room as my parents. It's a shitty idea because to them I'm an abomination and an embarrassment, but Martin won't take no for an answer. I was in a shitty mood and wanted to talk to you is all."

I cross my arms and stare at him. A kaleidoscope of different emotions flashes around in his eyes.

"Oh, fuck. Don't do that. Don't start to feel sorry for me or romanticize me. I'm not some kicked puppy who is heartbroken due to family issues. If you're going to feel anything about me right now, I'd rather it be desire. I don't know...blow me or something."

"Oh my God." Gary rolls his eyes at me, but I can see the amusement on his face. "I'm not romanticizing you, and I sure as shit don't see you as a puppy—though puppy play sounds fun. I'd be a real obedient puppy."

I cock a brow at him. He never ceases to surprise me. "I'm sure you would be."

"I was just thinking about how shitty life and family can be...and that you never really know what people are dealing with. You're gorgeous and confident."

"Keep going." I smile, and it earns me one from him.

"Conceited, too. But I guess I never imagined you dealing with shit like that, which is stupid—I realize that—but it's true. And I guess I'm surprised you called me when you felt that way."

Yeah...yeah, I am too. "Well, you *are* my fake boyfriend. I should get some benefits out of that."

He frowns. "What? My ass isn't enough?"

"Superass is definitely enough." We both laugh and Gary sets the laptop on the nightstand. He changes positions so his whole body is now facing me. It's strange, sitting here with him like this. Talking with him like this. I sure as shit never saw this coming when I woke up in his bed—hell, not even when we started this stupid farce. "What's your biggest sexual fantasy?" I ask him.

"What?" Gary drops his head backward and laughs. "I'm not answering that. Hell, I don't even know."

Well, that's a damn shame. "Fine. I'll let that one pass. Tell me why you're such a beast when we fuck, but you had mediocre sex with Peter."

He hasn't straight up come out and said that to me, but he makes it obvious. Otherwise he wouldn't be so surprised by the way he goes at it with me.

His cheeks flush pink and he turns his head. I hook a finger beneath his chin and turn his head so he's facing me again. "You skipped my last question; you're not skipping this one. I don't care if I have to force it out of you." I nod my head at him as though I'm waiting for him to test me. "I'll do whatever it takes to get what I want, Gary."

His Adam's apple bobs when he swallows. "Jesus, that kind of got my dick hard."

"Only kind of?" I reach down and grab his stiff cock, but only briefly because I'm really not going to let him skip out on this question. "Tell me."

He shrugs. "I don't know...I guess I just didn't feel comfortable letting loose with Peter."

Huh. I didn't expect that...and I don't fully understand it either. "But you feel comfortable with me? We hardly knew each other the first time we fucked." In a lot of ways, we hardly know each other now, but it doesn't feel that way. Somehow, I feel like I get Gary and like maybe he could get me.

"Maybe that's why, because I hardly knew you. Or maybe it's because you're so fucking sexual or I'm so attracted to you. I don't know why it is, I just know that I feel that way, which surprises me. How you can intimidate me and yet make me feel confident at the same time."

I'm not sure how much I like everything he just said to me. "I intimidate you?"

"Not like that." He waves his hand in the air as though I'm being ridiculous. "Not like I'm scared of you. I just mean because you're so sexy, and you have the perfect body. You're confident and experienced and everyone wants you. You're so damned gorgeous, how could I not be intimidated by you?"

My pulse speeds up in a way I'm not familiar with. I've had too many men to count tell me I'm attractive, but it feels different coming from him. "Stop selling yourself short. You're sexy as hell. You keep my dick hard. I want to toss you around and fuck you every time I see you. Hell, I'm not even screwing anyone else, and I'm satisfied. You need to give yourself more credit."

He looks away, and I let him this time. The tension in the room switches, changes into this awkward heaviness. I suddenly feel like lines are blurring between us, and it makes unease settle at the base of my spine. "Are you going to blow me or not?" I ask, trying to lighten the mood.

"Are you going to go?" he asks when he looks at me. Somehow, I know he means to the birthday party.

"I haven't decided yet," I answer honestly. "I don't want to let my parents dictate what I do. Martin is my brother and I love him, but that's what makes me feel like it's best if I skip it. I don't want to ruin his day." My biggest fear is that I won't be able to keep my cool and it will only hurt Martin and Liz. I also can't believe I just told Gary that.

"You won't," he says softly. "You won't ruin his day, not by being there. He wants you there, and you'll keep your cool because you care about him, and that's the kind of man you are."

I open my mouth, but nothing comes out. No one has said something like that to me before, especially not some guy I'm fucking. He sounds so confident in his words though, confident in me. I don't know how I feel about that. "I'll think about it," I tell him, but it doesn't feel complete there, so I add, "thank you." Patting my lap, I say, "Come here. Straddle me."

Gary moves swiftly and fluidly until he's sitting on my lap, one leg on either side of me. Part of me feels like I need to get the fuck out of here. Like I need to put some space between us. This moment feels raw in a way I'm not used to. Still, I add, "Good boy. Now, kiss me." Not sure if I'm going to stop it right after the kiss, teasing us both, or show him just how fucking hot his ass makes me.

I grab ahold of his waist. My hands are big around it. I glance down at his bulge, right before he does as I said—leans forward, and presses his mouth to mine.

I thread my fingers through his hair, push his face closer so I can kiss him deeper. My cock throbs, and I want nothing more than to take his hole, but I feel too raw tonight, like I need to get my ass out of this bed and get the hell out of here as quickly as I can.

Tugging his hair a little, I pull him away. "I'm gonna go."

His forehead wrinkles in confusion. "Okay...I thought you wanted me to blow you."

A smile pulls at my lips. *Jesus, this guy does something to me.* "I always want you to blow me, but it's better if I go." *Because I feel too close....*Right now, I feel too close to him and that has my head spinning.

Gary nods and crawls off me. Turning his way, I take his mouth one more time, because he tastes so fucking good, before I force myself out of the bed. I pick up our mess from dinner, the computer, and ask, "I'll see you tomorrow, right? Gotta keep this shit looking good for the fundraiser."

Gary smiles and tells me, "Yeah, of course. Though I don't think you have anything to worry about." There's a moment where I consider climbing back into bed with him and fucking him until we both lose our minds. Or maybe more than just fucking him...maybe I think about talking to him some more too, or laughing with him. That's my cue to get the fuck out, so I wink, turn and walk away while I still can.

21
Gary

Water sprays from the showerhead, hitting my chest and slapping against the tile floor beneath my feet. Travis massages my shoulders from behind, his thumbs pressing into my muscles. His touch feels so good, especially on my right shoulder, which I strained when I was using the bench press a few days ago.

"Feels better, doesn't it?" he asks.

"So much better. If you keep this up, I might start finding more reasons to hurt myself."

He chuckles. As he loosens me up, I roll my head back, enjoying how good it feels, reveling in his touch the way I might if we were fucking.

"I'm just glad we only have a week until the fundraiser," I say. "At least my body still looks decent from all the gym time we put in."

I can't believe it's already been two weeks since we were trolling through our Facebook friends for volunteers for the fundraiser, which has become the Summertime Boys Boxers and Briefs Strip-Off. The drag queen we hired, my primary care physician, suggested the name.

Travis stops massaging and trails his fingers down my back, around to my torso. He gropes and fondles my new muscles. Not massive but just a little more defined than usual.

"What are you doing?"

"Shhh," he whispers, his breath hitting behind my ear just right. "Just let me enjoy this hot body you've been working on."

He works his skilled hands. Those hands that have learned their way around my body as we've fucked our way through our preparations for the Boxers and Briefs Strip-Off.

The past few weeks have been busy as fuck. From contacting the hotties who'll be stripping to creating promo material and posters to hang around town, we've had plenty of work to do, and we've done it all together. Other than that, we've spent every spare moment we've had fucking each other's brains out...but the thing is, we've done a lot of talking too. And laughing. And watching movies. It's confusing as hell.

Travis moves closer to me, his chest pushing against my back, his hard dick pressing up between my ass cheeks.

"I just blew you not even five minutes ago," I say, shocked that he's as hard as ever.

"That was just to get rid of the morning wood. And I wouldn't have let you do it if I'd known how much it was going to hurt your neck. You have to tell me these things."

As he continues caressing my torso with his hands, I find my own dick stirring to life again.

Being with him like this has done wonders for my self-esteem.

He tucks his face close to me and whispers into my ear, "Wouldn't be a crime if we had another go. I can never keep my hands off you."

I roll my head back as warm sensations rush to my cheeks.

When we first started hooking up, after we fucked, I'd go back to my place, or he'd go back to his. But one night I managed to fall asleep on his bed while we were working on finding stock images for the event poster. After that, it became a no-brainer that we'd spend the night when we were together at whosever place we ended up at. Not cuddling or anything. It was just about convenience. Not that I haven't imagined him accidentally rolling up close to me and holding me the way he did the morning we first met. But this morning was one of many where I woke up at his place instead of mine.

"No," I say as he nips at the back of my neck. "You know I gotta be at my parents' in an hour."

I finally managed to schedule some time to see them for lunch today. This is something I've avoided for far too long, especially since we've gotten so busy with the fundraiser. It's been a great excuse to delay something I'm not all that excited about anyway.

Travis wraps his arms around me and holds me close. "You have to go. I know." But the way he kisses behind my ear, it's like he doesn't.

I pull away from his grip and spin around, the running water hitting my back. I scan over his body, taking in those muscles that have blown up even more since we've started hitting the gym hard for next weekend.

"Fuck you and this body," I say.

He smiles. "What?"

"You do a bicep curl and your muscles swell up like you have an allergy to working out."

He laughs. "I put on muscle pretty easily. And don't act like I'm the only one getting all fit here. All those bench presses certainly haven't hurt you."

He grabs my pecs and squeezes.

"They have hurt me, remember?" I set my hand on my right shoulder. Although I acknowledge, as he has a grip on my muscles, that it hasn't taken them long to firm up. Still, unlike him, I don't have the body of a fucking god. Not that I'm complaining. Because if I can't have it, at least I still get to fuck it.

"Just hurry on back for dinner with Steven and Raymond. We need to make sure we have everything in place for next weekend, and then we can reward ourselves with a little treat."

"A treat?" I ask.

He moves forward, his body pressing against mine as he grabs my ass cheeks firmly in his hands.

"This ass has needs, Gary."

"Oh, you think I'm just going to be your permanent bottom?"

"You can do whatever you want to me as long as you promise not to cut me off from that sweet ass. Although I don't feel like you'll be cutting me off anytime soon."

I push him away. "I hate a man who knows how good he is in bed."

"I get that," he says. "It's hotter when they don't realize it."

I can tell by the look he makes he's referring to me, and I can't stifle my grin. The feeling his compliment fills me with is concerning.

It's just sex.

I've had to repeat that to myself far too often. It's become more difficult to separate the fake relationship from whatever the fuck we're doing now. It was easy to not worry about liking him when I didn't know him. When I didn't know he likes to eat waffles for breakfast and he likes listening to nineties grunge music. That despite it being older, his favorite show is *Friends*, but he tells everyone it's *Goldrush*. He's not just some conceited guy I'm pretending to be in a relationship with anymore. We've spent so much time together. Hitting the gym in the afternoon to share gossip. Heading to bars at night, me moaning about all the messes Eric makes at work and Travis telling stories about some of his clients. He's more than a fuck buddy now. He's a friend.

His gaze shifts quickly, as if he's suddenly uncomfortable. As if he's on to what I'm thinking about.

He opens the glass door to his shower, grabs one of the two towels hanging off a rack on the wall, and dries off before heading into the bedroom to change.

What have I gotten myself into?

I know what's happening here. We aren't coded the same way. I'm programmed to think of things in terms of a relationship. He's coded to just want to fuck. For all I know, when I'm not around, he's off fucking other guys all over town. Although we haven't had much time apart and he told me he wasn't. I don't imagine he has a reason to lie, but there's that part of me that's insecure because of Peter.

I finish up my shower, dry off and throw on some fresh clothes that I brought in my laptop case, which I also packed my toothbrush and deodorant in. Not even in case I stayed over. Because I knew I would.

I finish dressing before him in his bedroom. He lies on his stomach, his laptop at the foot of the bed as he types. He glances at me occasionally, but neither of us speaks. Something weird happened in the shower there. Could he tell what I was thinking about? That's stupid. Why am I making such a big fucking deal out of this?

It's just sex.

There it is again!

"Guess I'll see you tonight," I say.

"Cool," he replies.

I grab my laptop case, leave, and walk down the hall. As I'm about to head into the nook where the elevators are, I hear the door open. I turn and see Travis heading toward me, just the towel around his waist. I wait, curious as fuck.

"You forget something?" he asks.

He holds out his hand, my keys dangling from his fingers.

"Oh, fuck. Shit. I'm such a fucking dumbass."

He smirks.

I take them from him and turn to enter the nook. Travis grabs my arm and turns me back around.

He moves forward and pushes me against the wall, kissing me.

A wave—like fire—rushes through me. The explosive energy I feel when he ignites that spark within me—one that spreads fast like a wildfire—leaves me shaking as my body recovers from the intensity of its power.

Overwhelming as it can be, it feels so fucking good.

I wrap an arm around him and grab the back of his head with my other, pulling him close as we kiss in a frenzy, as if we're about to be separated for weeks rather than a few hours.

We've spent too much time together. We shouldn't be doing this, but I just want a little more. That's what I keep telling myself. Only a few more fucks and kisses. But I know it's not this sexual chemistry that's the problem. It's the other shit. That I actually enjoy spending time with him. That I like being at his place or him being at my place. That I crave spending my days with him even more than I crave this hot sexual chemistry I feel when we touch.

He pulls away from our kiss and whispers, "Get your ass back quick so that I can give it what it needs."

He leans forward a bit, and I think he's coming in for another kiss, but he smacks me on the ass and winks.

"Later."

He heads back to his condo, and I enjoy the show as his ass shifts about beneath the towel he wears. I'm still recovering from the desire he's stirred...and more importantly, my fucked-up thoughts that are scrambling to make sense of what the hell we're doing.

***

"So, what have you been up to that you couldn't come visit your parents?" Mom asks as she picks at her baked beans with her fork.

We sit at the dining table in the same house I grew up in. In the kitchen where we used to all have dinner together.

All four of us.

Now there's only three people at a table that seats eight. Dad sits at the head of the table, Mom in the chair adjacent to him, right beside me. That leaves three empty chairs on the opposite side of the table. One of those used to be where Caroline sat.

Since I got here an hour ago, they've beat around the bush. While Mom set the table with grilled cheese sandwiches, baked beans, and french fries, Dad talked about the last Braves game. But I knew we'd get around to the question I've been avoiding—the question I'm always avoiding.

What have I been up to? Well, I'm gay and pretending to be in a relationship with a guy who likes my ass and who'll move on as soon as I've finished helping him get the money he needs to take his business to the next level.

"Nothing much," I reply. "Work."

Mom and Dad glance at each other. It's clear they aren't satisfied with my reply.

That's always been the answer. Because they don't know who I am. They don't know anything about their son. Haven't for a long time. Ever since I realized I was attracted to guys. Ever since I started seeing guys. Hell, I was in a five-year relationship that they knew nothing about.

"Haven't you met any girls?" Dad asks, his voice filled with concern.

"What?"

"You're all alone downtown."

"And you're always working," Mom adds. "Don't you think it's time you started seeing someone?"

This is not the fucking time for this conversation. Although this is what they typically say, so I'm not surprised.

"I'm fine," I say.

I can tell they're agitated. To them, I've just been living downtown on my own for so long. Working, but not having anyone to share my life with. They're concerned about me, but in some ways, I have the added pressure of their stress about Caroline's loneliness.

"Just don't work too hard," Mom says. "You've always been such a loner, and that worries me sometimes."

I haven't been a loner, Mom. I've just never been able to talk to you guys.

Not because they're awful or bad parents. But because they've had enough to deal with. Because I can't bear to see them look at me the way they used to look at Caroline when she upset them.

This is why I've procrastinated making plans with them.

I don't like being around them and living this lie.

And now I have my sexuality and a fake relationship to worry about. Lies are so goddamn frustrating...and confusing. Hell, I think part of what's fucking with my brain with Travis is that I've lied for so long that I'm actually starting to believe it.

It'd be nice if I could talk to my parents about everything I'm going through, but I can't. And that makes me sad.

"I went and visited Caroline the other day," Mom says, I figure to change the subject.

"And?" I ask, relieved to talk about anything but me.

Mom catches me up. Lets me know Caroline might be getting out on probation sooner than they expected. As she talks, though, I can sense her discomfort—and Dad's, too—not just about my sister, but about me. I've let them down. But I'd rather just let them down than for them to feel like I'm a failure. Like they created two kids who couldn't function like normal people in the world.

22

Travis

My door opens behind me, and my lips automatically stretch into a smile as I turn around. "Decide you want a quickie?" I ask right before I see Cody standing in the doorway instead of Gary.

"Nah, I'm good. I don't think your boyfriend will like that," he replies, closing the door.

"Fake boyfriend," I remind him.

"Oh, sorry. I didn't know we still believed the fake part. My mistake."

The fucker hasn't stopped giving me shit about Gary in weeks. It's starting to drive me crazy. "I'm going to kick you out. Don't make me kick you out."

Cody walks over and plops down on my couch. "You wouldn't kick me out. You're all talk, Travis. Pretty soon you'll realize it."

I have a feeling he's not talking about booting him and referring to Gary. That's not something I want to think about, much less talk to him about because as fucked up as it sounds, the lines have been a little blurry lately. We're not in a legitimate relationship. I'm not a Peter and I never will be. The reasons we're faking it are two of the people we're having dinner with tonight—them and his ex-dickhead, but I'd be lying if I didn't admit I like him more than I thought I would. He makes me smile even when I don't feel like smiling. I want to touch him all the time, just because I like that I can, and I like the way his skin feels beneath mine. He makes me feel an ease I didn't know I was missing, likely because he's such a simple man. Even if the only place I do admit it is a dark place in the back of my head that I can easily ignore.

"Let me go get some shorts on. I'll be right back," I tell Cody.

"Why? I've seen you in a towel before. I've seen you in less than a towel before." He winks at me like an idiot.

"Have you always been this annoying? Jesus, I'm going to kick your ass."

But the truth is, if Gary happened to come back, he'd lose his fucking mind if he saw me in here wearing a towel with Cody. He would try to hide it, but all those insecurities from Petey would show up when he's been doing so fucking good about ignoring them lately. Plus, rumors around here fly around worse than high school. It wouldn't surprise me if someone has their binoculars out, watching us from the other tower right now.

I head into my room, pull on a pair of boxer-briefs and some basketball shorts before heading back into the living room with Cody. "What's up, man?" I ask as I sit in the smoky-gray chair across from him.

"Nothing, really. I just haven't seen you in a while. You've been busy with your boyfriend." When I cock a brow at him he changes it to, "Your *fake* boyfriend. Though you know it would be okay if you lost the fake part, right?"

"Huh?" My skin feels tight all of a sudden. Relationship talk makes me itchy. "Because of you?" We've fucked once. He's my friend. *What in the hell is he getting at*?

"No, jackass. Because of *you*. Because of that *me tough man, don't need anyone* bullshit you believe. It's okay to like someone. To want to be in a relationship with them. It's okay to believe you're enough, T."

The tightness in my skin intensifies. Shoving to my feet, I head for the kitchen and start some coffee. "I don't know what you're talking about, and this conversation is over."

Cody is the only person who knows about some of the shit with my family—not all of it, but he knows my parents have nothing to do with me—mostly because he's a nosy motherfucker but also because he's met my brothers, and I might have gotten too drunk around him when I got into a fight with my parents one day.

"Tell me to mind my own business, and I will." Cody stands up, walks to the bar and leans over it.

"Mind your own business. And you're wrong. Haven't I already told you this is only about Peter, my job, and the fact that I like fucking him? I don't want to say it again."

"Yes, sir!" He gives me a mock salute, and I can't help but grin at him. "How are things going anyway? Do you have a feel for what Steven is thinking?"

"Fuck. I don't know." I run a hand through my hair. His question reminds me how important this is to me. "Raymond likes Gary a whole hell of a lot. That's gotta be a plus, especially since most people don't like me much."

"People like you. Shut up."

"Aww, that's the sweetest thing anyone has ever said to me." I tease him but I'm not in the mood. "I'm nervous. We're going over tonight to finalize fundraiser shit. Thanks for participating, by the way."

Cody rolls his eyes. "Please, baby boy. Like I need a reason to take my clothes off in front of people."

He's got me there.

We talk for a few more minutes about the fundraiser and some guy he took home last night. As soon as he leaves, I ignore the coffee I just made, head to my room, and fall face-first onto my bed.

I'm not thinking about what Cody said about relationships, getting hurt and all that other bullshit.

I'm not.

***

"You look nervous," Gary tells me as I pull my car up in front of Raymond and Steven's house. Inwardly, I groan because it looks like the house I grew up in—where you have to hide who you are and be absolutely perfect all the time.

"I'm not nervous," I grit out, annoyed at myself.

"Yes. You are. You get little crow's feet by your eyes when you're stressing or nervous." Gary reaches over and rubs my temple, but I jerk away.

"Did you really just tell me I have crow's feet?"

"Only when you're worried. It's not like you need Botox. Just need to relax, so you can continue to look gorgeous as always."

I realize then that he said it on purpose just to get a rise out of me and to help me relax.

"It's just dinner. You'll be fine. I know that's easy for me to say since you're actually doing this fake relationship thing for a good reason instead of just to make your ex jealous like me, but you'll be great. I know it. The fundraiser will go well, and I have no doubt Steven is going to invest in you. I would if I were him."

His words bounce around in my chest like a pinball machine. *I would if I were him....You'll be great.*

And somehow, those statements help, even though I don't like that they do.

"Oh no! What happened now? You looked fine, and now you look even more nervous! Should I blow you real quick?" he asks and I wish like hell we had time for that.

"No." I get out of the car, fully aware that I'm in Grumpy Travis mode. I have to get all my asshole behavior out before we head inside.

Gary gets out behind me, and I make myself stop to wait for him. When he reaches me, I thread our fingers together as I lead us to the front door. After ringing the bell, I look his way and mumble, "I'm sorry. I'm nervous, and I don't know how to deal with it."

He sighs, sets his head on my shoulder, and says, "I know, Travis."

I sort of freeze up at the intimacy of the moment just as the door opens, and we're standing here, holding hands with Gary's head on my shoulder, and I hope I don't look like I'm going to throw up.

"Aren't you two the cutest! I remember those days when Steven and I first got together!" Raymond reaches out, hugging Gary first and then me.

Raymond shows us into the living room. Steven is sitting on the brown, leather couch with a coffee table in front of it. He stands and as I walk over, holds out his hand, which I clasp with my own. "Hi, Travis. It's good to see you again."

"Thanks. Same to you."

He shakes Gary's hand next. Raymond sits in one of the chairs across from Steven and then Gary takes the other so I sit down beside him on the couch.

"Let's see where you are," he says. Gary and Raymond pull their seats closer, so we can all see well, while I pull out the papers and start going over all the details with him.

Every so often, Gary will jump in with a thought or an idea. At one point, his cheeks flush, and he apologizes as if he doesn't have the right. Reaching over, I squeeze his knee. "No, it's fine. I couldn't have made it this far without you. I value your opinion." Which is the God's honest truth. Gary has likely saved my ass in more ways than one recently.

Steven and Raymond both seem impressed with all the things Gary and I have to say. Once we're done going over everything for next week, we head into their dining room where Steven brings out the lasagna he made for dinner.

The conversation flows well. There are laughs and not many lulls, especially when Raymond and Gary start going off about musicals again. The night has a strange vibe to it that's unlike anything I ever thought I would experience. It reminds me of dinner parties my parents used to have with other couples, only no one here is an asshole, except likely me.

When the evening is over, Gary and Raymond are talking as I walk with Steven toward the door. He stops me with a hand on my shoulder. "I'm proud of you, son. You and Gary have taken this idea and run with it. I'm excited to see what other work we can do together in the future. Once we're finished with the fundraiser, let's have a meeting so we can further discuss working together."

"Thank you...I...thank you." I can't find words other than those. My heart pounds, jumps, as my head spins. That means he wants to work with me, right? It's not a guarantee, but it sounds pretty fucking close.

I can hardly contain myself as we get into the car and pull away. The second we're out of sight from the house, I pull off to the side of the road, grab Gary, and yank him into a tight hug. "I think we did it. Thank you, Gary. Thank you. Thank you." Again, they're the only words that seem to come to me.

23
Gary

Flirt is packed with hotties. Not just the guys who signed up to take off their clothes. It's hotties and friends of hotties and friends of friends of hotties. All that social media promotion the volunteers worked on clearly paid off.

Despite the successful turnout, I'm stressed as fuck. While Travis rallies up the participating boys, I scramble around to finalize some last-minute preparations. Putting out fires. The ice machine broke down, so I had to make an emergency run to the nearest QT to pick up enough bags of ice to last the bartenders through the night. And the guy who was supposed to collect donations at the door backed out ten minutes before we needed him, so I had to find a replacement while I manned the booth. As soon as I found a friend who was willing to help out, Miss Laurie Firebomb—AKA my primary care physician, Dr. Martin Crawley, who'll be hosting the event—accosted me. Evidently, the DJ didn't have any of the songs she wanted to use in his playlist, so Laurie Firebomb needed me to fetch a CD from her car. As she said to me when I tried to get out of it, "These boots aren't made for walking!"

After I hand her the CD, I start looking for Travis to make sure he's gotten to all the guys. I fight my way through the crowd.

Someone grabs my arm and pulls me to the bar.

It's Hayden, who I haven't seen since the pool party. He wears his pinned-on #6 badge, indicating his place in the lineup for tonight. Travis and I made the badges a few nights ago, taking occasional breaks for BJs and buttsex.

"You look stressed as fuck," he says as he adjusts his glasses. He studies my expression.

"Look at *you*," I say. "In a little short-sleeved button-up and jeans. Guys are going to lose their shit when you get up there. I'm surprised your man wouldn't do it."

"Oh, God no. He's weird about stuff like this. He's even uncomfortable about me doing it. Hell, even when I went to the pool party, he was uneasy about me wearing a stupid speedo."

Funny his boyfriend would be that way. Hayden is the quiet one, and Lance is the loud, fun-loving guy who's always looking for attention. But when I asked them, it was Hayden whose eyes lit up like this was a great opportunity to unleash the secret exhibitionist within.

"He seemed kind of mad about it earlier," Hayden continues.

"He'll be fine," I say. And I certainly can't blame Lance for being uneasy about Hayden participating, considering I'm not sure how I feel about Travis removing his clothes in front of everyone. Not that I have a right to be bothered by it. I'm just glad I've had enough things to keep me busy that I haven't really had time to focus on it.

Hayden spins back and calls out, "Derek!"

Derek is just a few guys away from us, wearing his #9 badge as he texts someone on his phone. He has a concerned expression on his face. Like something's wrong. It reminds me of the conversation I had with Eric about the guy Derek's supposedly been seeing in secret. I'm a crappy friend. We haven't hung out much since Travis and this fundraiser started taking up all my free time. Although Derek hasn't reached out to hang either— likely because he's been just as busy with his secret relationship.

"Derek!" Hayden calls again. "You want shots?"

"Yeah, yeah," Derek replies.

Hayden orders three tequila shots from the bartender. Hayden and I drink ours right away.

"Hey, you," says a voice behind me. I spin around. Travis grins, looking charming as ever in an indigo-colored polo. He runs his hand through his dark brown hair, and I notice it falls right back into place like there isn't a goddamn thing he can do to make himself appear less attractive.

We stand there, gazing into each other's eyes. But I don't want to stop.

He breaks the silence with, "So I don't want to spoil your night, but Peter and Evan just got here." He points them out.

The rectangular bar takes up most of the room—obviously designed so that no matter where you are in the space, you can order a drink. We're in one corner beside the restrooms, while Peter and Evan sit on stools in the opposite corner, in front of the platforms we've set up to create a stage. The area's typically where everyone dances as soon as they've had enough drinks to forget that life is sad and hard.

Seeing Peter with his man, at an event where I'm about to totally expose myself to everyone in town, makes the blood in my face drain.

I snatch Derek's shot off the bar and down it.

"Hey!" Derek exclaims. I turn to see his arm stretched out like he was reaching for it.

"Peter and Evan are here," Hayden explains to him.

I finish the shot and set it back down.

"Can we not broadcast it to everyone?" I ask.

He wasn't loud enough for anyone to hear. I'm just on edge about it.

Hayden orders another shot.

"Don't I have enough on my mind as it is?" I add.

"You okay?" Travis asks, his expression filled with concern. He reaches out and rubs his hand up and down my back.

"Yeah. Just freaking out a bit."

"Don't look at them. Don't even think about them. They're nobodies, okay?"

But Peter's not a nobody. He was the first guy I let in. The first guy I opened my heart up to. The first guy who ripped it out of my chest and shattered it to pieces.

"This'll take your mind off them," Travis says, handing me my badge. I check and see that it says #1.

"What the fuck?"

"It was the last one I had."

I glare at him before snatching his badge from him.

"Okay. Deal," he says.

I check it. "Number two? You were planning this all along!"

He arches his brows and smiles. "Not gonna let you chicken out of this."

The bartender sets down Derek's shot. I steal it, throw my head back, and pour it down the hatch. I swallow quickly, cringing as I pray to God some of this alcohol will kick in soon.

"Seriously?" Derek asks.

"Get another, Number Nine," I say.

Travis chuckles. I should punch that cocky grin off his face.

"It's Raining Men" starts playing, and as Miss Laurie Firebomb takes the stage, I know it's too fucking late for me to back out now.

Travis grins. "Guess I got a show to put on."

He grabs my waist and pulls me to him, kissing me hard. That same energy I always experience with him is even more powerful in this moment, possibly because it's mixed with my uneasiness about what we're going to do.

Standing beneath our official Boxers and Briefs Strip-Off banner and flanked by helium balloons tied to either side of the stage, Miss Laurie Firebomb delivers her spiel about the fundraiser and the cause before setting a bucket for tips on a chair in front of the stage and saying, "The boy who collects the most tips for Seconds Chances is declared the winner of the Boxers and Briefs Strip-Off and receives a thousand dollar bar tab from our sponsor tonight, Flirt!"

The packed bar cheers and applauds. Even Hayden and Derek are clamoring with excitement. My legs are tense, as though they're saying, *You can try to get to the stage all you want, but we won't be helping you.*

I'm totally getting fewer tips than Travis. I fucking know it. And it's going to be embarrassing when I get up there and totally wig out.

I want to back out, especially now that I know Peter and Evan will be watching me front and center.

"Please welcome our first boy to the stage," Miss Laurie Firebomb says.

The music changes abruptly to Britney's "Toxic."

Everyone goes crazy as Travis steps onto the stage, totally owning his strut. The guys in the bar gawk at him. They must know by how his polo fits that whatever he's about to show them is gonna look good.

Travis moves to the beat like he's a fucking stripper. And an incredible one at that.

He grabs the hem of his shirt and pulls it off over his head, displaying the physique I've gotten to enjoy again and again these past few weeks. He whirls the shirt around his head before tossing it into the audience. A hand reaches up and snatches it. He's never seeing that polo again.

He undoes his belt and zipper and turns around, lowering his jeans enough to reveal a neon pink jockstrap beneath them.

"Holy shit," Derek says.

Clever bastard.

He didn't warn me about that.

A crowd of guys rush to the edge of the stage, pulling out dollar bills and holding them out eagerly for Travis, who pulls down his pants slowly as he kicks off his shoes and then tosses the jeans to the guys before him.

I'd be worried about how he was going to get home without his clothes, but my face is red with what I know is jealousy. Up until now, I've had him all to myself. And now here everyone else is, getting to enjoy that beautiful body. I wish I didn't feel this way. He's not even mine.

He turns back to the audience, who can now fully enjoy the bulge in the jockstrap, and that feeling that everyone else is enjoying that massive cock puts me even more on edge.

The crowd grows as more people join in, and Travis goes all *Magic Mike*, getting on his knees at the edge of the stage and moving his body to the beat in the way that best displays his abs, his chest...his fucking everything. Everyone's shoving cash into his jockstrap, and in a matter of moments, I know he's already made at least a hundred dollars.

The music finally stops and Miss Laurie Firebomb walks up the two steps that lead up to the stage. "Oh, I see you liked the little warm-up," she says into her microphone. "This is a preview of what we've got for you tonight, boys." She makes a big production of collecting the money from Travis and putting it in the tip bucket that no one bothered to use for Travis's performance.

I'm going to be the laughingstock of Midtown for the next year, if not longer.

"I'm so glad I'm not going next," Hayden says.

I glare at him. "Sorry, dude," he adds.

I pin my badge onto my shirt, and as I glance around to gauge the audience, I notice Peter looking at me from the opposite side of the bar. His expression makes me think he pities me. Like he's sure I'm gonna get up there and make a complete idiot out of myself...and I might. He doesn't think I can do this. But between his skepticism and a competitive spirit that's risen from Travis's performance—not to mention the jealous feelings that rage within me—I'm determined not to go down without a fight.

I still have a pair of scissors in my pocket from when I was putting up decorations this afternoon. I pull them out and cut a slit vertically down the center of my shirt collar.

"If he wants to play strippers, then let's play strippers," I say, setting the scissors onto the bar.

Hayden and Derek look at me like I've lost my mind, and maybe I have...or maybe the tequila is starting to kick in. Whatever the reason, I'm giving this my all...putting the beast that comes out in the sack into motion on stage.

Miss Laurie Firebomb chats up a bit while Travis hops down from the stage and turns back to me, winking. It's like he knows nothing I can do could top his performance.

"So, let's get this going with another boy, shall we?" Miss Laurie Firebomb says before announcing me.

I head for the stage as Nicki Minaj's "Super Bass" starts up.

I bob to the beat, and I kick off my shoes and start up the steps.

I offer a little tease, pulling up my shirt, and the guys, clearly hyped up because of Travis, scream out for more.

I notice a guy right at the edge of the stage. He has dark hair, nearly as dark as Travis's. His bright blue eyes are lit up with interest. And the look in his eyes gives me an idea. I'm not Travis. I can't take on this whole audience like he did, but I can work it with a guy who's into me. Travis has taught me that much, at least.

I grab the tip bucket and the chair in front of the stage. I place the bucket on the edge of the stage and the chair in the middle.

I turn back to the guy who can't keep his eyes off me, approach him, and beckon him with my forefinger.

He glances around, obviously surprised that I singled him out.

When I reach the edge of the stage, I squat down and grab him by the collar of his polo.

I pull him onto the stage and guide him to the chair, which he sits in.

I face the audience and spread my legs, squat down, and give him a lap dance. I move my ass in circles on his pelvis. Show everyone how I work this Superass.

The guys and girls in the audience lose their shit, throwing their dollar bills onto the stage as I grab my shirt collar and rip so it tears down the middle.

I check Travis's expression, wide-eyed. He appears impressed, and now I feel like I'm putting on this show for him more than anyone else.

I pull out of the sleeves of my ripped shirt and toss it into the audience before turning around and working my ass against my volunteer's lap, continuing my dance.

His expression is all the reassurance I need, as he looks me up and down, feeling lucky as fuck to be here right now. Like Travis makes me feel when we're together.

I unbutton my jeans and unzip my fly before standing up, turning around, and stepping back so my ass is right in the guy's face. Squatting, I reach behind me, grab his hands, and hook his fingers in either side of my jeans before urging him to pull them down.

He slides them down halfway. I stand and let them fall to my ankles, revealing my gold-banded black Calvins. I slide my feet out of my jeans and give him another lap dance, facing the audience. I place his hands on my torso, encouraging him to feel me up, which is driving everyone insane.

The dollar bills are flying onto the stage, and I lean back, keeping my balance as I grip the bottom of the chair. I turn to him, our lips inches from each other. I can tell he'd kiss me in a heartbeat, but the tease is what's driving the audience insane.

He starts moving in like he's going to, so I turn my head, but continue to let him enjoy groping me, fondling me.

This is so freeing. So liberating.

And as the dollars continue collecting on the stage, I can tell I've made more than my share of cash.

"Well, wasn't that steamy?" Miss Laurie Firebomb says, but she can hardly be heard over the applause.

The music cuts off, and I turn to the guy who's been helping me, thanking him for participating. He seems eager for more, but I thank him again and step off the opposite side of the stage Travis is on. Clearly, the tequila's hit my system now. And I'm overwhelmed by what a frenzy everyone's still causing over my silly little scene.

Peter and Evan are standing in my path to Travis.

"Hey, boys," I say as I reach them. I grab Evan's cocktail and take a sip before returning it to him. "Sorry," I say. "Was that yours?"

The expression on Evan's face, not conceited or annoyed, but sad, makes me think I may have taken out my frustration on the wrong guy. He didn't cheat on me. Peter did.

I smile at Peter before moving along, the guys in the crowd parting for me like I'm fucking royalty.

Travis stands on the other end of the stage, still in only the pink jockstrap, his eyes wide like he's impressed.

24
Travis

A burst of pride swells in my chest, an unfamiliar feeling since it's not myself I'm proud of right now. It's also not the only foreign emotion twisting at my insides, but it's a whole hell of a lot easier to deal with. Because as proud as I'd been watching Gary up there, seeing him fucking shine full of the confidence his sexy ass deserves, there had been a point where I wanted to rush the stage. That I'd felt anger that it hadn't been me getting a lap dance from him. That a room full of other men had seen Gary let loose and be free in a way he typically only does with me.

Ain't that some fucking shit?

"Hey!" Gary says when he reaches me, his breathing labored, likely from adrenaline.

"That motherfucker is looking at you."

"The guy I danced with?" Gary turns to check out the scene, sounding a little more excited than I'd like to hear from him, and then I have the urge to slam my head into a pole because that shit shouldn't bother me.

"No. He can look at you all he wants. He has the right to look at you, and touch you or whatever the hell else you want to do with him. I'm talking about Peter." But honestly, I really don't like the other guy wanting him either. That's a bit of information I'll just keep to myself.

"Oh," Gary says, a hint of disappointment in his voice.

"Did you want that guy looking at you?" I ask him.

"That's not what I meant."

"Did Peter say something to you?" Jesus. I sound like a Neanderthal all of a sudden. Like I'm going to go over and defend his honor or something. *What the fuck is wrong with me?*

"What? No. And even if he did, I can handle it myself."

I know he can. I think Gary can handle a whole lot more than he gives himself credit for. "I know, but it's still fun to piss him off. I'm your boyfriend. I have the right."

His eyes go wide, and he looks like he's going to swallow his own tongue. I'm not sure why he's freaking out. We're both in this fake relationship together. He knows I have to play it off for everyone. "Let's go." I grab his hand and head toward Peter and Evan. Peter has his eyes firmly on us, fire blazing as Evan leans against a wall with his arms crossed. *What a fucking slimeball.* I can't believe Gary was ever with him.

"What the hell are you doing, Travis?" Gary asks as he stumbles along to keep up with me.

"No fucking clue." Which is the truth. I've hated Peter since this shit started, but right now, I'm just angry and confused and pissed about being angry and confused, so I want to stir up shit. No one ever said I'm the most mature guy around.

But the truth is...I want to stick up for Gary. I want Peter to know what he passed up. I want everyone to know how incredible Gary is, Gary included.

"You were here to try and rattle him, and I don't like it," I say the second we step up to Peter and Evan.

"Oh fuck," Gary groans out beside me.

"No, I'm here because we come here often, and there's a fundraiser. You might not know it since this is your first, but this is what I do. I'm involved in making people's lives better, but then...I guess you are too. A little rub here and there does a body good."

"Motherfucker." I advance on him just as Gary's arms wrap around me. My chest heaves in and out. My head feels like it's going to explode, and, Jesus, what the fuck is wrong with me? I feel a tornado of different emotions, the

172

winds picking up and lifting more and more shit for me to feel.

"Let him go, Gary. If he wants to act like a Neanderthal, let him." It doesn't escape my attention that Peter just used the same word to describe me as I used about myself.

"Don't. I'm serious, Travis. He's just trying to get a rise out of you." Then softer, Gary says, "Steven and Raymond are here."

That's when all the pieces shift into place. Peter wanted to cause problems. Wanted to piss me off or embarrass Gary because he knew Steven and Raymond would be there tonight. Because he doesn't like the fact that Gary has moved on, and he wants to hurt Gary by hurting me.

And Gary just saved my ass.

The tension in my body loosens, obviously enough for Gary to feel it because he relaxes his hold on me. Looking Peter right in the eye, I say, "You're not worthy of him. You were never worthy of Gary. He's a million times the man you are, and a million times the man I am too. I won't fuck it up like you did, though." Because he's my friend. Because I would never hurt him. Even when this charade is over, I want to keep Gary in my life.

Turning my gaze to Evan, I say, "If I were you, I'd run as far and as fast as I could."

I grab Gary's hand again, raise it, and kiss his palm. "Come on, baby. And you were fucking incredible out there tonight."

At first, when I attempt to tug at him, he doesn't move. It's as though his feet are rooted to the floor. His pupils are blown wide; as he takes me in their hue darkens.

There's something in his eyes I can't read. Shock is there, for sure. But that's not all and for a brief moment, my stomach drops out, making me feel empty because I don't think he's going to go with me. Did I just fuck up worse than I thought?

Or maybe he thinks I'm overplaying it? That I just took this gig a little too far.

He might be right.

Silently, I plead with him. I don't realize that's what I'm doing at first, but it is, and then my gut switches and feels too heavy. Even fake relationships are a whole hell of a lot of work.

"Come on," I say again and this time, he does. Gary walks with me. People are screaming and yelling for whoever is on stage right now. I find a quiet corner, pull Gary into my arms, and nuzzle his neck, so I can easily say, "That was good, huh? I played the protective boyfriend really well back there." Only for a minute, it hadn't felt like an act.

His return hold on me slackens slightly. There's a short pause before he says, "Yeah...yeah you did."

"Thank you." Pulling back, I try to smile, but he doesn't return it. Hooking a finger under his chin, I tilt his head up so he's looking at me. "Hey, did I screw up? Are we okay?"

"No. You didn't screw up, and we're okay." But his words aren't real convincing.

"Are you sure? I know I'm acting a little unhinged, but I'm hoping that was a good thing." How, I don't know. "That's what a boyfriend would do, right?" No, no they wouldn't. And then because my head is a jumble of too much shit, I add something else to the mix. "You really were awesome out there. You had every dick in the building hard."

"I don't know about that..." He tries to look away, but I don't let him.

"Hey. I saw them, not you. People were going crazy for you, and you sure as shit had my dick hard. But then, you always do, Superass. You turned into Sex-God Gary like you do when we're fucking. I swear to Christ, every man you're with after this ends is in for such a fucking treat." For reasons I don't want to dissect, those words taste bitter on my tongue, so I decide to have Gary's taste there instead.

I crush my lips to his, don't go slow as I push my tongue into his mouth. He melts against me as he always does, and I want to savor the feeling, to ingrain it into my body. Kissing him deeper, I hold the sides of his face in my hands, suck on his tongue and grin against his mouth when he nips at my lip.

"Mmm. You're a good kisser. I've never been a huge fan of kissing. I think I appreciate it more now."

"Somehow, I doubt that."

"Don't do that," I tell him. "I hate it when you do that. Don't put yourself down. Fuck anyone and everyone who doesn't see your worth, and you need to start seeing it yourself."

I have no fucking clue why I'm getting so mushy all of a sudden.

"Come on. Let's go make an appearance and talk to Steven and Raymond. Oh, and you know I want one of those lap dances, right?"

Gary nods, but something feels a little off with him. I figure he just needs to work through it the way I would, so I hold his hand again because that feels like a boyfriend thing to do, especially after your man grinds his ass on someone else's cock. I totally should have thought of that shit.

We put our shoes on, what's left of our clothes, and a bartender gives us some spare shirts left over from a fundraiser before we end up in the middle of the room. Gary's in front of me, my arms wrapped around him from behind as we watch the rest of the show. Steven and Raymond join us for part of it, tell us how well it's doing, how impressed they are with us...what a good team we make together.

I let my gaze travel to Gary when they say that. I've never played real well with others, so I'm not sure I've made a good team with anyone before.

We have a few men tallying up money as the show goes along. When it's over, Miss Laurie Firebomb takes the stage to announce the winner: "Number two! Gary, get your sexy ass up here!"

He doesn't move. Everyone starts clapping and cheering. I'm laughing as I give him a little shove and swat the sexy ass Miss Firebomb was just talking about. "Go on. Get up there. You deserve it," I tell him, and damned if that pride doesn't fill every inch of me again as I watch Gary go.

25
Gary

We have several more shots before leaving Flirt—victory shots provided by Steven and Raymond and some other guys I didn't even know.

After I claim my thousand-dollar bar tab prize, everything becomes a bit hazy as my thoughts scramble to make sense of all that happened with Travis. He kept calling me his boyfriend and telling me how special I was. He fucking stood up to Peter for me. But then he said he didn't care if I'd gone home with the guy I did the lap dance for.

I sure as fuck didn't expect that. I was kind of hoping it'd make him at least a little bit jealous, but I guess he'd have to feel like I'm more than a fuck buddy for that to happen.

We head back to Metropolis, and soon, the taste of vodka on his tongue and lips mixes with the tequila on mine as Travis pushes me up against the door to his condo.

"God...you were...fucking amazing out there," he says between kisses. "You made all those other guys, even me, look like fucking amateurs."

He starts kissing at my throat. I glance around because we're still in the hall. We need to get into his condo, but I don't want to stop the feeling his mouth against my flesh stirs.

It all feels so good. Not just this kiss. Tonight. Being with him. And the worst of it, the most unsettling part, is when the thought crosses my mind: *Why does it have to be pretend?*

Why does he have to be a good guy? Why can't I keep seeing him as the conceited guy I thought he was when we first started this?

It was so easy then.

But this has gotten so hard because I don't like that it's a lie anymore.

His lips return to mine.

I just want a few more. That's what I keep telling myself. What got me into this mess. I want him. Crave him. I keep thinking that the more we fuck, the less I'll need it, but the intensity hasn't waned. It just keeps getting better and better. Because now that he's someone I like as a person, what was already hot sex has turned into even better sex—something I would never have even thought was possible.

He pulls away and looks into my eyes.

Can't he see everything that's going on in my head right now? Can't he tell how confused I am?

I can't look at his face without saying, "You're so beautiful, Travis."

It's not a compliment. It's a realization that nothing I could ever do could make someone like this want a guy like me. Reminds me that Peter couldn't have settled for me when he could have Evan.

He smirks like he's proud of himself and kisses me some more. "I don't fuck ugly," he says between a kiss.

That's not what I need to hear right now, and he must sense it because he pulls away again, those hazel eyes shimmering.

He moves his hand to my face, caressing his thumb across my cheek.

"Gary, I don't know what Peter, or whoever it is, did to fuck you up like this, but I have the hardest time understanding what's wrong in your head that you can't see what everyone else sees."

I know what he's trying to get at, but I can't handle a compliment right now. Not from him. Not when I'm so confused about what the hell is even going on between us.

I turn away to avoid those beautiful eyes of his, but he moves his hand to my chin and pulls on it so that I'm forced to look at him again.

"You're gorgeous, Gary. And I'm not just talking about this hot body that all those guys were drooling over tonight."

He moves in closer, whispering, "You've got everything. Beautiful face. Tight body. That ass...I can't find any flaws with it."

I chuckle, and I'm glad he made a joke because I needed it right now.

"But you're actually a good person, too. I owe you the fucking world for everything you've done for me."

"You helped me out, too."

"But you didn't do this just for you. I know that. You never had to say yes to helping with the fundraiser. I don't like it when people help me because it makes me feel like I owe them something, but you never make me feel like there are conditions. Like you really want to help because you're a good person. And it's because you are. Thank you. You're incredible."

A powerful sensation sweeps through me as goose bumps prick across my flesh.

"Don't say that," I say.

"It's true, and every time you doubt yourself...or you say something self-deprecating...it fucking...it makes me want to smack you until you get it into your dumb head just how special you really are."

His lips are on mine in a moment.

Sweet, sensuous kiss.

He wraps his arms around me and pulls me close, pressing me up against the door.

In the back of my mind, I keep replaying the conversation about how he didn't care if I hooked up with that guy I brought onto the stage, but his words and this kiss...they promise so much. And it's so easy to get lost in the moment.

He retrieves his keys from his pocket and unlocks the door. We kiss, fondle, and undress each other on the way to the bedroom.

We've fucked a lot, but the sensations crawling through me tonight are so much more powerful than ever before.

Soon, we're naked, my legs pressing into the mattress on either side of his hips.

I feel so safe with him. So comfortable.

Each kiss pulls me further away from all those worries that raced through my mind before as I become engrossed in this experience. In the pleasure. In everything that Travis is.

I kiss down to his chest, offering licks as I crawl down his body, until I'm at his hard cock.

So fucking hard.

I like it when it's this hard because it makes me feel like he means it when he tells me I'm hot. Or beautiful.

I take it into my mouth, sucking and teasing the tip with my tongue, offering him the pleasure he deserves.

I pull it out for a moment to lick my fingers. I slide two between his cheeks and navigate them into his hole as I open my mouth and take his cock again.

His groan lets me know I'm doing a good job satisfying him.

It's the only thing that reminds me of how fucked I am.

Fucked for how much I want this. For how much I want him.

I continue pleasuring him until my cock is too hard for me to resist. I pull back, a burning question on my mind. I force it out before I have a moment to second-guess myself: "Do you mind if I top you tonight?"

He tilts his head.

"Never mind."

"What? No. That'd be great. I'm just surprised you asked."

"Peter was always weird about it. I'd ask, but he was never all that excited about it."

He grins. "I'd be happy to take that cock of yours."

His invitation makes me smile. I fetch a condom and lube from the nightstand before readying myself. After working into him, he smiles before I descend, kissing him as I thrust.

He groans into my mouth so I can hear his pleasure. It makes me even harder.

"Oh, fuck, Gary," he says, and my name on his lips drives me crazy.

I fuck him as he throws his head back to the pillow, twisting his body as he cries, "Oh, fucking God, Gary!"

I want to keep fucking him like this so he'll keep saying my name.

As much as we're enjoying this, I want to take him from behind, so I pull out.

"Get on your knees," I instruct.

And his eyes light up with the lamplight coming from his nightstand. They're excited. Eager.

And so am I.

He gets on his knees, facing the headboard.

Peter was never this adventurous. With Travis, I always feel like he's game for anything. Totally willing to explore and experiment.

That's so freeing.

As I work back into him, he tosses his head back, moaning once again, sounding totally uninhibited as he revels in his pleasure.

I wrap my arm around him and caress my fingers through the grooves between his firm muscles—those muscles jacked from all the work we've put in for the fundraiser. Leaning forward so that my chest is pressed against his back, I rub my cheek against his. He turns and kisses me. He reaches back and cups the back of my head in his hand.

I feel so close to him. Closer than I've ever felt to him before.

These kisses aren't like the kisses when we were first hooking up. They're so much more.

This can't just be in my head. Or can it?

"You feel amazing, Gary." My name on his lips takes away all my concern.

I just want him right now.

I reach around and grab his hard cock, stroking it, some of the lube from when I was putting on the condom still wet on my hand.

"God, you're making me so fucking hard. If you keep doing this, I'm gonna fucking blow, Gary…"

I love hearing my name so much, and it keeps me building and climbing. My balls contract. I'm so fucking close.

"You have no idea how fucking amazing you are," he says before kissing me again, slamming his mouth against mine. It's not anything like a kiss we've shared before. Something more intense that sends the vibrations shaking through me as I erupt in the condom.

I feel his dick pulse, and he curses as he spews on his pillow in front of him.

Our sweat-soaked bodies pressed together, we breathe heavily as we come down from the high. I rub my hand through the sweat on his abs, enjoying the sensation of being so close to him.

We stay here for so long. Too fucking long before he starts to move. I pull out, and he spins around, offering me even more kisses.

We relax on the bed together, continuing to kiss and fondle.

I enjoy his body and he enjoys mine.

I don't ever want it to end. Can't I have this forever?

But in the back of my mind, I know better.

***

"Fuck."

I wake to a throbbing headache.

Why the fuck did I drink all those tequila shots?

I force my eyes open. I'm gonna need to grab some ibuprofen, but I notice Travis has his arm around me.

I freeze. This hasn't happened since that first morning when I woke up to the stranger in my bed. The hottie across the way who I'd watch run on his treadmill or do sit-ups and push-ups in his living room occasionally.

Only now we're in his bed. Together.

My head hurts like a motherfucker, but I like the feeling of his arm around me. In a way that I know I shouldn't.

I've come down from the high of our experience last night, which was so much more than fucking. For me, at least.

But I know it wasn't that way for him. He didn't care about the guy I was dancing with. I could have gone home with him, and Travis would have been high-fiving me this morning.

He stirs. I close my eyes and pretend to be asleep. I wait for him to pull his arm off me, but he doesn't, and I'm glad.

Does it mean something?

It has to, doesn't it?

But I realize once again I'm the one who's kidding myself.

"Morning, sexy," he whispers into my ear before offering a gentle kiss.

His words sound so good again, but they remind me this can't last.

That I can't go on like this. It doesn't matter to him, but it matters to me, and if we keep on, I'm going to get hurt. So fucking much.

I wish I could say it was just about the sex. I wish I could go back to thinking he was some cocky prick.

But it's too late for me, and I know what I must do.

26
Travis

It's almost as if I'm outside of my body, watching myself, seeing myself lie here with Gary, holding him, whispering in his ear...and wondering what in the fuck I'm doing.

But still, I don't let go. I nuzzle his neck, feel his stubble on my face, and let my hand run down his body to wrap around his cock. "You're fucking good with this thing. Maybe I should let you top me a little more often. I'll still want your ass, but you know how to work that dick too."

A tremble rocks through him, vibrating into me.

"I love the effect I have on you," I tell him. "I never would have thought this game would have turned out to be so fun." That I would like spending time with him so much. That his accomplishments would feel like my accomplishments. That it would make my chest ache and piss me off so damn much when he doesn't see how incredible he is.

"On that note. I need to go to the restroom." Gary slips out of bed, and I let him, watch his tight ass move as he walks away.

"Awww, come on, baby. Things were just getting good!" I tease him, but he doesn't come back with a sarcastic comment, or hell, even acknowledge what I said at all.

That sends a little prickle of nerves through me, though I don't know what in the hell I would have to be nervous about.

Gary closes the door behind him. I wait for him, my mind drifting back to last night. I still can't believe how proud of him I was. What it felt like to watch him, a mixture of satisfaction and possessiveness making a cocktail inside of me I'd never experienced before. And if I'm being honest, one I'm not too keen on feeling again.

It takes Gary a couple of minutes in the bathroom. When he comes out, he picks up his underwear and pulls them on, making me frown. "What's going on with you?"

"Nothing." He starts walking around the room. "Where the hell are my pants?"

"I think I took them off you in the hallway. Seriously, what the fuck is wrong with you?" He never gets dressed and takes off like this anymore unless he has to be at work, has an appointment or something like that.

"I need to talk to you, and I need to do it with my clothes on. Would you put your clothes on too? That would help."

The hairs on my arms start to rise, and I sit up, a strange feeling creeping through my veins. "No, I won't. Get your ass over here and tell me what's going on."

"That's not going to work." He shakes his head, finds his shirt, and pulls it on. "Being all sexy and bossy just makes it worse."

"Makes what worse?" A throb begins in my temples and spreads across my forehead. "Please, come here. Tell me what in the hell is going on."

Gary sighs, then walks toward me in his T-shirt and briefs. He reminds me of Tom Cruise in that movie from the eighties, but I'm not sure if now is the time to bring it up.

He stops next to the bed, in front of me and says, "I can't do this anymore."

It's as though my insides crystallize, freeze, and then break apart. "Do what? What can't you do?" Is he going to drop our act right as I'm about to get what I want? No...that's not Gary. He wouldn't do something like that.

"This. Us." He points back and forth between the two of us. "The sex. It's just...it's not working for me anymore."

Now it's heat taking me over, blazing anger scorching through me. Why would he do this? Why would he call this off at the last minute? "It sure as fuck worked for you last night when you had your dick in my ass."

I shove off the bed and head for my dresser. He had the right idea about clothes. After grabbing a pair of boxer briefs, I pull them on. "I can't believe you're pulling this shit on me at the last minute. What the fuck, man? We're almost there, almost fucking there. Is it all the work with Raymond and Steven? Do you feel like I'm not putting in as much effort? Whatever you need, I'll do it. I'll turn up the act, seek your dickhead ex out more if I need to."

"No. Jesus, no." He runs a frustrated hand through his hair. "That's not what I mean. And I won't stop pretending to be your boyfriend. We can keep that up as long as you need to. I still want to be your friend, Travis....It's the sex. I just...I just don't think it's a good idea for us to continue sleeping together, that's all."

That should make me feel better, but for some reason, it doesn't. My anger is still a ticking time bomb waiting to detonate. Why would he tell me this now? What changed? "Why? Come on, Gare. You're not that guy. You got my ass, and now you're done? That's not you. What changed?"

"Nothing. It's not a good idea. I'm allowed to change my mind. Where the fuck are my pants?" he says again as though I didn't already tell him where they are. "You're still my friend. I'd like to keep spending time with you—working out or whatever, and I won't go back on what I said. I'll do whatever it takes to help you with Steven. I just can't have sex with you anymore. That's all. There are plenty of men out there who can't wait to get into your bed. You won't miss me."

But the truth is, I will miss him. I haven't thought about fucking anyone else in weeks. He's been everything I need.

"I'm going to go, okay? We'll…we'll talk soon." Gary walks past me.

I don't know how far he makes it. My back is to him when words I don't plan on saying push past my lips. "Did I do something wrong?" My voice comes out soft, a whisper, but not as soft as his when I hear him quietly curse behind me.

"No, you didn't do anything wrong."

I turn around. He's in the doorway, facing the hall, when I ask, "Then what is it?"

Gary sighs. I imagine he has his eyes closed. "I want more." His words echo through me as blood rushes through my ears. *I want more….I want more….I want more….*

Why in the fuck would he want more with me? He knows that's not what I'm about. Plus, Gary deserves a whole hell of a lot better than me. I'm not sure I'm much better than Peter.

"Nothing to say about that, huh?" He turns to face me. "I didn't plan for it to happen. You're not who I expected. You're kind and funny and protective. You make me feel things I didn't expect to feel, and that's not what you want. You can't give me what I need. I didn't want to need it, but I do. So, it's better if I stop pretending I'm the guy who can sleep with you and talk to you and then not care if you fuck someone else. I'm already trying to manage enough lies in my life as it is."

"Is that what this is about? Me fucking other people? Jesus, I told you I wouldn't screw anyone. I spend all my fucking time with you."

"Maybe not now, but eventually you will. You have that right. Can you honestly say you can give me something more?" he asks. He knows I can't. I hear it in the finality of his voice.

It's not him. I can't let myself trust anyone completely. I don't know how.

"That's what I thought. It's okay. It was my fault for thinking I could do this. I've kinda always known it had to end like this. I'm not the kind of guy who could hook you."

"Fuck that!" I say louder than I mean to. "Jesus Christ, Gary. Don't do that shit. I swear I want to kick your ass every time you put yourself down like that. This is *my* shit. This is who *I* am. There's nothing wrong with you."

He gets a small grin on his face, and I'm wondering what he has to smile about right now. "You're so much more honorable than you think."

I roll my eyes because now I know he's full of shit. I am who I am, and I'm okay with that. "So, we're really doing this, huh? We're explosive together. We're really going to shut that down?"

He looks at me sadly. "I have to. We're just coded differently."

I close my eyes and blow out a deep breath. Jesus, why the fuck does this hurt so goddamned much? Why does it feel like he's twisting a knife in my back? *Because it feels like he's walking away...like he's telling me I'm not good enough the same way my parents did.*

I open my eyes and say, "I'm going to miss that super ass of yours."

"It's going to miss you too. And we're still friends, right? I know we weren't before but—"

"We are now," I cut him off. "And we still will be. I'm definitely not going to stop dragging your ass to the gym with me, or making Petey jealous. He's so fucking jealous. You know that, right?"

Gary rolls his eyes as though he doesn't believe me. "I'm going to go, okay? Call me if you hear anything from Steven."

I nod at him, but don't reply. He pauses for a second. When I don't say anything else, he walks out of the room. I hear him in the hallway, putting his pants on, his footsteps walking away, and finally the front door closes. After walking over to my bed, I sit on the edge, elbows on my knees and head in my hands.

This doesn't feel pretend. It feels like I've been broken up with, like I lost someone I care about, and I'm not sure what to do about it.

27
Gary

I check my phone again. Eleven o'clock.

I won't get any sleep tonight; I know it. I keep expecting to look over and see Travis lying next to me. We didn't spend every night together, so this shouldn't be strange, but I think my body is recovering from the shock of knowing I won't get to have him anymore. That I'll never get to experience those hot, sweaty nights...those nights of such intense passion that left me shaking in ecstasy. Even worse, the mornings of seeing him lying peacefully next to me in bed.

We're still friends.

But that's not enough. Not anymore.

I set my phone back on my nightstand, and it vibrates. Again...and again. I grab it quickly.

Travis?

I'm destroyed when I see it's a Facebook message from Hayden. Last time we chatted was when I messaged him to help us with the fundraiser.

HAYDEN: *You guys free?*

ME: *I am.*

HAYDEN: *You out? Lance went to Kansas City for a work thing. Wanna go to Ten?*

I don't want to do anything. Not after what happened this morning with Travis. It wasn't a breakup, but that's what it feels like. And it hurts. So fucking much.

It won't help me to spend the night feeling sorry for myself. Not gonna get any sleep anyway. I agree and meet him outside. He walks over from Viewpoint, and we walk to Pump together. It's where most guys start drinking before heading to Flirt, which is on the opposite side of the street. Three guys head down the sidewalk toward us. The man in the middle's arms are slung around his friends' shoulders as they help him along. "And if I want another one," he says, slurring his words, "I should get to have another one."

"Not anymore, buddy," says one of his far more sober-sounding friends.

Once they pass and are out of earshot, Hayden glances behind us and says, "Oh, he is trashed."

"Right?" I force a chuckle to seem amused and not so defeated.

When we get to Ten, we head to the bar in the main space where everyone's hanging and drinking. We catch up about work and life while we have our first cocktail when he finally asks, "So what was up with you and Travis that day at the pool party?"

He has a suspicious look in his eyes. "It's a long story," I say. "One I'll have to tell you when we aren't in public."

"Fair enough."

Once we finish our drinks, Hayden glances around. "I'll get us another cocktail and meet you on the dance floor." I smile because I like the idea of dancing with him, escaping from all this bullshit that's stressing me out. That's what we used to do together when Peter and Lance would hang with guys at the bar to chat. I walk into the adjoining room, where the dance floor is. People crowd it as they dance to Whitney's "I'm Every Woman," which plays on the TV screens behind the bar on the other side of the room.

Derek stands at the end of the bar. He scratches at his arm like he's uneasy about something, his expression more serious than I've ever seen it before. Luke Henley, who I recognize from some events he's talked to Peter at, stands in front of him. A tall guy in his forties, he wears a tight tee that shapes around his impressive, toned body.

Even though I'm not near them, I know the conversation they're having. I've seen it before. It's the sort of conversation I've overheard hundreds of times just by being within the proximity of a couple in the bar.

He's getting dumped. It reminds me of how Travis looked when I told him I didn't want to hook up with him anymore. Although it's not the same. He's just going to miss the sex. I'm going to miss a hell of a lot more than that.

Derek's face lets me know how devastated he is. I recall his concern at the fundraiser when he was texting someone—surely Luke. He obviously knew things were heading this direction already.

I'm glad I came out tonight. Neither of us need to be alone right now.

I push my way through the dance floor and reach him while Luke walks over to a small group of guys, who I'm assuming are his friends.

"Hey, man," I say to Derek.

His eyes are on the TV screen like he's trying to look anywhere but toward Luke.

He turns to me, his eyebrows twitching as blue light from the TVs sparkles in a fresh tear forming in his eye. He runs his hand through his lengthy blond bangs.

"Hey," he says, his voice cracking.

"You okay?"

I think my question just made it worse because the tear releases and starts down his face. He shakes his head.

I want to hug him right now, but I don't want to cause a scene that Luke and his friends would notice because within my periphery, I see they keep looking over here like they want to see how Derek is reacting to the news.

Hayden approaches and hands me my drink.

"Hey, man," he says with as big a smile as I imagine he can make. "What's up, Derek?"

I glare at him and shake my head.

Derek glances around. He looks like an animal caught in a trap, trying to find a way out.

"Can you guys help me?" he asks. "I just need to get out of here."

A tear falls from his other eye, down his face.

"I don't want them to see me cry," he adds.

Hayden's expression shifts from playful to serious in an instant, and he stumbles forward, spilling both our drinks and falling onto me.

"What the fuck?" I ask.

He moans as he presses his palms against the bar, grasping around awkwardly like he's as wasted as the guy we saw being dragged home by his buddies.

Then it hits me.

Clever, Hayden.

I wink at Derek, and his eyes light up, suggesting he gets what's going on.

I wrap my arm around Hayden and help him up, putting his arm over my shoulder.

"We'd better get him home," I tell Derek, who wraps Hayden's other arm around him.

We guide him through the bar, past Luke and his buddies.

"Where are we going? Why are we leaving?" Hayden slurs in an all-too-convincing voice.

He stumbles. Groans. And it takes us a bit of effort to get him out of the bar.

Once we're halfway down the block to Metropolis, I say, "You can cut the act now."

"Who's acting?" he teases as he glances behind us to make sure the coast is clear.

"That was really good," I acknowledge. "I'd give you the Academy Award."

"I've taken a few acting classes," he says with pride.

As we turn to Derek, I see the tears are falling one after the other. That's how I feel right now. I'm doing a better job of keeping it inside, but I've had all day to get my shit together.

I step between them and wrap my arm around Derek.

"I think we need to have a guys' night," I say. "What do you think about that?"

Derek nods.

We head back to the condo and order pizza and Chinese. When they arrive, we take the food and a bottle of Chardonnay I had in the fridge into my room and turn on *Mean Girls*, which I have on DVR in case I ever need a good pick-me-up.

"I met him on Scruff a few weeks ago," Derek says before taking another large gulp from his glass of Chardonnay. He sits on my bed with his legs folded, the containers of General Tso's and sesame chicken open on top of the box of pizza that is set between us. Hayden lies at the foot of the bed, stretched out, chopsticks in hand as he devours some sesame chicken and fried rice from a bowl.

"I thought things were heading somewhere, but he told me I'm not relationship material," Derek continues. "I'm young, and he just can't see me that way. Maybe he's right."

"That's such bullshit," Hayden says. I notice the Chinese food is gone, so I remove the containers and open the pizza box, retrieving a slice.

Hayden and Derek race to get their own slices. It's like we haven't eaten in months. Probably true because I bet we've all been starving a little to look good for the strip-off.

"I don't want to talk about it anymore," Derek says. "Why don't you tell us about you and Travis? That's a much happier story."

My eyes water. "Not all that great, actually."

"Really?" he asks. "For a fake relationship, things didn't look all that fake at the fundraiser."

"So, that's what all that was about," Hayden says.

Now that we're on the subject, I start at the beginning, explaining what really happened that day at the fundraiser. I tell him about what we thought we were getting into. What I realized I was getting into. And how I had to call things off.

"I told him we can still be friends," I say, "but I'm really not sure I can even do that."

"What do you mean?" Hayden asks.

"It's how I am. I know every time I'm around him, I'll be wishing we could be something more. Something we can't be. And that's not fair to him."

"So, you calling it off?"

"I made a commitment to help him. I'm not going to leave him hanging when his entire future depends on me pretending to be with him. I know it's going to hurt...a lot. Knowing I care so much, and he just...he's missing a good lay. Because I really like him...a fucking lot. More than I've ever liked anybody else. I don't know how to turn this off."

"This is the worst night ever," Derek says. "We need to get on Grindr right now."

He reaches into his pocket and pulls out his cell.

"I don't think that's the solution," Hayden says.

"Easy for the guy who's getting laid constantly to say," Derek retorts.

Hayden's expression shifts to one that nearly matches Derek's. "Not so much."

"What?" I ask.

"He's mad about the whole fundraiser thing. And we've already been having some...issues, so that didn't really help."

"I'm sorry," I say. "If I'd known you guys were having problems, I never would have asked you to help out."

"It's not your fault. He just gets weird about stuff like that. It makes me sad because I actually had a lot of fun."

"Lance's a fucking prude," Derek says playfully. He's clearly trying to get Hayden to crack a smile again. And Hayden does.

Derek reaches into the pizza box between us.

"What the fuck?" he asks.

The pizza's gone.

"Holy shit," I say.

"And the Chinese?" Derek says. He puts his hands to his face, his eyes wide with horror. "Oh my God. What have we done?"

"I haven't had carbs since the summer started," Hayden says.

"I was starving for the fundraiser," I add.

"We gotta go back out and get drunk enough to throw this all back up," Derek concludes, more as an order than a request.

"Shut up," I say. "As if carbs even affect your twinky body."

"I'm not a twink," he insists. "I weigh less now than I did in middle school. They used to call me Chubby D."

"That's awful," Hayden says.

"I know! I have to be careful." But as he grabs the bottle of Chardonnay off my nightstand behind him and refills our glasses, I can tell his reaction was more an act than anything else.

We keep on chatting. Teasing. Laughing. As we start watching the movie again, we take turns quoting different parts.

I wish I'd been better friends with Hayden. Or that I hadn't stopped hanging with Derek so much. Tonight's just what I needed. And it's nice seeing the light return to Hayden and Derek's eyes as we tell stories about bad breakups and hookups gone wrong.

I needed tonight. I needed to remember that even though I don't have Travis—*can't* have Travis—at least I can have some amazing friends.

It's not going to be easy, but I'll get over him...eventually.

28
Travis

"What's new with you?" Vincent asks as I knead his shoulder muscles. He's always chatty when I give him a massage, asking about life at Metropolis, hanging out at Flirt, and things like that.

"Not much," I reply because it's the truth. Gary and I have chatted on the phone a few times and went to the gym together twice in the past week and a half. Aside from that and an awkward appearance at a Fourth of a July party where we pretty much avoided each other the entire time, that's really been the extent of it.

He wasn't asking you about Gary, dumbshit. He likely doesn't even know about him.

I shake my head, annoyed that my train of thought automatically headed for Gary station. That's been happening at the most random times, and I don't fucking like it.

"Why did you stop massaging?" Vincent breaks through my Gary musings.

Shit. "Sorry. I guess a lot has been on my mind."

"Sounds like you need something to take your mind off it. Get laid. That's always the best way. Nothing helps like a good fuck."

Yeah, don't I know it, only Gary has decided we can't sleep together anymore.

Earth to Travis, Gary isn't the only man in Atlanta. Gary and I weren't in a real relationship, and now that we're not fucking, there's even less reason why I shouldn't go out and get ass somewhere else. As long as I'm discreet until we figure out how much longer we have to keep this fake relationship going, it shouldn't be a problem.

"You're right." I run my fingers down either side of his spine. "Sex is the cure for everything." Like trying to get your mind off fake boyfriends who whistle when they work out, like to fade into the background but let loose when they're in the sack with you...or on a stage at Flirt. "I need a good lay."

"I happen to know one," Vincent replies, a little husk to his voice.

Chuckling, I tease, "Do you now? I can take a wild guess on who you mean."

When I feel his hand run up my thigh, I realize he's not joking. "You're fucking hot. I always figured you played on the side."

My body immediately tenses up. I grind my molars together. This isn't the first time a client has tried to hit on me—male or female, and every time, it's like spiders crawling through my veins. I like sex as much as the next guy, but there's more to me than that. "Because obviously, a guy like me would fuck his clients, right?"

"Obviously," Vincent replies as his hand slides around to my ass.

"Drop your hand, man. That's not what I'm here for."

In his defense, Vincent does just that, but then he turns his head, looks up at me and says, "Want me to suck you off? You flirt enough, and let's not pretend I haven't heard stories about you. I also heard you're trying to get money for your own place." His hand goes to the button on my jeans. "I know a guy who might be interested in helping with that."

There's a voice in the back of my head that tells me I should go for it. Steven said we would talk and now he's making excuses why we can't meet. Maybe everyone is right. Why not fuck to get what I want? It's something I'm good at.

You're so much more honorable than you think.

It's Gary's voice I hear in my head when I grab Vincent's wrist. *What the hell is wrong with me?* I've worked my ass off to get where I am, not sacrificing that for anything, and I sure as shit don't plan to start now by letting this guy suck me off for money.

"I don't do that shit. We can finish the massage or I can go. Don't touch me like that again."

When I let go of Vincent's wrist, he pulls his arm back and rests it on the table again. "My mistake. I just thought you might be interested in having a little fun," he says, anger making each one of his words stab at me.

The rest of the massage is uncomfortable. When I pack up to head out, I'm pretty sure I just lost a client, which is shitty in some ways because money is kind of important, but not enough to deal with this. My career is the one place in my life where I can prove people wrong about me...prove my parents wrong.

When I get to the car, I don't think about what I'm doing when I call Gary.

"Hello?" he answers on the second ring.

"You said we're friends, right? Hang out with me tonight. Not at the gym or some shit like that. Just come chill with me, Superass." I didn't mean to use the name, but I don't take it back either.

There's a pause before..."Yeah...yeah, I'd love to hang out with you tonight. That's what friends do."

***

We're Ross and Rachel. It's the stupidest shit to think, but those are the words that travel through my mind as Gary and I awkwardly sit on the couch in my apartment with shitty wine and lasagna in front of us.

If we had a lot of mutual friends, I feel like they'd have to choose sides. The whole time I think about how awkward this is, I have to keep reminding myself that we weren't in a real relationship. We stopped fucking; that's it. After Cody and I messed around, things never got weird between us.

"How's work?" Gary asks.

"Good. It's work." I almost tell him about Vincent today, but I hold back. I don't want him to ever think I'm that guy—screw someone I met at Flirt or on Grindr, yes. Fuck on the job, no. He likely already wonders about that, and the thought of Gary seeing me that way makes a vein on my forehead throb with anger.

"No news from Steven?" He takes a drink of his wine and looks over at me, those blue eyes of his expressive, even though I'm not sure what they're saying.

"Nope. He keeps making bullshit excuses. He cancelled our meeting." He says it's nothing, but I've learned that when people say it's nothing, it's usually something.

He sets his glass down, a slight frown pulling at the corners of his mouth. "Did you ever think maybe they're not excuses, Trav? Maybe he's busy. Maybe something came up. You're going to get that money because you deserve the money. You worked your ass off, and I can't wait to see all the good things that happen to you because of it."

"*We*," I say.

"We what?"

"*We* worked our asses off. Don't pretend I could have done this without you, and you called me Trav."

His cheeks pinken slightly, making me chuckle. "I've fucked you in a hundred different ways, and you've had your dick in my ass too, yet you're embarrassed that you called me Trav?"

"Just because you mentioned it!" He rolls his napkin and tosses it at me.

"Just because I thought it was cute." I shrug. "You've never called me Trav before." It's this, I realize, that I missed. Talking to him, laughing with him, spending time with him without the awkwardness that his deciding not to fuck me anymore injected into our friendship.

But then I pretty much see Gary shut down. See the tension bleed back into us as he turns away and takes another bite of his food.

"Okay, seriously. We need to have this shit out. We were supposed to be friends and now you're acting like I kicked your puppy every time I see you."

His forehead wrinkles. "I don't act like you kicked my puppy. I'm fine. You're overreacting."

"*I'm* overreacting? And maybe you're not acting like I'm a puppy-kicker but you're treating me like I'm really an ex."

"Maybe because it feels that way to me! Did you ever think about that? God, I never should have done this. I should have known this would happen from the start."

He tries to stand, but I reach out and wrap a hand around his wrist to stop him. "My dad's not really my dad." The second the last word leaves my mouth, I want it back. What the fuck am I doing telling him this shit?

"I'm really confused right now," he says, that crease still above his brows.

"I don't know why I said that...why I told you. What the fuck it means right now...it's just..." *Just that I've always felt like I don't fit in...like I don't belong, even when I pretend I do. Even when everything looks perfect on the outside, my edges just never connect with others the way they should.* "I guess I was kind of set to be the family fuck up from the start. My mom slept with another guy—just once. Biggest mistake of her life, she'll tell you. She told my dad, my stepdad. He forgave her. They hoped I was his. I wasn't. We don't speak about that, though. We pretend I'm his, so no one talks. He pretends to love me the way he does Martin and Malcolm, but he doesn't. She pretends to forgive me for not being his, but she doesn't."

"But you always call him Dad."

"Because he's the only dad I've ever known. He's my dad even though I'm not biologically his."

"I'm so sorry, Travis. I had no idea." He reaches out and squeezes my shoulder.

"That's because you're the first person I've told. I don't know why I'm telling you now." Or maybe I do, and I just can't admit it. Because I'm scared I won't be what Gary wants me to be either. That I won't fit the person he wants me to be or thinks I should be. It's easier not to give a shit. "It is what it is, though. There's no changing it so why stress about it?"

His frown grows deeper. "It's okay to hurt, ya know? It's okay to admit something or someone got to you."

But really, it's not. I'm tired of letting people down— not being Dad's, being gay, not following in my dad's footsteps like my brothers. "I don't want to talk about this anymore. Just...don't be weird around me. I've gotten used to having your sexy ass around, even if I can't have a piece of it." I wink at him, but he doesn't take the bait. He's not going to drop the subject.

"Are you going? To your brother's girlfriend's party?"

I fall against the back of the couch. Me and my big-ass mouth. "No."

"Travis, your brothers want you there. They love you. Don't let your parents get in the way of that!"

My anger spikes, and I shoot back up so I'm sitting forward. "Are you shitting me right now? Are you really going to give me hell about my family when you're not even out to yours? You don't know what in the hell you're talking about."

For a split second, he looks as though I hit him and then he's shoving to his feet, his anger matching mine. "Our situations are completely different, but at least I'm not a fake the way you are! You pretend to have your shit together—confident, don't give a fuck attitude, screw anyone who doesn't like me the way I am, but it's all a façade, isn't it? At least I'm honest about my weaknesses rather than walking around with a chip on my shoulder and pretending they don't exist."

"Get out," I say before clenching my jaw so tight pain shoots through it and up to my ears. *Weak.* Did he really just call me weak? And after what I just told him, shit I haven't told anyone else?

"Travis...I—"

"Get. Out," I tell him again. He pauses, then turns and walks away as I tell myself it's better this way.

29
Gary

I need someone to talk to, and this isn't the kind of conversation I can have with Derek. I don't need jokes and quips. I need a voice of reason.

The first person who comes to mind is Hayden. We don't know each other well, but he's always been the kind of guy I felt comfortable talking to. And after the other weekend, I feel like I can reach out to him without it being weird.

When I send him a message, he replies that he's free. I walk to his condo building, my mind jumbled with confusion from everything that just happened.

My chest is tight with discomfort, my face red with fury as I take quick, shaky breaths.

While I tell Hayden about the fight—leaving out the most personal part Travis told me—he brews some coffee and mixes some batter for cookies. Evidently, since the fundraiser, he's been treating himself with snacks, and I feel like I could use that today.

"What right does he have to tell me I should be out to my parents?" I ask him as I get to the part of our fight that set me off. "There are plenty of guys who aren't out to their families."

Hayden checks on the cookies in the oven. In sweat pants and a tank top, it's clear he was having a bed day, and I kind of feel bad for interrupting. He removes his glasses and sets them down on the kitchen island, the overhead fluorescent light glistening off the lenses. He takes a sip from his coffee mug as he sits on the stool beside mine.

"Are your parents super-religious or something?" he asks.

"No. It's just...I have this sister, and she's always gotten into trouble. It's a long story. I don't want to upset them."

"You think they'll be more upset about you being gay...or about never having really known their son?" His words hit me hard. They remind me of how little I tell them because I'm gay. All I can think about is those looks in their eyes as they seem to beg for me to talk to them about my life, to tell them I'm happy and not just sad and alone in my condo.

"Maybe you need to figure that out," Hayden says. "But it sounds like you guys were fighting about more than that. You said he hasn't heard anything from this guy who you both have been working hard to please so he'd invest in Travis's business, and he has this big party coming up that obviously, for whatever reason, stirs up family shit—shit you probably don't know anything about."'

The problem is I do know about it.

I should have been more sensitive. Travis was feeling vulnerable. I know how he gets—defensive. I'm normally good at keeping my cool when he gets that way, but tonight, he hit such a sore subject that I lost it. Got defensive right back at him.

"It sounds like you were pushing him to do something you knew he didn't want to do," Hayden says, "so of course he was going to do the same to you."

"You're right," I admit. I take a sip of my drink. "We've never had a fight. Not like this. I mean, he was *pissed*."

But I know him well enough to know that when he gets angry, it's because he's hurt. And knowing I hurt him tears me up. I should have been there for him after he told me that stuff about his father. I should have set aside my own insecurities and soothed him.

"I should've kept my stupid mouth shut."

"It's not a crime to have a fight, Gary," Hayden says, seeming amused by how seriously I'm taking this. "Considering all that you guys had going on, it was bound to happen. It sounds like you're both trying to figure out where you stand now that your relationship is totally different."

Relationship? There's a word I don't want to hear right now.

As I start to breathe normally again, already feeling relaxed chatting with Hayden about this, I feel kind of silly for having forced my bullshit on him.

"I'm sorry," I say. "I shouldn't have come here. I know we haven't talked over the years, but—"

"Oh, shut up, Gary. That's the way it goes. You run into people in similar circles, but being in a relationship, you have obligations. Certain people that you have to hang with. Me and Lance are the same way. You and me have always had a good time together, and I wouldn't go running off to have a guys' night with just anybody. This is what friends are for."

I smile at him referring to himself as my friend.

"I don't have a lot of those," I admit. "When I was with Peter, I ran with the circles he ran in. Sort of took on his life rather than making my own. Derek was the only friend I had outside of Peter's friends. Oh, and Peter hated him so much. Although Derek was never his biggest fan either."

I smirk as I remember some of the clever insults Derek would use against him.

"We're in the same boat then," Hayden says. "I'm always hanging around Lance's friends, but I never took the time to make my own, and now he's gone so much for work, and I sit here by myself. Gets lonely."

"Why don't you hang out with his friends?"

"Those assholes?" he asks, a playful expression on his face, but I can tell he's serious. It's how I've always felt about a lot of Peter's close friends.

"It's hard to find good people in the world, Gary. But when you find them, you have to keep them around."

He's a sweetie, and I appreciate how at ease he's made me just listening to my rant about Travis.

"So now that we're basically old-time friends," he says, "you want my real opinion of this Travis shit?"

"Rather than your fake opinion?"

"Don't be a Derek," he teases me as he offers a glare.

I smile.

"You really like him. And from what you told us the other night, I think you're bothered that he doesn't feel the same, so you weren't lashing out at him about your parents, but about the fact that you feel like every time you're around him, he's rejecting you."

It's true. When we're talking, I still feel these things for him...and it hurts knowing he doesn't feel anything more.

"I just don't understand how he can be the way he is. I'm not even sure I'm mad at him as much as I am myself. I started hooking up with him so confident this wasn't going to happen. I was fucking determined, and he wasn't my type at all...and not even the kind of guy who would ever give me a second glance."

"What?" Hayden sounds shocked.

"You've seen Travis. He's like a ten."

"And what do you think you are?"

The expression on his face reminds me of how Travis looks when I say something self-deprecating. Peter never used to get like this. If anything, if someone said something about me being cute, he'd just say, "Gary's doable." It was always said as a joke, but it got to me.

"I'm not playing this game," I say.

"No, I want you to tell me where you are on this little scale you have in your head."

"It's not important."

"I think it is."

"Oh my God. Like a six point five. Seven, maybe."

He chuckles. "Oh, wow. Peter fucked you up real bad."

"That's average!"

"The guy who was dancing on that stage at the fundraiser didn't think he was average."

He's right. That guy and the guy who fucked around with Travis never felt average, but that's not how I feel most of the time. I feel like...I'm just Gary. And obviously, I wasn't enough to satisfy Peter.

"Can we stop talking about this?" I ask. "It makes me uncomfortable."

"As your new friend, it's kinda my job to make things uncomfortable. Travis would be lucky to have a guy like you. An honest, attractive guy who—based on what you said the other day—gives him some mind-blowing sex."

"Saying it isn't going to make me believe it."

"Well, if we're going to make some real headway on this, I'm gonna need to get a degree, and you're going to have to start paying me an hourly rate."

I smile again. Hayden is better at having serious conversations and making me laugh than Derek, who would prefer to avoid serious conversations altogether.

"What do you really want with Travis?" he asks.

"I can't have that."

"Okay...rephrase...knowing he doesn't want you that way, what do you want?"

"I want to be his friend."

"Even after the fight?"

I nod.

"Can you do that?"

As I imagine being around him like I was tonight, my face twitches and my eyes tear up.

"I don't know," I say. "I miss him, Hayden."

A tear stirs in my eye. It reminds me of when I saw Derek the other night.

"I don't like that I get like this, but I wake up now, and it's weird not having him in the bed with me. It feels so empty. And not like it did with Peter. When Peter left, it felt like I missed him out of habit. Like missing having a piece of furniture. With Travis, it's like, I want him there in case something exciting happens. So I can celebrate with him if Steven calls. Or in case something happens with work and I want someone to talk to. It's stupid stuff, and I know he's not responsible for not feeling the same way about me, but then he says shit like I'm amazing or like I deserve someone incredible, and it just pisses me off because I don't understand how I can be so amazing if he doesn't even want to be with me. And I know it's not his fault, but that doesn't keep it from hurting...so fucking much."

I wipe at my face, spreading what tears have fallen on the back of my hands.

"So now are you ready for the million-dollar question?" he asks. "Do you want to cut him out of your life for good?"

Just hearing those words makes another tear slide down my face.

God, I hate myself so much for how much I care. How much it hurts.

I shake my head. "I want to be friends, but I don't fucking know how to do that. I look at his face—that fucking beautiful face—and it's like this switch turns on in my brain that I can't turn off. I think that's why we started fighting...because he keeps saying these things about me being awesome and it gets to me. He even told me something really personal that he's never told anyone, and I don't know how to process that. What does that even fucking mean? It makes me mad because it's like he's doing it on purpose. Like he's trying to drive me insane. But then I get out of it, and I know it's all in my head."

"It's not a crime to feel this way," he says. "You can't help that you like someone, and if he doesn't get that, he's an asshole. But I think he does, and if you care about being friends with him, then you have to push through those feelings. You're going to have some fights. It might be a little weird for a while, but you have to struggle through it."

"You think it'll get easier?" I ask.

"Fuck if I know," he says with a smile, his eyes lit up.

"Look, there're a lot of things going on with him right now. He's stressed about the money he may or may not be getting. He has this big thing coming up with his family. He's frustrated. Give him some space, and you need space, too. Wait for him to reach out to you."

"What if he doesn't?"

"Then you know how he really feels about being friends with you."

Scary as his words are, I know he's right.

30
Travis

I fucked up, and I know it.

Gary didn't deserve for me to lash out at him the way I did. If anyone understands what it means to be outted before you're ready, it's me. To put him in the same situation and call him out for not telling his parents was a dick move. He deserves better than that.

I push the weights up again and again, hoping the strain in my arms will help with the built-up tension rushing through my body, but then that just makes me wish he was here working out with me because it's a whole hell of a lot more fun with his goofy ass beside me.

I am so fucked.

Once I finish lifting, I set the bar back and sit up. Sweat runs down my forehead and stings my eyes.

"Where's your man?" some guy that I've seen around Metropolis asks. I don't even remember his name, yet somehow, he knows I'm with Gary...only I'm not with him. He just thinks I am.

"He has shit to take care of." I stand up, not really in the mood to talk to anyone. After wiping my face with my towel, I head to the showers and clean up before I meet my brothers for lunch. My ass really doesn't want to go there. I know there will be a last-ditch effort to get me to go to Liz's party, and as much as I know it makes me a prick, I really don't know if being there is the best idea.

The place we're meeting is within walking distance from the gym. When I get to the little pub, I already see Martin and Malcolm sitting in a booth toward the back of the room.

"What's up?" I ask as I slide into the brown, leather bench seat beside Malcolm.

"Not much. I ordered you a beer to start with," Martin says just as the waitress shows up with a frothy mug of beer. Fucker is bringing out the big guns. He knows how I like my dark brews.

"Thank you," I say. She asks if we're ready to order, and I go ahead and get the biggest burger and fries on the menu because I'm not ready to get back into eating well. I deserve this shit.

The second she disappears to put our order in, Martin starts in on me. "The party is this Saturday. You're going to go, right?"

"Jesus, don't I at least get to enjoy the beer you ordered for me before the harassment starts?"

"Nope." He winks at me. I ignore him for a moment and take a drink, letting the cool liquid slide down my throat before leaning back in the booth.

"Did you tell Mom and Dad you want me there?"

He gets a sad look in his eyes, and I know what their response was without him having to say it. "I did, and I don't give a shit how they feel. They love you, Travis. I know they do—"

"Don't." I hold up my hand to stop him and thankfully he listens.

When his phone rings, he looks at the screen and excuses himself, leaving Malcolm and me alone.

"I know this is hard on you, Trav. I can't pretend to understand. I hate that this is the way it is, but don't let them stop you from living your life."

"I don't," I tell him. "I make it a point not to."

"Maybe outside of the family you do, but not with this. You go about your life, which is great. You should, but then you ignore that we are also a part of that life. I know you want to be there...I know you do because that's the kind of man you are, big brother. You want to be there for

214

Martin because it's important to him. You'll regret it if you don't go."

"Fuck," I curse quietly because I know he's right. I want to be there. I don't want to let my parents keep me from spending time with my family.

"It's okay to let yourself be loved, ya know? I'm not sure if you realize that's what you do, but it's true. I know they let you down, but not everyone will. I won't. Martin won't. I'm sure you have friends who won't let you down either. Let us in."

It's okay to let yourself be loved.

I know they let you down, but not everyone will.

I'm sure you have friends who won't let you down either.

"Don't let yourself have regrets. You deserve better than that, and you're stronger than that. Bring backup if you need to. What about your friend Cody?"

It's then that a pair of blue eyes pop into my head—shy but sexy and confident when he's not thinking too much. An infectious smile, and those throaty noises he makes, and the way he looks at me like I'm king of the whole goddamned world.

It's not Cody that I'm thinking of right now...it's Gary.

Oh fuck.

"What's the smile for?" Malcolm asks, and I realize it's not the first time someone has asked me that question when I'm thinking about Gary. Because somehow, I know he's the backup I want in my corner. That he's the person who would make the night bearable.

"I gotta go." I push to my feet.

"Huh?" Malcolm asks.

I don't know...Jesus, I don't fucking know, but my head and gut are in knots and..."I need to apologize to someone." Because if I don't, Gary will be a regret, and the thought of him being that feels like something is eating through my heart.

"Right now?" Malcolm asks.

"Yes, right now. Sorry... I...tell Martin I'll call him later." My footsteps are heavy as I make my way through the pub. Gary's office is only a few blocks away, so I head directly for it. It's as if I'm suddenly possessed by some kind of something I don't understand. I feel like I'm always thinking that when it comes to him because I realize now that Gary makes me feel things no one has made me feel before.

I head into his building, and I must look like a man on a mission because people move out of my way as I go. I put my phone to my ear as I pace the lobby, waiting for him to answer his cell.

"Hello?" he says tentatively, and it's like a knife to the chest. He sounds the way he did when we first started talking....He sounds like he does when he speaks to Peter, and there's no one to blame but myself.

"I'm in your lobby. Can you come down? Or can I come up?" There's a neediness to my voice that I can't deny.

"Yeah...sure. Come up. Fifth floor. I'll meet you by the elevator."

It feels like it takes an eternity for the elevator to reach his floor. When the doors open, Gary's standing there, his head cocked and so many damn questions in his eyes.

He leads me to his office, and the second the door is closed I say, "I'm sorry," only to have the same two words spoken by him at the same time.

"What are you sorry for?" I ask him.

"For not voicing how important what you told me is. For letting my own insecurities and feelings block out the pain you were feeling."

I close my eyes and shake my head before opening them again. "You're such a fucking knucklehead. Of course, you would take the blame on yourself." And let's for a moment forget the fact that I just called him a knucklehead. *What the fuck is wrong with me?* "I shouldn't have pushed you. I shouldn't have taken my family shit out on you. You're...fuck." I run a hand through my hair and walk away from him, stopping when I reach the window. "Somehow you became my safe place where I can admit things I don't usually admit, which makes me take my frustrations out on you because..."

"Because you trust me?"

I shove my hands deep into my pockets. "I want to. I want to so fucking much."

That maybe is the most real thing I can say to him. It's not any kind of promise—those are mostly empty anyway—but it's the desire to want to do better...to be better.

"I don't..." his words trail off, and I turn to look at him. "I don't know how to do this—whatever this is. One minute you're talking to me about me going home with someone else or saying you don't feel the same, but then you say shit like that. I'm trying, Trav. Trying so fucking hard to keep the line intact because I don't want to lose your friendship, but you make it so difficult. I don't understand how you can say things like that but then not give a shit."

"No one said I don't give a shit. I'm here. This is a big fucking deal for me to be here like this. I just...I don't want to lose you either." I take a step closer to him...then another. "My thoughts are all over the damn place. I think about you all the time, even over stupid shit. I'm trying. No one has made me want to try before you."

It's like he's frozen in place—his eyes wide.

"I know, right? I can't believe I just said that either."

He cracks a smile then, and it lures me in, pulls me to him, a force I can't control.

"I don't want to get hurt," he tells me.

"I don't want you hurt either." Then because I need to be real with him, "And...I don't want to get hurt either."

He sucks in a shocked breath, and Jesus, I want my tongue in his mouth. Want to bite his lip and twist my hand in his hair and hold him close. Kiss him until he can't breathe anything in but me.

"Can you go with me?" I ask him.

"Go with you where?"

"To Martin's party for Liz. I don't want to miss it. I want to be there for my brother, but I don't know if I can do it alone."

Holy shit, this being vulnerable stuff is hard. I sort of want to melt into the ground admitting that.

"Of course, I'll go with you. I'm going to show you that you can trust me, Travis." He doesn't voice what I see on his face...that he needs me to show him that he can trust me too.

31
Gary

The party crowd is gathered on the balcony behind the Hartley Inn, a large "Happy Birthday, Liz" banner hanging across the back entrance. Everyone's dressed like they just got out of church. Travis looks adorable in his fuchsia button-up and powder-blue bow tie. His impressive biceps fill out his rolled-up sleeves nicely. Since we started hitting the gym together, I've noticed he fits his clothes even better than when we first met. But as good as the top looks on him, I can't keep from glancing at his ass, tight in the black dress pants he wears. His clothes are always so right for him. He knows he looks good and he flaunts it. In my gray button-up and black tie, I look like I'm getting ready for a funeral. I'm dressed so plainly because I've always worked to blend in with everyone. That's always been my goal...until I met Travis. Since we started hanging out—since he started forcing me to see I'm more than I give myself credit for—I'm starting to feel more and more uneasy with the old me. Even these clothes feel wrong. Like with our sex, I want to explore. I want to experiment. I want to do something wild and different. Not just keep pretending to be this guy I'm not.

Travis and I stand in a line at the bar.

"You okay?" I ask Travis as he glances around uneasily. I figure he's either scoping the place out for his brothers or nervous about running into his parents. Maybe both.

"I'm fine," he says.

Being here with him, for something I know is so important, gives me some hope—hope I've had since he said he didn't want to lose me the other day. That he thinks about me all the time. That I make him want to try.

Could this really be happening? Could he actually like me as much as I like him? I'm in shock, a little bit. After our fight, I sure as fuck didn't expect him to come running to my office to tell me he was feeling something for me. Ever since that happened, I've been excited but scared as shit. Maybe he's just not a relationship guy. Maybe even though he wants to make this work, he doesn't have it in him. He can't force himself to be someone he's not, and I wouldn't want him to because I like him for who he is, not for someone I want him to become. What if this whole fake relationship thing confused things for him as much as it did for me?

That's not my biggest concern right now. If anything, my relief about Travis's confession has transformed into tension on Travis's behalf over this party.

"Hey, Travis," comes a man's voice from nearby.

I turn and see two guys walking along a brick path that wraps around the house.

As they approach, Travis says, "Hey, guys, this is Gary. He's my...well, he's my Gary."

I figured he was going to introduce me as his friend, but I like that he didn't. Maybe I even like it a little too much.

"Hi, Gary, I'm Martin and this is Malcolm. I'm sure you've only heard amazing things about us."

Even though I recognize their names, it's nice to put faces with them. Up close, it's easy to see their differences from Travis. They have blond hair and brown eyes—not the dark hair and beautiful hazel eyes like Travis.

"Mom called and said they're going to be a little late," Malcolm says, giving Travis a heads-up. Both of his brothers keep glancing my way, like they can't believe Travis brought me here.

Welcome to the club.

"But everything's going to be good," Martin assures him with a broad smile, but I can see the tension in his expression. Like he's really not confident about that. "Remember what I said: if they have a problem, *they* can leave. It was nice meeting you, Gary. But I gotta go get these bobby pins to Liz or she won't be coming out of the bathroom for her own birthday party."

He pats Travis on the back, and Malcolm excuses himself as he trails behind his brother.

I can only imagine how Travis felt growing up with the two of them, who I'm sure he loves, but seem more connected at the hip than he does with either of them. Hell, their names both even start with the letter "M." It's like his mother was trying to single Travis out.

As we reach the front of the line at the bar, Travis orders a cocktail and drinks it quickly, as though he needs it to work up the courage to face his parents. I sip on mine, but as we step out of line, I notice he's still distracted.

"It's gonna be fine," I assure him. But that doesn't seem to help. Judging by the look in his eyes, I don't even think he heard me.

I take his hand.

"Hey," I say.

His gaze shifts to me. It's the first time he's made eye contact with me since we got here.

His tension dissolves. And as always, I love being captured in his gaze.

"I'm right here if you need backup."

He almost looks shocked by my words. Like I snuck up on him. He must be really out of it.

"Thanks," he says curtly, scanning my face.

"Do I have toothpaste on my lip?" I ask, licking my lips.

He chuckles.

Even though I don't know why he's acting this way, I'm glad he's starting to relax a little.

I keep trying to think of something to say. Some way of putting him at ease, but that's the best I've got. I keep his hand firmly in my grip.

When he finally turns away, he looks around and something catches his eye.

I follow his gaze to a woman who stands outside the French doors that lead to the terrace. Her hair in curls, she wears an olive-colored dress. Clutching a purse close to her, she stares at us. And judging by the shocked— maybe even horrified expression on her face—I can tell this must be his mother. A man steps onto the balcony behind her. He has that same blond hair as Malcolm and Martin, but his is much thinner—with a few long gray strands in it. He plays on his phone before he notices the woman and follows her gaze to us.

That's them. They have to be.

Travis's hand shakes against mine. I doubt it's from nerves, though. More likely the pent-up anger he's held in for so long—toward his mother, toward his father...well, stepfather.

I want to soothe him. I want to pull him out of this. To shake him and tell him that they don't matter. That nothing they think about him matters. But I'm distracted by the foul expressions on their faces.

Suddenly, it hits me.

We're still holding hands.

I would pull away just to protect Travis—so he wouldn't have to deal with their judgment—but a lot of good that'll do us now.

"I'm still here," I whisper so he knows he's not alone.

I'm not even sure he can hear me.

He looks like he's checked out. Like he's back at that night when they walked in on when he was so vulnerable and made him feel so ashamed for who he is.

"Trav," I say.

He snaps out of his daze and turns to me.

"This is gonna be even more interesting than I thought," he says.

"Like Martin told you, if they have a problem, they need to leave. We're not doing anything wrong."

He grips my hand. "You're right. I'm not going back to that night. They're not going to make me ashamed of who I am ever again."

"Come on. Let's just have fun."

I smile at him, and it takes him a moment, but he smiles back. "Yeah," he says before guiding me around the party. He doesn't let go of my hand even as we start chatting with Malcolm and some of his friends. I glance around occasionally as we socialize, noticing that his mom and dad keep eyeing us as they make their way around, laughing and chatting up other guests like nothing's wrong, but clearly, they're not okay with us being here.

After we meet Liz and her friends, we head to the front yard for a breather. When we head back through the house together, Travis's mom and dad step inside through the back door.

"Travis," his dad says, his face reddening, as though he's been holding in all his hostility and rage while he and Travis's mom put on their most hospitable performance for the rest of the party.

"Yes?" Travis asks, and I can tell by the tone in his voice that he wants this encounter to happen.

"We need to have a talk," he says.

"By all means."

His dad leads us into an adjoining room.

I'm amazed at how brave Travis is, willing to stand up to his parents who he knows hate him for being gay.

I admire him for that. I'm a fucking coward. Here I am worrying about what my parents will think of me when he already knows what his think and is still willing to get into a fight with them about it.

As soon as we enter the room, Travis's dad blurts out, "It's one thing to come here. It's another for you to bring *that* with you."

His dad's face is red from rage...some deep-seated anger he has against us for who we are. It's easy to see how a man like this would have looked after he caught Travis with some guy pants-down in his apartment.

"*That* is my boyfriend," Travis says in as serious a voice as I've ever heard come from him.

Now my face is filled with heat for a whole other reason. Travis just called me his boyfriend, and we're not even pretending for Steven's money or to piss Peter off.

It shouldn't feel so good to hear him say that, especially under these circumstances, but it's reassuring.

It reminds me I care way too much way too soon. Travis told me he's feeling something too—that he can give it a try, but he can't understand where I'm at...he's not capable of caring the way I do.

No. He's just trying to piss his father off. Get revenge on him for what a bastard he was to him all those years ago.

"And you're gonna show my boyfriend some fucking respect," Travis continues.

I'm excited about him calling me his boyfriend again, but terrified by his tone. He sounds like he's about to launch himself at his dad and beat the shit out of him.

This is Travis's revenge. For the night when he couldn't fight back. For all those years when he didn't get the chance to let him know exactly how he felt.

His dad's face is even redder than before, and he steps to Travis, saying, "I don't know where you think you get off bringing your abomination of a relationship into a respectable party...for your family. I raised you as my own and this is the thanks I get?"

Travis tenses up at that last part.

"Really," his mom adds. "This is not appropriate, Travis. Some of your family is here, too. And you're making a spectacle, holding hands, so everyone will be talking about us."

"Mom! Dad!"

I turn to see Martin standing in the doorway, Malcolm right behind him.

Martin's face is tense.

"What's going on?" he asks, though it's clear by the expression he's making that he already knows the answer.

His mom and dad eye each other uneasily.

"Martin, I don't think it's appropriate to have these two coming in here, making a mockery of your relationship and—"

"Seriously?" Martin asks, glancing between them and us. "This isn't about you guys," he says to their parents. "This is about what I want today, and I want Travis and his boyfriend here."

Will people stop calling me that? This certainly isn't going to make whatever the fuck it is we're doing make any more sense. Things are complicated enough as it is.

Travis grabs my hand again, clinging tightly. I know he's probably doing it to prove a point, but it gives me some confidence. Makes me feel like I'm not on my own in this horribly awkward situation.

I've been such a coward all these years for not telling my mom and dad the truth. Here Travis is, so brave and standing here fighting for me...for us...and even if it's just because he's trying to make a point, it reminds me of how stubborn I've always been about not telling my parents how I feel...who I really am.

32
Travis

I should leave. It's not fair for Martin and Liz that this shit is going down now, but it's so fucking typical of Mom and Dad to do it here—but to do it out of the way because God forbid they make a scene. People might not think we're the perfect family they want everyone to believe we are.

"Travis...this day is about Martin," Mom tells me. "You're making it about yourself. If you didn't *flaunt* your boyfriend it would be one thing."

Her words are sandpaper, rubbing raw the thick skin I've tried so hard to keep. "Flaunt him? Jesus Christ, I'm holding his fucking hand!"

"Lower your voice," Mom says between pursed lips.

Of course. Someone might overhear. "I care about him. He's my boyfriend. Is that so bad?" I realize then that he really is. Maybe this started out as some fucked-up lie, but it's transformed into something else. I tried to keep it contained, but this shit grew anyway, and I realize I want more. I'm scared, and I might fuck up, but I really do want more with him.

"It's not right, Travis. Don't ask your father and me to accept it." Mom crosses her arms, blocking out all her emotions the way she's so fucking good at...and I'm tired. So fucking tired.

"Mom. Dad. I'm going to have to ask you to leave," Martin tells them, but I can hear the pain in his voice. As much as I fucking hate it, as much as I really want to be here for Martin, I can't come between him and our parents.

"No," I say before they can reply and feel Gary squeeze my hand in support. "I'm just going to go."

"Stay," my brother tells me, but I shake my head.

"I won't be good company anyway. Tell Liz I wasn't feeling well and I'm sorry I had to go, okay?" I turn to walk away, but I'm stopped by the fact that Gary won't budge.

I turn back to see him looking at my parents. "You don't deserve him. Either of you. He's a good man. The kind of man who sees someone struggling and jumps in to help. The kind of man who would stick up for someone just to help make them feel better about themselves. He makes me feel like I can do anything. Like maybe I'm something special. You don't deserve him, and one day, you'll regret the way you've treated him."

And then it's Gary who's moving and me who is rooted to the floor. My chest feels full, like it's reached capacity because of the man standing beside me right now. I know how hard that had to be for him, for Gary to draw attention to himself...and he did it for me.

"Who do you think you are? Don't talk to my wife like that, you—"

"Stop right there. Don't say another word to him. Gary, let's go." I toss a look of apology to my brothers and then Gary and I are walking out of the building. My whole body is shaking by the time we make it outside. The second we're out the door, I'm backing Gary against the brick building, and I'm on him, my mouth devouring his.

I grind my pelvis against his. My fingers dig into his hips and his hand knots in my hair. In this second, I think I would crawl inside of him if I could.

I'm hungrier for him than I've ever been for anyone before. The desire is so strong it overpowers any fears or worries or overthinking.

"Jesus, I need to be inside your ass, Gary. Please...I'll beg you if I have to." I've never begged for sex in my life, but in this moment, I would do it. For him, I'd get on my fucking knees and beg.

"Yesss," he hisses out just as a car drives by and honks at us. "Maybe not here, though. We'll likely get arrested," he teases. I chuckle as I grab his hand and tug him away.

Then we're in my car and parking at Metropolis. I nearly drag him to the elevator, and once the doors close, my mouth takes over his again. There's a slight taste of vodka on his tongue, but he smells like Gary and feels like Gary, and Jesus fucking Christ, I'm losing my goddamned mind over him right now.

When the elevator dings, we're practically running down the hallway, laughing as we make our way to my condo.

"What's gotten into you?" he asks as I unlock my door.

"Don't know, but I know I'm about to get in you." I wink at him, and he laughs at my ridiculous cheesiness.

We fumble our way into my apartment. I feel this overwhelming giddiness that would embarrass me if I wasn't so fucking needy for him.

Nothing else matters in this moment—not Steven or the money. Not my parents or the fact that I'm scared to fucking death that I can't be what Gary needs.

I'll try. I can't not try.

"You look so fucking hot in this bow tie," he says as he starts to loosen it on our way to my room.

"I'll wear it for you again."

"Just for me? Aren't I lucky?" He gives me shit, and then we're pulling at each other's clothes, and I'm running my hand over his bare skin, loving the feel of his flesh against mine.

"What the fuck are you doing to me?" I ask him as I lay him on my bed. Lying on top of him, I nuzzle my face in his neck. "I wanna take you rough and dirty, slow and sweet. I can't decide which one I want more."

"Oh fuck. Jesus, that's sexy." Gary trembles beneath me.

I kiss my way down his chest. He arches off the bed as though he can't get close enough to me. "Travis..."

I squeeze his hips, lean over and let my tongue circle the head of his meaty dick.

Kneeling between his legs, I push them back. "I missed having this hole." I rub my finger over his pucker and Gary damn near lurches off the bed. "Missed fucking it. Tasting it. I don't know if I want to fuck your ass or eat it."

Gary's breathless when he says, "Fuck now. You can do whatever else you want to it later."

He looks at me, my eyes on him as well, and I can't hold back the truth that rolls off my tongue. "I missed you too. Not just fucking you. I've never had that before."

His eyes water, and I'm so damn scared I'm doing the wrong thing. All this shit is bottled up inside me; it's there waiting to burst free, but what if I fuck it up? *What if I hurt him? What if he hurts me?*

"You're killing me, Trav. Do you know what hearing you say that does to me?"

Instead of replying, I cover his mouth with mine. Kiss the hell out of him before pulling away to grab a condom and lube from my bedside table.

I cover my aching dick and wonder what it would be like to sink inside him bare. To feel his tight, hot hole with nothing between us.

I squirt lube into my hand and stroke myself before putting more on his hole. I push a finger inside.

"Travis..." Gary says as his hands tangle in the blankets, as he arches toward me.

"Gonna fuck you good," I tell him. "Gonna love you good."

He opens his legs wider for me as I push at his hole with the head of my cock. I work my way inside him. I shudder and he quickly does the same. I feel so fucking raw in this moment. Like he can see everything inside of me.

We both let out a deep breath when I push all the way inside of him, but don't move.

"Fuck me, Travis."

"Tell me again."

"I thought you were the one begging me?" he teases. I can't hold back anymore. I pull almost all the way out and thrust forward again. I lean over him, kiss him as I rut into him.

I take him hard and fast, then soft and slow. "God damn this hole. So fucking addicted to it," I tell him, my face in his neck as I thrust into him over and over.

His blunt nails dig into my ass, his quick, sharp breaths in my ear. I kiss my way down his neck, lift his arm and nuzzle my face in his pit.

I lick his collarbone. Bite his neck.

"Harder," he tells me, so I take him harder. I spit in my hand and stroke his swollen dick. "Oh fuck. Right there. Christ, Travis, right there." His cock spasms in my hand, his body arching off the bed as a rope of come spurts out of him, on his stomach and into my hand. I keep stroking, keep fucking as he shoots some more.

His hole tightens around my dick, and the build-up becomes too much, so I let loose. Bite into his neck again as I thrust through my orgasm, emptying my load into the condom.

Then I fall on top of him, pull out, but don't have the strength to move.

We breathe together for a moment, reality making its way back into my world. "Thank you."

"What are you thanking me for?" Gary asks.

"For having my back." It didn't escape my attention that he used the same words I thought. "For telling my parents I'm a good man."

For the first time, it's Gary tilting my head up so I'm looking at him. "You are. You're not who I thought you would be, Travis. You're so much more."

I kiss him again, and it's slow and exploratory. A kiss with emotion, something else I've only shared with him.

"I don't trust very easily."

He chuckles softly, his body vibrating against mine.

"Yeah...I guess that's pretty obvious."

"It makes sense that you don't. The people who are supposed to love you the most have let you down. I won't let you down, Travis. I promise. I won't try to change you. You're exactly who you're supposed to be...who I'm falling for."

"I think I'm falling in love with you," I tell him, but the words don't feel strong enough. Like the *think* doesn't belong in there. Jesus, I'm shit at this.

"What did you say to me?" Gary asks, a tremble in his voice.

"I think I'm falling in love with you. I'm all twisted up when it comes to you."

And then it's Gary kissing me with so much fucking hunger and need. When he pulls away, he says, "I love you too. Just...don't hurt me, Trav. I can't handle you hurting me."

I couldn't live with that either.

"We're getting entirely too sappy. Give me a minute to recoup and then I want to see Sex-Beast Gary. I need some more Superass before this night is over."

And then we both dissolve into laughter, and I think if this is what being in a real relationship is, I should have gone in with him sooner.

33
Gary

We stand in line at the ticket booth for the production of *Avenue Q* that's being put on at Boulder Crest Park. I hold Travis's gym duffle bag, which has a blanket and some snacks in it. We saw the signs for the event on our jog through the park yesterday, and Travis mentioned it as a great opportunity to have our first actual date.

We've been on dates and spent plenty of nights together, but that was all before we talked about how we felt. It was to perpetuate the fake relationship we were trying to convince everyone of. Now, not only is it official, he fucking said he thinks he's falling in love with me. And I love him.

I knew that's what I was feeling all along. I didn't want to use the word because it scared me. Because to call it that knowing he didn't love me back—*couldn't* love me back—would have been too painful.

But hearing those words coming from his mouth was magical.

Every bit of anger and frustration I carried with me from the party last Saturday dissolved in an instant. And the night we shared, kissing, caressing, loving...was amazing.

We've had an incredible week together, and I haven't felt like I've had to hold anything back. I like getting cute texts from him while I'm at work. I enjoy waking up to him having his arm around me like I did that morning when he scared the crap out of me...and the morning when I was scared for an entirely different reason.

"You're hot as hell in that shirt," he says, standing behind me.

I went out with Hayden and Derek after work to H&M and picked out a blue polo. It's a much brighter blue than I would have bought in the past, but when I tried it on, it was the first thing I've ever seen myself wearing that made me think, *That's me*. And Hayden and Derek eagerly agreed.

"That's the third time you've said that," I say, recalling how his eyes lit up when he opened the door. Right before he attacked me with a kiss.

"And I'm gonna keep saying it until we get out of here so I can rip it off you."

He wraps his arm around me and nuzzles his nose against the back of my neck.

I lean back against him. I could melt into him right now.

We get our tickets and head to an open area, finding a spot next to several other blankets where we'll be able to get a good view of the stage.

"This was a perfect idea," I say.

"Well, I know you love musicals," he says. I turn to him and he winks.

I laugh as I recall the drunken night when I was singing *Les Mis* in the hall outside my place after we had dinner with Steven and Raymond.

We set up our blanket a few rows of people away from the stage before I get out some sandwiches I made before meeting up with him. Travis lounges on the blanket, clearly happy it's Friday, and he doesn't have to deal with any clients for the weekend.

I sit down beside him, and we remove the sandwiches from Ziploc bags before I pull out some bottled water I brought with us. Everyone around us is doing the same thing. Having some pre-show snacks. By the time we finish, the performers come onto the stage for a mic test, each singing something popular from the radio, getting the audience excited about the performance.

"These are good," Travis says after he swallows a bite of his sandwich. "What are they?"

"Just ham, cheese, mustard, and mayonnaise. My personal favorite."

"It's really good," he says before glancing around at all the other people here. "This is kinda cool. I didn't realize they did this."

"Neither did I. We'll have to check and see if they'll be doing any more plays this year."

His gaze settles on a family a few rows in front of us.

An older woman sits on a lounge chair beside a young man who wears a rainbow wristband. She tells an older guy on a blanket next to them, "Oh, my son has been dying to see this show for a while now. He's all over the theater department at his school. He's the head of their LGBT Alliance group—"

"*Mom...*" her son says, dragging out the word in an annoyed tone.

"Let me brag on my boy," she says.

She goes on, but I'm too focused on Travis to hear what she's saying. I can tell, as he looks at them, he's bothered by how at ease she obviously is about her son being gay.

"Must be nice," he mutters. "To not be afraid of being judged. To be accepted. Encouraged, even."

I'm thinking the same thing. I'm still stunned I could stand up to his parents last weekend. If someone had been shouting at me like that, I would have walked away. Wouldn't have stood up for myself. But since it was Travis, I couldn't stifle the impulse. I had to do something...because they didn't have a right to make someone as incredible—as wonderful as Travis—feel like there was something wrong with him.

There's nothing wrong with him. Even when I didn't think he wanted me, I knew that. As I reflect on how Travis is with his parents, I'm reminded of what a wuss I am with mine.

When the show starts, our attention is pulled to the production. The first act is phenomenal with fantastic songs and hilarious one-liners. The actors are incredible, and I'm thinking we need to get a subscription to the local theater that puts on these productions. That would be a fun, datey thing to do. I like that I'm sitting here, appreciating the show, already planning out future dates with this awesome guy who I'm so fucking lucky to be with.

When intermission starts, I notice we've both finished off our bottles of water. I offer to get drinks from the concession stand, and Travis asks me to grab him a Twix while I'm there. I think I'm gonna have a snack too. We've both been really lax about eating. I'm comfortable with Travis, and he doesn't seem like the kind of guy who'd care if I gained weight. And I doubt him eating would do much more than help him pack on muscle.

After I grab a Twix, and a Butterfinger for me, I head back to our blanket when I hear, "Gary."

An eerie sensation creeps up my spine as I tense up and turn to Peter, who approaches me a little too eagerly, a cocky smirk on his face.

"Where's your new boy toy?" I ask. I feel unusually confident. Showing him how much I don't need him at the fundraiser must be at least partly responsible for this feeling.

"Around," he says. "I noticed you guys were a few blankets away from us, so I thought I'd swing by and say *hey.*"

"Well, hey."

"And I kind of wanted to talk to you about something." I can tell by the expression on his face that it's not good news. I wonder if he's heard something from Steven about the money he said he was considering investing in Travis's business. Steven called Travis to tell him he had to go out of town for work and that he wants to chat with Travis as soon as he gets back. Travis thinks Steven might be blowing him off. I keep assuring him that's not the case, but I'm nervous too. And I can't help but wonder if maybe Peter heard something through the grapevine. "What is it?" I ask.

"It's about your man. I know you don't trust me for shit right now, so I'm just...give me a second."

He pulls his phone out of his pocket and keys in his code. I notice a Grindr message on the screen before he closes the app and opens Facebook Messenger. He hands it to me.

"I don't know what you think you're about to show me," I say, "but—"

"Just read it."

It's a message from some guy named Vincent Schwartz: *Yeah, and that Travis guy that your ex Gary's with sure never has a problem letting me suck him off. We have kind of an arrangement. Got me a real good massage today, if you know what I mean.*

My face flushes.

I check the date. It was sent to Peter yesterday.

We've only been together a week.

Could he really still be doing stuff with other guys? After we said we loved each other, we talked about being totally exclusive, but if this is true…I don't even know what to think if this is true.

But why would this guy send Peter this message if it wasn't?

It would be one thing if it was just Peter's word…but this…

A tear stirs in my eye.

I turn slightly because I don't want my d-bag ex to see me like this. He doesn't get to see me cry like he did the night I confronted him about Evan—the night that I was so furious but the tears flowed even through my rage because of how much he wounded me.

I hand his phone back. "You can act like you're helping me out all you want, but you don't have any fucking good reason to have shown me that."

"I'm doing you a favor," he says.

"I bet. By the way, I saw your Grindr app on your phone. You might want to hide it better before someone tries to do Evan a favor. Fuck you, Peter." I hardly get a chance to appreciate the guilty expression on his face as I storm off.

I head back to our blanket.

Travis is lying on his back, his elbows propping him up slightly.

"Hey, Superass," he says with that cocky smirk on his face. "Where's my chocolate? I gotta work on putting on some love weight."

My hand shakes as I give him his Twix.

His expression shifts from playful to concerned.

I must be wearing my anxiety…my confusion…my disappointment.

I can hardly process it all.

He said he loved me, but I know how he is. Sex doesn't mean anything to him. Maybe it's back to what I've thought it was all along. He can't do this...not like I need him to. Not without doing what he does best. But still...why did he fucking lie about it?

But it means nothing to him, so why would he lie? That doesn't make any sense.

He hops up.

"Hey, hey," he says moving close. "What's wrong?"

I step away from him because I can't be near him right now.

I put my hand in front of me. "Please, don't come any closer," I say.

I need a minute to think this through.

"Gare, talk to me."

Oh my God, I'm gonna fucking cry like a baby.

"Do you know a guy named Vincent?" I ask.

"He's a client, why?"

More evidence to confirm my suspicions.

"Do you guys have something going on?" I spit it out because I need an answer right now. Is my world totally about to fall apart? Or is it all a lie?

"Vincent?" The way he says it, it sounds like the most ridiculous thing in the world. Although when I accused Peter of fucking around with Evan, he was just as convincing—so convincing that if I hadn't had the messages to prove he was lying, I might have believed him.

"Have you been hooking up with any of your clients...or anybody?"

"No!" he insists. "I haven't even hooked up with anyone since we started pretending."

The tears start rolling down my face.

"Where is this coming from?" he asks, approaching me again.

I step back some more.

"Peter—"

His jaw tightens at that. "Oh, Peter said something? Big fucking surprise there."

"No. There was a message on his phone from Vincent who said you guys had some sort of arrangement...something involving blowjobs."

He looks at me, stunned. Is it because I caught him?

I'm so fucking confused right now.

His gaze drifts down.

"So, that's what you think of me? That I'm a liar? Another Peter screwing around behind your back?"

No, I don't think that. But I need to hear you say it.

I can't believe he would do this, but he could have, and this has activated all those insecurities that Peter left me with.

"I'm asking because I deserve to know the truth."

"If you think that's the kind of guy I am, then I don't even know why we're doing this."

His words cut me deep.

"Vincent's a fucking client who tried to make some moves on me. Yeah, it happens sometimes. And you know what, people talk all kinds of shit about their massage therapist to brag-it-up, but obviously that's a problem for you. And if one fucking rumor is enough for you to question everything that we've had for the past few months...if that's all it takes for you to want to run off, then I think I was fucking wrong about what was going on here."

What's happening right now? I went from thinking tonight was going to be this sweet, wonderful evening...and now it's a nightmare.

"I think I should go," he says.

He tosses his Twix onto the blanket and starts off.

"It's probably better this way," he mutters.

I turn toward the stage as Act II begins. It's a loud musical number. Puppeteers rush onto the stage, hopping as they sing the next song. Travis and I should be laughing our asses off right now, but I sit on the blanket, the tears rolling down my face.

Is it over? It makes sense that he'd have clients like that, but he knows what happened with Peter. Didn't I deserve an explanation? Don't I at least deserve him staying and not walking away? He's my boyfriend. He's supposed to help me through my insecurity, not lose his shit over it. Travis of all people should have understood what I was going through after Peter showed me that.

At the same time, I'm relieved in a way. Seeing the text, even considering the possibility of Travis doing something like that, terrifies me. I don't want to go through that again. I don't want to trust someone, give them everything to find out it's all a lie. What if I wake up again to discover he's fallen for someone else? Someone more attractive. Someone younger. Someone more worthy of him than me.

Tonight needed to happen, I know that. Because considering Travis's line of work and my history with Peter, it'll always play on my mind. I'll constantly be wondering if he's really going to see a client or if he's fucking some guy behind my back.

Do I want to open my heart to someone else so I can spend my life wondering if he's going to break it?

34
Travis

Sweat runs down my forehead, stinging my eyes, but I keep going, keep pushing past the burning, not only there but traveling through my muscles as well.

My cell is resting on the lip on the front of the treadmill where I can see it as I beg it to ring. I've been doing that for days, and as pathetic as it is, I can't seem to stop. When it does buzz, it's never Gary...it's never Steven. As soon as those thoughts start coursing through my head again, I push the button to accelerate the speed on the treadmill because it seems to be the only way to work out my frustration.

He left....I can't believe he fucking left.

"Goddamn it." I try to shake those thoughts from my brain. This isn't me, and I don't like it.

Pumping my arms, I look out my living room window toward the other tower, the TV playing softly in the background. The past couple of months, my life has been so consumed with Gary and working toward Steven investing in me, it's like I don't have anything tethering me to the earth right now. Like I don't know what the fuck to do, and as much as I hate the feeling, I can't seem to kick it.

He left....I can't believe he fucking left.

"AHHH!" I slow the speed on the treadmill until it stops, before leaning over, breathing heavily. I miss sex. I don't know why I don't go out and fuck whomever I want since apparently I can't control myself, according to the guy I was willing to make a change for.

I grab my sweat towel, wipe my forehead, and down a bottle of water, my muscles tired but my body still antsy as fuck.

As soon as I make it into my kitchen, and grab another water, there's a knock at the door. I set the bottle down, walk over, and pull it open, not surprised to see Cody standing there.

"You're going to fucking kill yourself running on that thing. That's all you've been doing when you're home."

Without replying, I turn and head for the living room and sit down, letting him take care of the door.

It closes softly behind me. When he's in view again I say, "I don't need a babysitter."

"I beg to differ, baby boy. You're a little fucked up right now." He goes down beside me and pats me on the leg, making me wonder why I'm friends with him. The truth is...I *am* screwed up, and I know it. I can't seem to work through all the thoughts bouncing around inside my head.

"You know it's okay to talk to me, T. I'm your friend. I've been your friend for a long time."

"I don't talk." I cross my arms, realize I look like I'm pouting, but don't give a shit.

"You talked to Gary though, didn't you? I have a feeling you did."

"Because that did me a whole hell of a lot of good? You're doing a shitty job of talking me into opening up."

Cody laughs, and I can't help but do the same. "Ugh." I lean forward, resting my elbows on my knees with my hands in my hair. "What the fuck is wrong with me? I don't like this. I think it's because of Steven. That has to be what has my mind all twisted up. I knew, fucking *knew* he was going to give me the money, and now he's avoiding me."

"Or, you know, maybe he really does have shit going on. That's a possibility too, but I'm not going to pretend that's what's really wrong with you right now. You miss Gary."

Yes, I miss him, and I hate myself for it. "No, I need to fuck. This relationship shit is too much work. Do you want to have sex? You know I'm good at making you scream." Cody and I definitely enjoyed each other's bodies, and those friendship lines wouldn't get blurred between us. Maybe that's what I need.

"Sure," Cody replies and then reaches for the hem of his shirt and starts to pull it over his head.

My hand shoots out and grabs his, stopping him. "No. Don't. I can't." *Motherfucker.* Gary broke me. I can't even have no-strings-attached sex anymore.

"I had a feeling you were going to say that. For the record, I wasn't going to fuck you. I just needed to prove a point. You're hurting, T. It's okay to hurt. It's okay to admit you're hurting. It doesn't make you weak. It doesn't make you less of a man. You fell in love."

"And this is exactly why I didn't want to let that happen!" I push to my feet. "This is exactly why I didn't want to give someone that power over me, and I did it, I fucking did it and look at me!" *I feel the same way I did when my parents walked away from me. When who I was, wasn't enough for them.* I was right all along. When you let someone in, they let you down.

"I never should have trusted him." I pace the living room, wishing I could just jump back on the treadmill and try to replace the pain in my chest with pain in my muscles. They seem to be able to handle a beating better than my heart does.

"Yes, you should have. That's what love is."

"He betrayed me."

"No...he didn't. I know it feels like that, but he's scared too. Peter fucked around on him for years."

I stop moving, narrowing my eyes at my friend. "Are you really taking his side?"

Cody shakes his head. "No. We're not twelve. I'm not taking anyone's side, and you know if I did, it would be yours. Always. But I'm keeping it real. He's insecure. Just as insecure as you are, only he doesn't hide it quite as well as you think you do. Thinking you cheated on him plays on every one of those insecurities, but you know what? Even if that didn't happen, something else would have broken you up."

"Jesus." I fist my hands, really wishing I could hit something. "So this is my fault? And if something would have broken us up regardless, what the hell is the point? You fucking suck at uplifting, best friend conversations, Cody. I'm trading you in."

He sighs, then stands and walks over to me. "No, it's not your fault. It's life's fault, and if you love him, then there's your reason for trying right there."

"You've never been in love. You don't understand." I try to walk away, but Cody's hand shoots out and wraps around my wrist.

"This isn't about me. It's about you. When is the last time you've ever given up and walked away? When in your whole fucking life have you walked away? You worked your ass off to start a life of your own and to have your own business, without help from anyone. I've never known you to give up, yet the second shit gets serious with Gary and you have a fight, you just give in and throw in the towel? I don't think so. You're scared, T, and it's okay to be scared, but don't let that fear make you lose out on someone you love. Don't just take the first reason you have to walk away before you get in too deep. You'll regret it."

It would be a whole lot easier if I could ignore the part of me that knows he's right. That knows loving Gary scares me more than anything else because he has the power to devastate me. Because I'm scared to death he'll realize I'm not who he thought I was. That he'll decide who I am isn't good enough, the same way my parents did. The same way my real father easily walked away when my stepdad gave him an out. Just like Steven apparently did too.

But Gary didn't really leave me, did he? I'm the one who walked away. He just didn't stop me. I'm not sure if that makes a difference.

I walk away from Cody because it's easier not to look at him. I sit on the couch, my leg bouncing up and down as I tilt my head toward the floor. "I don't know if I can do it, man. I really don't know if I can do it." If I can trust him. If I can believe he loves me and won't let me down.

Cody doesn't let me take the easy way out. He sits beside me, wraps an arm around my shoulders. "You can, baby boy. I promise you, you can. Work through your shit. Do whatever you have to do to work through it, and then go get your man back. This vulnerable side of you is freaking me out."

I give him a soft chuckle, even though I don't really feel it. "You think you're so fucking smart now, huh?"

"I've always been smart."

He pulls me close and kisses my forehead. "You got this," he says, but the truth is, I don't really know if I do. I don't know if I have it in me to fix it.

35
Gary

I've had to push through this week. Hayden and Derek have done their best to cheer me up. They even suggested another guys' night, but right now, I want to be alone.

I miss Travis.

I thought things were actually heading somewhere— that we were getting closer to each other, but then it all fell apart.

It's not that I think he did something with that guy Vincent. After Travis left, as I thought about the sorts of assholes Peter knows and the bragging Travis was talking about, it made sense. Once he explained, I wasn't afraid he cheated. I was terrified of waking up one day and having to face that reality the way I did with Peter. I want to believe he wouldn't hurt me like that. I want to believe he *couldn't* hurt me like that, but I thought the same thing about my ex. I opened my heart once before, and I'm terrified if I do it again, the same thing will happen. And if Travis hurt me, I don't know if I could handle that. Even suspecting something might have happened at the park was too much.

Why go through all that again?

I sit at the dining room table in my parents' house, picking at baby carrots with my fork.

Mom and Dad cut their steaks, seemingly not noticing that I'm fucking dying right now.

"How are things downtown?" Mom asks, shaking me from my thoughts.

They've skirted around this question for a while, keeping the conversation on work and talking about some new television shows they're watching. As soon as the words come out of her mouth, tears well in my eyes.

I've always had a hard time keeping things from them. When I met up with them after Peter, it was difficult to keep it together, but I managed. This isn't the same. What happened with Peter upset me mostly because he made me feel like an idiot. And he made me feel like I wasn't good enough to make him happy. With Travis, I miss my friend. I'm sad I won't be there to help him with his loss if Steven never gives him the money. Or celebrate with him if he does. To tell him about my shit at work or about how Derek managed to embarrass me at the bar.

We made such a good team. At least, I thought we did.

"I'm not good," I blurt out.

Their eyes widen with concern as they're both totally thrown—the way I expect them to be.

"I can't keep doing this anymore," I say. "I can't keep pretending all the time."

"What's wrong?" Dad asks, and I can see the concern in his eyes—the same concern that's always been there—only because he's never known what's really been going on in my life.

"I never tell you guys anything, I know that. I've just been so scared for so long that if I told you the truth you'd be stressed out like you always are with Caroline. That you'd worry about me and think I'm a burden. But I'm tired of not being myself. And I'm tired of being such a coward. I'm hurting a lot right now. I broke up with someone I really care about. Someone I love. And right now, it's burning in my chest and feels like it's never going to go away. His name's Travis."

There. I dropped the bomb.

Mom puts her hand to her face.

"Oh my God," she says.

I can sense her disappointment. This is it.

My father has a disturbed look on his face too.

"It's a surprise," he says. "But it makes sense now that you say it. Why you never had any girlfriends. Why you never talked about your life."

"Gary, are you sure?" Mom asks, still appearing horrified.

Her question makes me chuckle. I'm amazed to be in the middle of this thing I feared and to have a sense of humor about it.

"Yes, I'm sure. I was actually in a long-term relationship with another guy who I met right after college. We're not together anymore, but it was a really big part of my life."

"Deb," Dad says, "I think now's the part where we tell him we love and support him regardless of who he loves."

"I just…I don't know what to think. I mean, all these years, and you spring this on us?"

"For Christ's sake, it's not that big of a deal," he says.

"Not a big deal that I don't even know who my son is? I can't even process this right now."

"Honey, I think he likes boys." He winks at me, clearly trying to diffuse what's becoming a tense situation. I can tell Mom's rattled, but it's nice knowing at least I have Dad on my side.

"Don't you understand how much harder his life is going to be now?" she asks him.

They get into it. It's the fight I feared. The sort of fight they might have had over some of the trouble Caroline might have gotten into.

But it's the fight I needed to happen. The fight I needed to face.

It doesn't take long before Mom shuts down and heads up to her room, but Dad pulls me aside into the family room and offers me a warm hug. For the first time in a long time, it's like he's hugging the real me.

"She's from a much more religious family," he says as he pulls back. "It's hard for her, but she'll come around. It was a lot for her to find out that her son hasn't been able to be himself around her all these years. But she does love you. You know that, right? I just wish you would have told us sooner. That you didn't have to keep this all bottled up to yourself for so long."

"Me, too," I say. Because it didn't hurt as much as I thought it would, and even though it didn't go great, at least now we can deal with it.

Dad and I chat a little longer before I head back downtown.

Despite Mom's spaz out about it, I feel relieved. It wasn't the best reaction, but it wasn't the worst either.

And I'm not stuck with that lingering fear about how they could have reacted…it reminds me of this fear I have about Travis. I'm so fucking scared of him hurting me like Peter did, and it's this demon I'm torturing myself with. I'm avoiding him for the same reason I avoided my parents.

I'm scared. Scared as fuck of being hurt. Being rejected.

But I've been rejected before and survived. I survived with Peter, and I survived tonight with Mom. If I've learned anything since I met Travis, it's that avoiding pain has never kept me from feeling it. It just makes it last so much longer. I can't keep torturing myself about what might happen. Can't let the frightening *what ifs* control my life.

36
Travis

I sit in my car in front of my childhood home. The last time I was here is when I left flowers for my mom's birthday—flowers she never once mentioned to me.

She doesn't seem to feel my loss the way I've tried to tell myself I don't feel theirs. It's a lie. I feel it. It weighs me down every fucking day of my life.

But Gary helped. He filled those empty spaces inside me, which is why I'm here.

I sigh, then push open the door before I do the easy thing and walk away, the same way I walked away from Gary. The same way my parents walked away from me.

The easy way doesn't cut it anymore.

I make my way down the cement walkway, surrounded by their pristine lawn.

When I make it to the porch, I raise my hand and knock, trying to ignore the tight fist around my windpipe.

It's only a moment later that the door pulls open, a frown creasing Mom's lips. "Travis...what are you doing here?"

"Why do I need a reason to be here? Regardless of how you feel about me, I'm still your son, aren't I?" *Say yes...I need you to say yes...*

"Of course you are. And please, don't put this off on me. We're in this situation because of choices you've made, not me. You're determined to shove your lifestyle in our face, which you proved at Martin's engagement."

My heart slams against my chest the same way my feet slammed against the treadmill daily since my fight with Gary. How can they not want me to be happy? How can they want me to hide?

"Who's at the door?" my dad asks.

"It's me. Your son," I say as I walk past Mom and into the house. I head straight for the study because I know that's where he is. Mom's heels tap against the tile floor behind me. "What about you? Am I still your son, too? You made a commitment to me when I was a baby. You've been the only father I've ever known. Why did you do that if you could so easily turn your back on me?"

He sits behind his dark, mahogany desk, a soft lamp lit on the corner of it.

"Don't be dramatic, Travis. You don't have to stop loving someone to disagree with them. We disagree with your lifestyle. You know that."

Every instinct inside of me is telling me to lash out, to walk away. Fuck them, because I don't need them, but...I do need Gary, if he'll take me back. And I can't have him if I don't do this.

Without being invited to, I walk over and sit on the leather couch across from him. Mom watches us, her eyes shooting back and forth between Dad and me.

"I used to want to be like you," I admit to him. "The kind of man who would take in a son who wasn't his. Who wanted his children to succeed. Who loved his wife with every piece of him...and then I realized that for me, it wouldn't be a wife, and my whole world came crashing down. Do you know what it feels like to grow up with two brothers who have the same father, while you feel like the outcast? It wasn't Martin and Malcolm's fault. I know they love me, but in here." I tap my temple. "And in here." Then my chest. "I just felt different. I knew being gay made me even more different, and I did everything I could to stifle that so I didn't stand out even more in this family."

"I never treated you any differently," he says, and there's a part of me that knows that's true.

"That doesn't change how I felt. It doesn't change the fact that I spent years trying to be someone I wasn't. Do you know what that does to a person?" I look at Mom. "It was eating away at me until I couldn't deny it anymore and then...then I didn't want to. What was so wrong with who I was? What was so wrong with what I did? You both answered that question for me when you found me with that guy in college. Everything that I knew would happen did. You couldn't accept me, and I think...because of that, I think there was a part of me that couldn't accept myself."

Mom gasps, which surprises me. My leg is bouncing up and down, and I drum my thumbs on my knees.

"I talked a good game. Made myself believe I didn't give a shit, that I didn't need anyone...but I do. I think we all need someone and I found him. I found him in Gary whether you both like it or not, because for the first time in my life...I felt like me. I felt whole, when I hadn't realized there was a part of me that was missing."

I push to my feet. "And I realize for the first time...that there really isn't anything wrong with who I am. The words I used to shove at everyone—that I didn't care what you thought and that if you couldn't accept me, it was your problem and not mine—I believe them now. They're not just words, and that's what I came here to tell you. That I'm in love. That I'm happy. That I have a career I love and that I'm good at what I do. That I'm a damn good man and...and if you can't see that, then it really is your problem and not mine. I'm not going to keep trying to make you love me. I'm not going to stay away from events in Martin and Malcolm's lives. I'm not going to sneak flowers on your porch on your birthday. I can't help that I'm not Dad's...I know you both wish I was."

Dad looks down.

Mom covers her mouth with a shaky hand.

But neither of them speak.

"I was so scared of getting hurt, I pushed Gary away. I walked away from him and told myself it was him walking away from me. I'm going to fight to get him back. You were always a fighter, Mom. I think I got that from you."

I walk to the door to the study, silently wishing one of them would speak....But they won't...and I know it. I have to be okay with it because that's on them, not me. "You'd like him, Ma. He digs musicals. He doesn't like attention on himself. He loves big. You both know where to find me if you need me."

And then I walk out, feeling lighter than I have in years. Like I can breathe, when I didn't know I'd been quietly and slowly suffocating for years.

Just one more thing to do. It's time to go get my man back.

37
Gary

As I get out of the elevator on my floor, good as I feel about confronting my parents tonight, I'm sad that I don't get to share this with Travis. Maybe I can wake Jacob up, and we can have a few drinks while I tell him about my new family drama.

I've already made up my mind to call Travis tomorrow. Maybe he'll have calmed down, and we can actually have a discussion about what happened the other night. Although I just keep thinking about how mad he was...how hurt. I pull out my phone as I consider texting. I've been considering it ever since I left my parents' place. Yeah, it's scary to open my heart again—to know Travis could hurt me, but I'd rather that than spend the rest of my life like I did with my parents, living in fear.

I don't want to live my life like that. Not anymore.

As I round the corner into the hallway, I see Travis sitting outside my door. With his arms around his legs and his head tucked low, he looks like he's lost in thought.

"Trav?" I ask.

Shit. I shouldn't have said his fucking nickname.

He turns to me and pushes to his feet.

"Gary."

We stand there for a moment, looking at each other awkwardly.

"Is Jacob not home?" I ask.

"He is. I was in there for a bit talking to him and then I left because I was going to go back home and think about how to do this, but then I changed my mind and just started pacing out here to think...and then, well, I decided to sit down and think some more."

"You've been doing a lot of thinking," I tease.

He chuckles. It feels nice. Breaks the horrible tension that still lingers between us.

"I came out to my parents tonight," I say.

"Really?" His eyes light up, then dull just as quickly, as though he's realized he can't really share this moment with me considering all that's happened between us.

I must be on a confident streak because I just go for it. "That wasn't very fair to me. Peter shoved that in my face, and it wasn't wrong for me to ask you if anything happened."

I notice it's one of the few times my gut instinct hasn't been to blame myself for an issue between us.

"I know."

He's not fighting?

"And after what Peter did to you," Travis says, "I know that played off all your fears and insecurities. I was just so thrown that you could think I would do something to hurt you. And it hurt me. It felt like you were accusing me and not even giving me a chance. Like how the fuck am I supposed to prove that I didn't do anything with that guy...or any guy who might say something about us messing around?"

"I know you're new to this whole relationship thing, but sometimes you have to trust that someone's telling you the truth, even if there's a possibility that they might not be. I know you, Travis. I know you're not like Peter. Hell, if you wanted to fuck around with guys, you'd go do it. You've always been open and honest about what you wanted. It was a lot hitting me all at once, and I admit, I got a little scared, not about what you did, but about what you might do one day."

"Gary—"

"But I realized, that's not the person I want to be. Life can suck sometimes, but I don't want to end up so afraid of getting hurt that I never really get to be me...or do the things I enjoy. I've spent too much of my life like that already. And I can't live my life afraid one day I'll wake up and you'll be with the next Evan—some boy toy who's so much hotter than me."

"He's not hotter, and you know it," he says.

"You've made it easier for me to believe that."

He smiles.

I like seeing him smile again.

I like seeing the relief in his eyes.

"But," I continue, "you really hurt me walking off like that. I know I hurt you with what I said, but this is the kind of shit we have to get used to if we're going to make this work. Sometimes we'll fight things out. It's not always easy. And we're not going to be this in love every single day, but we've got to be able to talk about shit when it comes up."

"I know." He pushes his hands into his pockets and looks down, more vulnerable than I've ever seen him. "I went to see my parents too."

I want to reach out for him but don't know if I should. Travis went to see his parents? I can't imagine what he would have said to them after what went down at the party.

"For years, I've been telling myself it didn't matter how they felt. Fuck them if they couldn't accept me, but...but I didn't really feel it. I hardened myself, created my own armor where I didn't let anyone in. And then you—this quiet, sexy man who doesn't fucking know how gorgeous he is—happened, and I was feeling shit I wasn't ready to feel. Things I didn't know how to deal with because I was scared, Gary. That's not easy for me to admit, but I was scared you would realize I wasn't enough for you."

This time, I can't stop myself from reaching for him. I grab his hand, pull it out of his pocket, and interlock our fingers. "How could you possibly think you aren't enough for me? You're everything, Trav."

"The same way you think you aren't enough for me. Or that you weren't enough for Peter. We have that in common, and we never realized it, and that's why I walked away. I needed to leave before you could hurt me. I'm so fucking sorry for that."

He lifts my hand to his mouth and kisses it. "So fucking sorry. I love you, Gary. I meant that when I said it, but loving someone is scary as shit. I've never had this. And it's freaking me the fuck out."

"It's freaking me out, too."

We have this strange distance between us.

I don't like how, after all we've shared—how many nights we've spent, our bodies pressed up against each other's—we feel so far apart...even though it's only a few feet.

"I love you too," I say. "You know that, right? No one has made me feel the way you do. You helped me realize it's okay to be who I am." It's important to me that he knows that. I didn't feel comfortable sexually before him, and I was insecure about my body and what people thought of me.

"Jesus, we're like fucking twins or something. But yeah...that's creepy, so no, but you did the same thing for me."

And that's the thing, we all react to the shit life throws at us in different ways. For Travis, it was becoming highly sexual and pretending he didn't give a shit about anyone.

For me it was burying the pieces of me that wanted to let loose. But inside? Inside, we were both killing ourselves.

He gives me a gentle tug, pulling me closer. "It's fucking killing me not to have my mouth on yours right now."

"Then I guess you better kiss me." I step back to the wall and soon his lips are on mine.

There it is.

The explosion of our passion that I've gotten so used to. We're like this bomb that's always seconds away from detonating, and we revel in the burn.

Here I am, once again—tasting him, wanting him, needing him.

We wrap our arms around each other.

I don't ever want to let go.

He pulls away from our kiss and gazes into my eyes. Then he moves close so that his nose rubs against my cheek. Raising his hand and gripping the back of my neck, he strokes his thumb across it. As his breath slams against my face, I feel so loved, so appreciated. "I missed you, Superass. Everything about you."

I can't stop the smile spreading across my face. "I missed you too. You wanna come inside?"

"Only if we're talking about your ass." His lips curl into a smirk against my cheek. I missed this, his joking playfulness.

We claw at each other's clothes as we make our way into my condo. Our kisses are frenzied. My body aches with my need for Travis, and I'm eager to remind him of who his Superass is.

EPILOGUE
Travis

Three Months Later

I walk through the door to what will soon be the new and first home of Magic Touch. Gary is standing on a stepladder, applying a pale blue paint to the walls. "You were right. It looks incredible." I hadn't been sure about the color, but he'd insisted it would look good. Leave it to him to always be right.

"That's why you should always just listen to me." He tosses a grin over his shoulder before getting back to work.

"Shut up."

"It's okay. You'll get used to it."

I roll my eyes at him. He's gotten awfully cocky the past few months, but really, I fucking love it. Love seeing him shine.

"How was lunch with Steven?" he asks, his back to me. Turns out Steven really did have shit going on a few months ago, a business emergency out of the country. When I thought he'd been blowing me off, he'd really been doing his job and getting shit done. As soon as he'd gotten back into the country, he'd invited me over to his place and made me an offer. It was everything I'd hoped it would be. Now, here we are, getting my place ready to open.

"Good. He and Raymond want us to go to a show with them next month, a musical or something. I don't remember the name of it."

Gary freezes, turns and looks at me like I just ran over a kitten. "How do you not know the name?"

"Um...because I forgot it?"

"Travis!"

"Gary!"

"I hate you," he says, so I walk over, wrap my arms around his waist and pull him off the ladder.

"Well, I love you." I have my moments of uncontrollable sap, which would be embarrassing if I didn't love the bastard so goddamned much.

Gary's arms knot around my neck and his lips come down on mine. I push my tongue into his mouth and wish like hell I could lay him on the floor right here and make love to him.

Before I can't control myself, I pull away and set him down. "It looks great, really. Thanks for helping."

"Of course I'm helping. We're a team now, remember?"

Yeah...yeah, I do. It feels good being a part of a team like this.

I grab the second paint roller and start helping him. We talk about the opening and Martin's upcoming wedding. My parents will be there, of course. We haven't spoken since that day at their house, but I didn't expect anything different. They're too set in their ways and that's okay. It's not the outcome I want of course, but that's life, isn't it? Everything doesn't always turn out perfect, but when I look at Gary, I'm reminded some things do. I hadn't gone there that day for them. I'd gone there for me...for Gary, and I'd done what I'd needed to do. Like I'd told Mom and Dad, they know where I am if they ever want to talk to me.

His family on the other hand, is a different story. It only took me about a week to meet his dad, who'd insisted. About two weeks later his mom had come around.

"My mom called to check on the progress," he says. "She's telling all her friends about her son's boyfriend's *massage clinic*. She fucking loves you."

"Is that really any surprise? I mean, I am me, right?" I tease, making Gary laugh.

"You're such a cocky bastard."

"Good thing you like cock." I wink at him, earning me a look that says I'm ridiculous.

We spend the next few hours working at the shop. Just as we're about to leave, Gary's phone rings. "It's Hayden," he says. "I need to get this." And then into the phone, he says, "Hello?"

Gary listens for a few moments, then closes his eyes and gives a soft, "Fuck. I'm sorry."

My stomach twists as I wait to hear what's happened, hoping everything is okay. Hayden is a good guy. He and Derek have been great friends to Gary.

"Do you want to go out? Trav and I can take you out?" Gary asks him, but I can tell by the look on his face Hayden says no. *Huh.* Must not be too bad if he's talking about going out.

He listens for another few moments and then says, "Yeah. We can hang out this week. I'll keep my eye open and let you know if I hear of anything. I can ask Jacob if he's looking for a roommate, but I'm not sure."

Ask Jacob if he's looking for a roommate? *What the fuck?*

Gary moved in with me. He's renting his unit to Jacob, and apparently Hayden is looking for a place to stay.

"Lance broke up with Hayden," he says to me when they get off the phone.

"Shit. I'm sorry for your friend." Hayden was really there for Gary when I had my head in my ass, so I definitely just want what's best for him.

"He'll be better off without him," he says. "I really believe that. It just sucks. He sounded really torn up about it. Asked if Derek and I wouldn't mind having a guys' night next week."

"You have all the guys' nights you need with them as long as you end up in bed with me."

I give him a quick kiss, and then we head out, locking up behind us. We only make it a few steps before I grab Gary's hand, turn back and look at the sign above what will be my place. My chest swells with pride. "I did it," I say softly. "I can't believe I did it."

"I can," Gary says from beside me. "We're going to have a good life, aren't we, Travis?" he asks me. Nothing went the way either of us thought it would. We each had a long road filled with way too many potholes, but when I look at him, all obstacles that brought me here were worth it. I know he feels the same.

"Yeah, we are, Superass....We are."

The End

ABOUT THE AUTHORS

Riley Hart

Riley Hart is the girl who wears her heart on her sleeve. She's a hopeless romantic. A lover of sexy stories, passionate men, and writing about all the trouble they can get into together. If she's not writing, you'll probably find her reading. Riley lives in California with her awesome family, who she is thankful for every day.

Devon McCormack

A good ole Southern boy, Devon McCormack grew up in the Georgia suburbs with his two younger brothers and an older sister. At a very young age, he spun tales the old fashioned way, lying to anyone and everyone he encountered. He claimed he was an orphan. He claimed to be a king from another planet. He claimed to have supernatural powers. He has since harnessed this penchant for tall tales by crafting worlds and characters that allow him to live out whatever fantasy he chooses. Devon is an out and proud gay man living with his partner in Atlanta, Georgia.

70223630R00152

Made in the USA
Lexington, KY
10 November 2017